PENGUIN BOOKS

In Harm's Way

Anthony Mosawi lives in London with his wife and son. *In Harm's Way* is his second novel, following *Trust No One*.

In Harm's Way

ANTHONY MOSAWI

PENGUIN BOOKS

PENGUIN BOOKS

UK | USA | Canada | Ireland | Australia
India | New Zealand | South Africa

Penguin Books is part of the Penguin Random House group of companies
whose addresses can be found at global.penguinrandomhouse.com

First published 2021
001

Set in 12.5/14.75 pt Garamond MT Std
Typeset by Jouve (UK), Milton Keynes
Printed and bound in Italy by Grafica Veneta S.p.A.

The authorized representative in the EEA is Penguin Random House Ireland,
Morrison Chambers, 32 Nassau Street, Dublin D02 YH68

A CIP catalogue record for this book is available from the British Library

ISBN: 978-1-405-92961-5

www.greenpenguin.co.uk

To my brother, Andrew,
and my sister, Eleanor.

PART ONE

I

The nightclub was packed.

Joe stood on the mezzanine balcony, staring down at the dance-floor, where several hundred bodies churned to the trip-hammer bass of deep house music. The drugs he'd taken were melting through his system, leaving him clench-jawed and shivery, his T-shirt sticking like cellophane to his damp torso.

He preferred to stand on the balcony level, away from the crowd. He was older than most of those there by a good ten years. And age wasn't the only separating factor. Whether it was the dancing or the youthful metabolism, they were all lithe, skin stretched tight around their bodies, like vellum on a drum. Unlike him. He knew he'd let himself go since he was decommed. There was a point to fitness in the army: it was about survival. Back in the real world, fitness seemed more about attracting the opposite sex, and the way Joe saw it, why waste the energy? That ship had sailed the day he'd got his facial burns, three months into his first tour in Helmand Province. In his early twenties, already six foot four and pushing twenty stone, he was a recruiting officer's wet dream. A decade later, the muscle now flab, the hard belly now a soft white sack, his face scarred and livid, he was most people's nightmare.

He loved to watch them, though. The young and the beautiful. Before he'd found the rave, his eyes had sought them out on the street each day. He'd imagined what it would be like being at their parties or sitting with them in pubs, next to girls in button-up summer dresses and boys with floppy hair and infectious laughs. But he knew these were fantasies. He knew who he was to them: the monster working behind the counter at the chemist.

He took a swig of his bottled water, then lifted it vertically and let the contents flood over his face, sluicing the sweat and re-drenching his T-shirt. It was like a furnace in the club. There was precious little ventilation. And he'd taken more pills than he usually did. He rarely got high on his own supply, but he'd felt itchy in his skin, a restlessness that began at his root and crawled its way up to his scalp. He shook his head, trying to dislodge the thoughts that were rattling around inside. At least no women in the club fitted the bill. The lack of temptation was half the battle, and the drugs were making him too unsteady for anything.

Find a channel for your anger, the counsellor had told Joe, after describing the unvirtuous circle in which he was trapped. His burns made people uneasy, which made him uneasy, which made him more isolated, which affected his behaviour, which made people more uneasy. When Joe heard the counsellor's prescription – years of therapy – he'd never gone back.

He'd found the rave quite by chance a few months ago. He always avoided his tiny flat at the weekends.

4

Dark thoughts teemed there, like spiders in a hole. Socializing wasn't an attractive option either: he quickly tired of the company of his older brother's boxing friends. When not punching each other in the gym, they took verbal jabs at each other over pints in the pub, and Joe was too easy a target. So, he walked most weekend nights, sometimes till dawn. He'd walk through endless neighbourhoods, each high street containing the same noisy pubs and crowded takeaways. He'd keep his pace, his army boots beating out a military tattoo on the pavement, the background rolling past him, like he was on a stationary treadmill. Sometimes he'd notice a woman who'd fit the bill – the right body type, right hair – getting off at a bus stop or staggering out of a chip shop, and alter his course, following her for a few blocks, building up his nerve. But the timing was never right – it all felt too exposed in the open air – and after getting one or two nervous glances from her, he'd peel off in another direction.

One Saturday night, he found himself walking near the river. It was almost four in the morning. He stopped and looked around at the darkened office buildings that towered above him, like trees in a deserted concrete forest. And then he heard it. A heartbeat. Like the city was breathing. But faster. More like heavy machinery on a repetitive loop. He followed the sound to the main road of an industrial estate, subsidiary lanes peeling off on each side, like leaves on a stalk. The warehouses at the end of each lane were identical, except one, which had a line of young people snaking around two sides and steam rising from the roof. He joined the back of the queue and, an hour later, walked into his own neon-lit fantasy. They were all here. Young and fit. Off their faces on pills. The same ones who crossed the road to avoid him during the day were stacked inside, pressed around him. The club was the great leveller.

It had seemed like destiny. A few weeks before, his job at the chemist had been a mundane means to a pay-slip. Now he felt like he was working at the Royal Mint. The pharmacist inventoried stocks each Friday and it was easy to skim from any oversupply before it was sent back to the distributors. He walked into the warehouse on Saturdays, his pockets brimming with pills: the currency of the rave scene. It didn't take long to work out a plan of action. Find a girl he liked, flash the baggie of pills, motion her to an exit door. She would assume he was a dealer, and would know security was vigilant inside the club, so his insistence to step outside would be believable. And once they were outside, he would say they needed to steer clear of cameras. He'd find an area cloaked in shadow. Stand close. Reach into his pocket. But instead of the MDMA, he'd pull out the hard vial with the aerosol top. He'd savour her confusion for as long as possible before squirting the contents into her face. It had worked like a dream twice, and he was savouring the prospect of a third time – but tonight the pills were stronger than he'd bargained for.

The music downshifted and below him the dancers responded, coalescing from isolated pockets to one bobbing mass. As a strobe light strafed the room, the downstairs appeared to Joe's melting mind like a sea of hands attached to an irregular mass of torso.

That was when he saw her. Drifting through the heaving mass. Even in a beautiful crowd, she stood out. Long mermaid hair reaching her lower back. Eyes closed, a look of rapture across her face. As she disappeared beneath the overhang, Joe leant over further, returning her to his view. It looked like she had been floating aimlessly, but her path wasn't random. Her arms trailed behind her, the tips of her fingers grazing the bare skin of each person around her. In the strobe-lit, heaving chaos, only he seemed to notice what she was doing. She was trying to touch everyone in the club.

She must have been in her early thirties, older than the other clubbers by at least ten years. He'd never seen anyone who looked like her in the club before. In the real world, women like her married football players or CEOs and drove Range Rovers. And the few times they walked into the chemist, they clutched their expensive handbags tightly for protection and avoided contact with anything or anyone. They didn't come to raves in Kennington. And they didn't try to touch strangers. But here she was. And on her own as well.

The familiar urge came to him suddenly, engulfing everything else. She wasn't a perfect fit, a little on the skinny side for Joe's taste, but this could be a way to take some revenge on all the stuck-up women just like her.

He took a step away from the balcony towards the stairs heading down, but the drugs made the floor tip back and forth, like a deck on high seas. He wouldn't make it, not without doing something stupid like falling over and drawing attention to himself. He gripped the balustrade, riding it out, and watched as she again disappeared under the overhang and was gone. His anger was back now, fully formed. Someone, anyone, would do tonight.

Next to him, a girl dressed like an X-rated version of a pixie, her white tutu composed of a ruff garlanding a minuscule thong, climbed onto a podium and began to move her arms languorously in time to the synthesized rhythms. Joe stared at her. Her long, toned legs were clad in white leather boots up to her knees, and on top of her head a white tiara was decked with fairy lights. She looked into the distance as she danced, detached, blissed-out, like she was dancing for her own pleasure rather than anyone else's. A dream made flesh. She would do just as well.

Joe enjoyed the stirring he felt as he stared at the dancer. The hunt had begun. Girls like her might look as if they were from a different planet, but he knew otherwise. He and she belonged to the same tribe. Everyone in here was broken, no matter what they looked like on the outside. Who else needed a salve for their soul at the end of a working week that was equal parts chemical high and crashing electronic music? They were the same. Understanding her gave him the edge. He just needed to wait it out. She would finish her shift eventually. He had the bait already in his pocket: twelve tabs of the best MDMA on the street. He still had four left. Popping eight tabs tonight had not been on the cards, but not one person had looked him in the eye all day and he'd needed something to numb the pain.

He looked at the dancer. Whatever she'd taken before she climbed onto the podium would wear off. She'd be looking for more. He'd approach her. Just the thought of it was turning him on. He'd soon have a much better way to numb the pain.

Something in his peripheral vision made him turn around. The woman from the dance-floor must have climbed the stairs because she was only yards away, on a direct course towards him.

He could see her more clearly now. Black jeans tucked into expensive-looking leather riding boots. An untucked blue shirt, three buttons undone from the top. A perfectly symmetrical face. She walked directly past the dancer, and the contrast was striking. The dancer now seemed gaudy, a cheap fantasy paid to dance on a podium. Joe dismissed her and turned his attention to the approaching woman. She was older, better-dressed, classier. Would the strategy work with her? Of course it would. She was in here, which meant she was broken too.

Her fingertips trailed the exposed shoulder-blade of a guy in a white tank-top. Her eyes were still closed. She was practically next to Joe now. Her hands were reaching out, looking for the next human contact point. Fingertips extended. Closer. If she touched him, it gave him the perfect moment to speak to her. It was either him or a kid next to him in a hoodie. Joe's eyes were on her hands. Where would they land? She was so close he could smell her now. A hint of citrus filtering through the fug of sweat and alcohol around him.

And then Joe felt her fingers lightly skim his forearm. In that moment, the drugs seemed to complete their final assault on his senses and the world muted. The only sound was his heartbeat, slow and steady. It was just the two of them in the club now. They were connected by the tips of her two fingers, an attachment feather-light yet it felt secure, like they were lashed together. The drugs must be playing with his emotions because he felt euphoric at first, and then the feeling evaporated, leaving him with a residue of shame. What had begun as a connection to her now felt like exposure. He felt raw, peeled open for her to see. Images were dredged up from his memory, sights and sounds he'd done his best to forget. He pulled away, breaking contact, and the nightclub came crashing back. Her eyes were now open and she was staring directly into his face.

Joe felt a sudden sense of vertigo, less from the drugs than from having a woman like her place her sole attention on him. He steeled himself, his fists squeezing into tight balls. Think of those women, he told himself. Think of their expensive heels clack-clacking on the floor of the pharmacy. Think of them pretending not to have seen him. Think of them queuing for the other pharmacist, even though Joe was available. He felt the anger surging in him again. He took a step closer to her, but he was still unsteady. He reached out for the balustrade but grabbed air and began to lose his balance, falling back against the railing, which vibrated with the impact of his weight.

'Are you OK?' she asked. Her voice was accent-less, like the ones Joe heard on the TV news. It confirmed his profile of her, but the attention she was paying him was unsettling, throwing him off-balance.

'Do you get high?' He wasn't sure whether it was the drugs or his facial disfigurement, but each word seemed to tangle with his tongue on the way out. She shook her head.

He was having trouble focusing. The dose made the dance-floor an impressionist smudge, random faces popping into focus, as if a magnifying glass was in perpetual swing through his field of vision. Joe's stomach tightened. He needed a new strategy. Now, before she disappeared again. But his mind was drifting in and out and he wasn't in control of his body. He hadn't expected anything to happen tonight, and now he realized he had dosed himself too much. Somehow, staying upright seemed the most he could manage at the moment.

'You look like you need some air,' she said.

Joe looked at her, dumbfounded, then nodded. Once again, the stars were aligning for him at the club. She smiled reassuringly and glanced around, then pointed to a fire door ten feet from where they were standing. She held out her hand again to him, but fearful of what had happened before, Joe reached and pressed a steadying arm against the wall, letting it slide along it as he lurched towards the exit.

She pushed the door open. A distant alarm sounded, ignored by the crowd around them, then she and Joe were walking into a wall of refrigerated air. Joe felt immediately more alert, as if his face had been splashed with ice water.

The door closed behind her. It was just the two of them now. They were standing on a metal gangway, three storeys up. His mind was back, processing. New strategies churning. Above his head, the black orb of a security camera was fixed into the brickwork. The first thing he needed to do was get off the fire escape, get her to the ground floor.

'Do you want some water?' She was holding a bottle out to him.

He hadn't expected her to be this kind. It was making him waver. Maybe she wasn't like those other women. She didn't seem afraid of him, like they did. She was standing close to him, which they would never do. The cold air turned her breath into a dragon's trail that swathed his head.

He found his anger receding. Maybe she was the wrong one. Even if he could commit to this part, he wondered whether he could go through with the rest. The dancer would be an easier target. He needed to get back into the club before her shift ended. The door they'd just walked through was exit only, no handle on the outside. He looked around for another, but instead found himself peering into a window. Standing next to each other, he could see them in the reflection: a grotesque parody of a couple. Joe gritted his teeth. There was no way she could see him as anything other than a monster. The only reason she was there was to toy with him. The anger surged in him again. He reached into his jacket pocket and gripped the vial.

'I need to get out of here,' he said. 'Can you help me?'

'Sure,' she smiled.

The car park behind the nightclub was filled with cars and buses, parked neatly in compact rows, drivers dozing or gazing into the wan light of their phones. Neither they nor the car-park security paid any attention to the black Mercedes van parked at the rear. Many of the buses were equipped with state-of-the-art entertainment systems, so the various antennae sprouting from the van's roof did not attract any undue attention. Its black domes and aerials were also designed to obscure their true nature. The surveillance van was Scotland Yard's latest model: it had roof-mounted ball cameras with thermal sensors, digital communication jamming equipment and a drone-operation system.

Robert Waterman shifted uncomfortably in the team-leader console in the front passenger seat. The vans weren't designed for people of his size. The bucket seat was meant to turn in a 180-degree rotation, so it could face the rear, but with Waterman in occupation, his knees were jammed together and twisted to one side after a quarter turn. Waterman did his best to dismiss his discomfort and peered at the monitors in the rear of the van by looking over his shoulder at ninety degrees.

In the back, Lewis, the van's operator, sat on one of two leather seats facing a console with rack-mounted data-processing units. His short, stocky frame was pulled tight to the lip of the console.

On one of the screens in front of him was a duo-chromatic green and black digital image of a woman descending a fire escape followed by a mountain of a man.

'OK, we're on,' said Waterman. 'Get us closer.'

'Can't get too close,' said Lewis, twisting the joy-stick. 'The drone's difficult to hide. Too close, he'll see it. Or hear it.'

The view on the monitor dropped as the drone descended rapidly. When the next flight of stairs was visible the perspective jerked to a stop, hovering in place. Waterman watched as the woman's feet, legs, then torso came into view. The man's feet and legs followed. He was leaning on the handrail. When his head was in the frame, Lewis screen-captured his face on the monitor. 'He's a pretty one. That should be enough for a facial ID,' he said.

Lewis stared at another monitor, which had split into two screens: on the right-hand side was the digital capture of the man, and on the left, a blizzard of driving licences and other government IDs flashed past at high-speed.

'Here we go,' said Lewis. A matched ID card appeared on the left-hand side. The words 'British

Army' ran in a thick font across the top. 'He's in the system,' said Lewis. 'Joe Briggs. Ex-army. In and out of jobs. Currently works in a pharmacy.'

'He fits the profile. A local dealer was one of our working theories for the perp. But it could be anyone with access to drugs. Is this a positive ID?' It was Green, the more senior of the two Special Branch officers in the rear of the van. They were both dressed in night-gear. Eyes as hard as ball-bearings stared through the letterbox openings of their black balaclavas. They crouched by the rear doors, ready to crank the handle. Various lethal-looking items were clipped to their belts. A handgun, a Taser, stun grenades.

Waterman motioned to Lewis. 'Close up on her right hand.'

Lewis dipped the joystick and the camera dropped again, catching the woman as she descended the next flight of stairs. It pulled in tight on a close-up of her hip. A small black lipstick tube was clutched in her hand.

'She's got the remote,' said Waterman. 'There's no ID until she pushes the button.'

'Why is she talking to him?' persisted Green. 'Why exit with a suspect if she hadn't made an ID?'

'Can you test the connection on the remote?' asked Waterman, looking at Lewis.

Lewis pointed to a green light on the console. 'It's in range. It's working. She hasn't pressed it yet.'

Waterman rubbed his beard, a nervous habit in times of stress. He'd rehearsed the operation with Sara. She knew the drill. Make the ID, press the button on the remote, step out of the way. She knew that a rapid response team was outside. Two girls missing in the last month, both last seen at this weekly rave. Traces of succinylcholine, a powerful muscle paralytic, found on the wall outside the club. The MO was similar enough that the abductions had to be connected. The last thing he had told her, when she had sat in the seat next to him less than an hour ago, was to take no risks.

'She's playing it out. Making sure,' said Waterman to Green.

He delivered the words with confidence but knew they were a lie. The file said Sara was never meant to have hunches. And never needed to play things out. The whole purpose of her intel was that it was meant to be instant and as reliable as fact. It had to be. She was unique, the intel something only she could experience. And with anything that subjective, it had to be 100 per cent reliable or it was useless. The reason for this operation, this *test drive*, as his boss had put it, was to see if Sara could perform *in theatre*. Whether she could produce tangible results. Yet here she was, having made physical contact with someone, flesh on flesh, leaving with him, and still no identification had been made.

A sense of dread was now roiling in Waterman's stomach. He had been a sceptic from the start. Who wouldn't have been? What the file described wasn't rational or scientific. It required a leap of faith that Waterman had been unwilling to make. If this had been his operation, he would have cancelled it without question. But his orders came from the top. Sara Eden was unlike any other agent, and this operation was about a lot more than Joe Briggs. If it succeeded, and that was a big if, it might rewrite the rules of his business.

'There's something you're not telling us,' said Green, becoming increasingly restless. He got up from his crouch and sat back on the bench.

'I'm the operational head of GCHQ,' said Waterman, avoiding his eye. 'There's a lot I'm not telling you.'

'This isn't right,' persisted Green, shaking his head. 'I was told military intelligence was being seconded to this operation. That you had an agent who might have a way to make an ID. But you're not running her like an agent. And she isn't behaving like one.'

Waterman didn't respond, his eyes on the monitor. Sara was about to reach the final set of stairs to the ground floor.

'That's a lamb to the slaughter,' pushed Green.

Waterman opened his mouth, then closed it. By the time he had formulated what to say, Lewis nodded to both of them.

'Look.'

Sara had reached the bottom of the stairs. Waterman stared in disbelief as, in full view of the drone's camera, she flicked her wrist and threw the remote into the space under the stairs. Then she stepped back, into the shadows by the nightclub wall, and was lost from sight. Briggs reached the bottom of the stairs and stepped towards Sara, into the darkness.

Lewis twisted the joystick, causing the camera angle on the monitor to veer back and forth.

'I can't get down any further,' said Lewis. 'Not without risking hitting the stair supports.'

Green glared at Waterman. 'What is going on?'

Waterman leant back in his seat and exhaled deeply. He was quiet for a moment, then nodded. He was about to tell them that Sara's safety was their priority, but Green and the other officer were already out of the door.

Waterman pushed open the same door and dropped down, landing awkwardly, twisting his knee. He limped-ran in a straight line towards the fire escape, needle stabs radiating up and down his leg. He stopped when his path was blocked by a wall that ran around the club. Waterman rerouted, speed-walking again, cursing silently until the words sounded like an empty mantra in his head.

The architecture of the club was labyrinthine, and he needed to cover the entire perimeter before finding his way to the alley that ran to the bottom of the fire-escape stairs. When he arrived, his lungs were screaming for air.

'Where?' he gasped, between breaths.

Above his head, the drone clanged once against the fire-escape stairs, wobbled and then pulled back to a safe distance. The area was empty, save for a row of dustbins. Sara and Joe were gone.

Green and the other officer pointed the beams from

their flashlights into the dark corner where Sara had been standing minutes before.

'There,' said Green.

The light shone on a section of the wall at Green's head height. The grey stucco surface was covered with what looked like a fine spray.

'Don't get too close,' said Green, holding up his hand to Waterman. 'The smell is strong. Probably the same chemical we found before, but we won't know for sure until a lab van arrives.' Green turned away from Waterman and spoke into the radio mic attached to his lapel. 'What's the ETA on backup? I want Briggs's face on all wires.'

Something caught Waterman's eye under the stairs. He squatted, reached an arm through a gap in the steps, stood up and was dusting off the object he'd picked up when he realized Green was talking to him.

'Does she have a GPS?' said Green, slowly, as if Waterman was hearing-impaired.

Waterman held up the object. It was the remote. 'The panic button was her GPS.'

The Special Branch officer said nothing, but his look was unambiguous. This was amateur hour.

Waterman turned away and walked to the perimeter wall. He took a deep gulp of air to push down his nausea. A buzzing sound distracted him and he looked up again to see if the drone was returning, but the sky was empty. He then realized it was his phone, vibrating in the inner pocket of his jacket. Waterman stared at the flashing caller ID. It was his old boss and mentor: Sir Charles Salt, former head of GCHQ, now elevated to chairman of the Joint Intelligence Committee, which oversaw GCHQ, MI5 and MI6. Salt was the most powerful person in the British intelligence community.

Waterman's finger hovered over the call button. This was his fault. He should never have agreed to be her handler, never have agreed to something he was not qualified to do. Never have agreed to any of it.

Waterman pulled back his foot and kicked the nearest dustbin with all his strength. It crashed into the other bins, felling them like dominoes and eliciting shouts of dismay from Green and his partner.

He'd had his chance to say no three months ago.

His security clearance was high enough for him to know who Sara Eden was. Or, in any event, who the British security service thought she might be.

Waterman had been sceptical when he had first reviewed the file. It was a truism of domestic security that the more threatened a country believed itself to be, the more likely it was to embrace unorthodox intelligence. The Eden file came bundled with a number of other bizarre secret projects: numerology and astrology research during the Second World War, LSD-laced truth serums during the Cold War, mediums to contact dead jihadists in the twenty-first century. They all had one thing in common: they were intelligence of the last resort. In Waterman's mind, the only thing that made colleagues willing to treat such projects seriously was desperation. Sara Eden, and whatever mysterious power her gene pool was meant to have, was no different.

The War Office had first opened a file on the family in 1940, when Helen Duncan, Sara's great-grandmother, was identified as a potential intelligence asset for the war effort. The precursor to MI6, the Naval Intelligence Department, cultivated her, trained her, and deployed her. But the experience was a disaster. Duncan showed little interest in spycraft. Having a trained asset they could not control was too much for the NID. When Helen unintentionally disclosed a state secret to help a mother searching for her son, she was arrested, tried and imprisoned. After her release from Holloway, the Duncan family went to ground, hiding for a generation. It wasn't until the chilliest period of the Cold War, when Soviet tanks were rolling into the satellite states of the Eastern Bloc, that the Security Service sought out the family again. In the spring of 1992 they found Phoebe, Helen's granddaughter, and her two children. They were living close to the poverty line and an offer of hefty financial support secured Phoebe's initial cooperation. Waterman's file was scant on detail, but somehow the spies identified her daughter, Sara, then only eleven years old, as the most gifted of the three. Waterman was shocked when he read the extent of the training programme: weapons education, live drills, close-quarter combat, enhanced interrogation techniques, covert action. They'd pretty much trained the pre-teen as an assassin.

But the experiment was short-lived. When the mother found out what was on the syllabus, she'd helped Sara escape and hidden her in the care system, so effectively that, for a decade, the Eden file gathered dust, MI6's quarry gone. It was only recently, in the mid-noughties, as suicide bombs ravaged central London, that the Service was once again on the hunt for their precious asset, now in her mid-thirties. But even though they hunted her, Sara was always one step ahead of them.

There had been only two demonstrations of the purported family power, both videotaped while Sara was in MI5 training in 1992. Waterman had watched them with a sense of suspended belief. They were shocking to see, but it was part of Waterman's job not to be taken in by appearances. Videos could be faked.

As the newly appointed head of GCHQ, Waterman had the luxury of dismissing the files after reading them. They were not part of his world. He was a technocrat. His territory was exaFLOP computer systems, surveillance satellites and undersea cable taps. More than 70 per cent of his workforce had a PhD. It was unlikely any of the Security Service's fringe projects would cross his path. So it had come as a surprise when he'd heard Sara's name again, during one of Salt's routine tours of GCHQ.

Salt and Waterman had been standing in the lift that ran from the ground level of GCHQ to the supercomputers housed in the basement when Salt had abruptly pressed the emergency button, causing the lift to shudder to a sudden stop.

'Let's talk about Sara Eden,' said Salt, without pre-amble. 'She's made contact. She wants to come in.'

Waterman hesitated. Despite his position now, and having known the man for almost five years, he was still, like everyone else, intimidated by Salt. His mentor was charismatic, and the spotlight of his attention could be overpowering. Tall, hawkish good looks, immaculately clad always in Gieves & Hawkes suits and what appeared to be a new pair of Church's black leather shoes each day, he looked like the headmaster in the jeans-wearing campus environment of GCHQ. Salt also didn't suffer fools and, given that he was always ten steps ahead of everyone else, his interactions were legendarily brief and more than occasionally short-tempered.

As always, Waterman thought carefully before responding. He remembered from the Eden file that Salt had led the MI5 team that had pursued Sara in the 1990s. Waterman had always imagined there was a complex ulterior motive behind Salt's need for her. His best guess was that Salt making China or Russia believe, at the right time, that someone like Sara existed could divert their resources to a wild-goose chase after a similar asset. Possessed of a first-class mind, and an effortless understanding of the intricacies of spycraft, Charles Salt was a master of the game. With such natural ability to excel at his job, his belief that Sara was what she appeared to be was unsettling, like finding out that the prime minister read a horoscope every morning before setting national policy.

'I thought it was odd that you'd asked to check the computers,' said Waterman. GCHQ was the listening post into Britain and Europe, with unimaginable detection power and the software to process it instantly. Due to the high-value nature of the facility, the architects had done everything in their power to make sure that the listening power could operate as much internally as outside. As a result, offices and corridors were not safe places to have private conversations.

Salt pointed to the roof. 'A little-known fact about GCHQ: the lift shafts are lined with aluminium and copper. Even if there was a bug inside, the transmission would be blocked. It's just you and I here. So?'

Waterman tried to focus his mind. Its natural state was unsettled, flitting from each of the threats he was overseeing, like a harried teacher keeping track of rebellious charges. Any one of the dozen early-stage situations the listening station was monitoring could advance to full-blown crisis at any time. It left him little bandwidth for dealing with matters that threatened to suck his time with little promise of return.

'I've got my concerns,' he said eventually, aiming for understatement.

'Let's hear them.'

'Fringe projects like Sara, they're . . .' started Waterman, wondering how freely he should speak his mind.

Salt finished his thought for him. 'More of a sign of desperate times?'

'Exactly,' said Waterman, relieved. 'There's no hard

evidence to show she's real. How can we rely on intel we can't verify?'

'Not just that,' said Salt. 'We can't risk anyone else knowing about her. Not until she's proven herself. So, we can't risk training her again. We have to take her as we find her. She may not be capable. And even if she is, we don't know if we can trust her.'

Waterman hesitated, wrong-footed by Salt's own criticisms. 'So why are we doing it?'

'You tell me,' said Salt, with a smile.

'I have no idea,' said Waterman, looking at his watch. He didn't have time for this. He was due in five minutes at a meeting on level one. The room would be full, and the top agenda item was the review of intercepts from a suspected terror cell operating in England. It would be a complex meeting, with representatives from the data-processing, legal and oversight departments attending. It was the sort of meeting that GCHQ held several times a day and its proper purpose. It was what he should be focused on, rather than being stuck in a lift discussing paranormal projects with his old boss.

'We have GCHQ,' said Salt, noticing Waterman's growing impatience. 'The Americans have the NSA, the Russians the Sixth Directorate, and the Chinese the MSS. All using the same technology, playing by the same rules. We have MI6, the Americans the CIA, and the Russians the GRU. All running agents, using the same tactics. My point is we're all using the same play-book. This family's ability is unique. It's a way of giving us an edge. That's why British governments have pursued it since the Second World War.'

'They pursued it because they were hoping it was real,' said Waterman, looking again at his watch.

'It is real.'

Waterman struggled to keep the cynicism out of his voice. 'You need proof. Tangible proof. Enough to convince a diehard sceptic.'

'And you're going to get it for me.'

'Me?' Waterman's voice climbed a few octaves and reverberated around the enclosed space.

'She's never been operational,' said Salt. 'We need to put her in some active operations and see how she performs.'

'What's that got to do with me?' asked Waterman. Human intelligence – HUMINT – was MI5's job. Waterman ran signals intelligence – SIGINT – for the government, a completely different intelligence field.

'That's the point,' said Salt. 'No one would ever suspect GCHQ of running a human asset. It's the best place to hide her. She has to remain a secret, Robert. Start her with an undercover operation. Something away from the purview of military intelligence.'

'Other than that thin service file, I don't know anything about her,' Waterman said.

'You don't need to,' replied Salt, with a level of finality.

Waterman had a sudden feeling of being outside his own body. He was suspended over the void, literally and figuratively. He could make as many arguments against

Salt's proposition as he liked, but it would all be for naught. 'But how do I prove something that isn't real?'

'That's the point,' said Salt, pressing the emergency button. The lift shivered and then resumed its smooth climb. 'What better person to prove this than a diehard sceptic?'

'It was my fault,' said Waterman.

He stood a discreet distance away from Green and his colleague, his hand cupped over the phone, speaking in a low voice. Raucous shouts filled the air. The club was emptying and the car park was gridlocked with vehicles ferrying exuberant clubbers home. 'I should have insisted. Doing his own diligence. On giving her more training. On better support.'

'Slow down. What happened?' The voice wasn't dry-mouthed from sleep. As always seemed to be the case, Salt was awake when Waterman called.

Waterman took a breath and described the events of the evening to Salt in short, staccato sentences, leaving nothing out. After he'd finished, Salt was quiet for a few beats, his voice preternaturally calm when it returned.

'Robert, the remote panic button, the surveillance van. They were all part of the cover we need with Scotland Yard. None of it is necessary.'

Waterman felt as if the edges of his world were falling in. 'I don't understand.'

'You're not there to protect her, Robert,' said Salt.

'You're just there to keep her secret. Now it's time to see if Sara can deliver.'

Waterman hung up. He'd thought he had nothing in common with Sara. But now he realized he did. They had both been thrown in at the deep end.

Joe watched Sara as her head moved woozily back and forth. She'd been out for half an hour now.

He put a hand against the exposed brick wall to steady himself. The world was tipping back and forth on its axis and a desperate thirst and raging headache were distracting him. He'd thought he'd turned a corner when they stepped out onto the fire escape, that the drugs were loosening their grip on him but, if anything, it felt like the strength was ramping up. His right arm pricked with pins and needles and his elbow was numb.

He was mostly unsettled by what had happened at the fire-escape stairs outside the club. He'd whipped out the vial and held it up to her face. Before his finger pressed down on the aerosol pump that would release the muscle paralytic, he could have sworn he heard her whisper something. She'd said it so quietly that he thought he'd misheard. But then she'd said it again, her eyes open, calmly staring at him. 'They're alive, aren't they?'

Her face was tilted up in expectation, like a worshipper expecting the sacrament. The contradiction between the words and her actions had thrown him. He'd almost dropped his arm again. But then he felt the familiar tickle in his belly, the imminence of a new captive, and squeezed the pump firmly, spritzing her with a fine spray. Her legs buckled immediately and she was out before she hit the ground. As he'd thrown her over his shoulder, he couldn't shake the feeling that he'd just been co-opted into a joint enterprise whose purpose was beyond his understanding.

He shook his head to clear his thoughts. What he'd heard must have been the drugs. He could feel them churning through his system, tightening his heart, as though an invisible fist was squeezing it, playing with his brain and vision, imbuing objects with trace-trails as he moved his head from side to side.

The good news was that he didn't have far to carry her. It had taken him a few weeks, but he'd finally found the perfect place for the girls.

He'd missed it the first few times he'd walked past it on his way home from the raves. The entrance was partially obscured by creeping vines, and the whole structure was barely larger than a family-sized car, butted up against the embankment wall. The hatch was rusted shut and it had taken all of Joe's strength to pull it open. Inside, it looked like a pump station, one of several along the banks of the river near Vauxhall. When he saw the manhole cover in the corner, his heart beat faster. He slid his fingers into the recessed handle and pulled. It came off cleanly. Mouth dry with expectation, he looked at the metal ladder leading down. He stepped inside, hoping. And it had been perfect.

Now, it was time to wake her. He knew where he would start. On that pretty face.

*

The flashing lights on the four police cars washed over the pockmarked grey walls of the nightclub. Waterman stood to the side, shunted back by what was now a police operation. Green and his number two were briefing a huddle of uniforms clustered around them. A spotlight had been rigged next to the wall where Sara had last stood and two crime-scene technicians, masked and gloved, took samples with tweezers and placed them in evidence bags.

Waterman could hear Green winding up his discussion. They made eye contact and Green walked over.

'We'll search the area around the club again. Just to see if there's something we missed. But we're assuming he had some form of transport. Which means the search area could be much wider. The next few hours are crucial,' said Green. 'After that . . . well, we're still looking for the other two.'

Waterman nodded, unsure of what to say. He then realized Green was staring at him. Waiting. 'Do you need something from me?'

The Special Branch officer looked irritated at having to spell it out. 'Look, I know there's some cloak-and-dagger going on here, but now is the time to tell us everything you can. Who she is, what she knew. Anything. The more we know, the better the chances of finding her.'

Waterman looked at the ground. Empty beer crates were piled up in the dustbin area. Flies buzzed around cigarette butts and food leftovers. This shouldn't be where it ended. He wanted to help Sara. Yes, she had volunteered, but Salt and Waterman had put her in this situation. He knew that anything he shared with Green might increase her chances of being found alive. Substantially. But he also knew, as head of one of the key branches of British military intelligence, he had an order to follow, even if it meant signing Sara's death warrant. He shook his head.

'I can't tell you anything.'

Sara shook her head groggily. She looked up slowly, taking in her captor. She could see him more clearly now in the bright-lit space. He was a giant. Filthy trainers, black sweatpants, old T-shirt. The clothes of someone who is never noticed. His missing upper lip twisted his face into a skeletal grimace. His face and hairless scalp were lobster-red, with red ridges where his eyebrows used to be. But the eyes looked like they belonged to someone else: hesitant, wide-open, pinched with pain.

They were in a windowless room, barely larger than a lift. Brick walls. He stood in the corner, watching her. The ceiling wasn't high enough for him to be upright, and his head was forced to tip forward, compounding his predatory look. She was on the floor, her knees pulled up, her back pressed to the corner of the far wall. How long had she been out?

'What time is it?' asked Sara. Her tongue was dry.

He picked up a thick length of metal pipe at his feet and jabbed it once with force into the wall, his strength profoundly evident. The rusty jagged edges left a circular bite mark in the brickwork two inches deep. He turned back to her, the pipe hanging loosely by his side.

'It's time for you to suffer,' he said, each word slurred and thick.

Sara rubbed her face. Her mind was still foggy from whatever he had sprayed her with. 'You're not a killer.'

'You sure of that?'

'The girls are still alive.'

'How do you know?' The pipe pointed at her, its ragged end approaching, like a distended mouth full of razors. He walked slowly towards her. She didn't let herself acknowledge the dried blood crusted to the serrations.

'I saw them. When I touched you.'

'What are you *talking* about?' He was snarling, working himself up to whatever he was planning.

'They're in a room next door, aren't they, Joe?'

A look of confusion tightened his features, and he stopped walking. 'How do you know my name?'

'I'm a psychic. I'm working with the police.'

Joe pulled at the collar of his shirt. His face was flushed and trickles of sweat ran down his forehead. He wiped his palm across it and laughed weakly. 'Some psychic.'

'I know you're not going to hurt me.'

He was perspiring heavily now, large damp patches on the stomach and underarms of his T-shirt. His feet dragged as he took his next step, tilling two furrows in the sandy floor. 'That just shows you're not much of a psychic.'

'Tell me the time, Joe.'

'Why do you keep asking about the time?'

'Just tell me, please.'

He kept flexing his left hand, squeezing it into a fist, then spreading the fingers wide. The whole left side of his body was beginning to tilt, and the corner of his mouth was twitching, as if an invisible string was tugging it towards the floor.

'It's the middle of the night. Twenty past four. There's no one around. No one can hear you.' He roared the last few words to prove his point, his voice cracking at the end, the sound deafening in the enclosed space. The shout reverberated around the room and afterwards the stillness was so loud her ears rang. His effort took a toll and he stabbed the pipe into the floor and leant on it as a support.

'Twenty past four,' said Sara. 'OK. Can we talk for a while?'

He stared at her, unmoved. 'They're not coming for you.'

'I know.'

'I searched you. You've got no phone. Nothing else they can track you by. You can't buy time. There's no one coming.'

'It shouldn't matter for you to talk to me then, should it?'

Joe hesitated long enough for her to continue.

'How did it happen? Your mouth?' Her voice was soft, empathetic. She wanted him to know it was a genuine question.

She could see his jaw muscles clench hard. A subject that was never mentioned. He hesitated, but she could tell he wanted to talk. Tears pricked in his eyes.

'None of your business.'

'You were in the army, weren't you? You were injured fighting for your country.'

'I fought . . .' He stopped. The left side of his face was sliding down, slipping like melting candle wax.

'I sought . . .' He tried again, louder, but the words were even more mangled. Gravity suddenly became overpowering and Joe fell down on one knee. One arm hung loosely by his side.

'Unn.' He groaned.

He fell onto his other knee, then tipped to the side, collapsing into the dirt, his hand clutching his chest. His sleeve fell, exposing a plastic wristwatch.

'Wass ha'ening to me?'

She came closer and knelt by him, looking into his eyes. She lifted the pipe from his hand and threw it into the corner of the room. She then checked the watch on his hand.

'You're having a stroke, Joe. It was the drugs you took.'

'Hep . . .'

Sara shook her head. 'There's no time.'

'Ama gun die?'

'Yes.'

The anger in his eyes was replaced with fear. He struggled to say something, but his mouth was no longer cooperating with his brain, and all she heard

34

was a series of sounds, choked out in an anguished tone. His eyes were imploring, both hands now gripping hers, pulling her closer. She leant in, her ear dipping towards his ravaged mouth. His words were barely a whisper now, but she could just about make them out. It was the same two words, over and over.

'Neck door.'

She tightened her grip on his hands and looked into his eyes as the light in them faded, the corneas filming to glass.

She searched inside his jacket pockets. The vial of knockout spray was in one pocket, and a handful of tablets in the other. She patted a trouser pocket, then reached inside and pulled out a small key. She stepped over his body and tested it on the padlock on the door. It was a fit.

Neutralize the threat. Protect the innocent.

This was the mantra she had learnt during her child-hood training. The first was the Service's contribution. The second was her own addition.

She stepped through the door and found she was in a storm drain. It was huge, the radius at least ten feet. The water was only ankle-deep. Behind her, the tunnel disappeared into darkness. In front of her, the entrance was less than ten yards away. There was no covering and she could see the lapping waves of the flowing river and the lights of the embankment on the far side.

There was another door a few feet away, identical to the one she had just stepped through. A padlock hung on the lock. She pressed the key she was holding into the lock, but it didn't fit. She slapped the flat of her palm against the door.

'Hello! Anyone in there?'

Silence. Sara banged her fist on the door this time, as hard as she could.

'Hello!'

Silence again. She was about to turn away when she heard a scraping sound coming from inside. Then whispers. Someone talking. Then a weary voice cried out, 'Who's there?'

'Hang on,' said Sara, frantically looking around the floor for something to lever open the door. 'I'm going to get you out.'

She ran back into the cell where Joe's body lay and picked up the metal pipe, then ran back. The padlock was attached to a latch fixed to the door and the frame. She repeatedly stabbed the jagged end of the pipe into the wood surrounding the latch, creating a rut under it. When it was deep enough, she wedged the edge of the pipe into the space. The latch came off with the first yank.

Both girls were inside. In their underwear. Both tall, both brunettes with long hair. They were on the heavier side, but Sara could see how the three of them might be echoes of some original fixation from Joe's past. They had flinched when Sara had opened the cell door. Their faces and exposed skin were caked with so much mud and dried blood that it was impossible to tell what their injuries were.

'It's over,' she said. 'It's time to go home.'

Sara took off her jacket and put it around the shoulders of the nearest girl, the smaller of the two, who was shivering violently. She led them out of their cell and helped them down into the tunnel, pointing in the direction of the river. It looked like a short drop into the water, less than ten feet. She'd be able to swim to the nearest stairs or jetty and from there get help. As they passed the cell where Joe's body lay, both girls looked in, hesitating.

'You're safe,' said Sara. 'He's dead.'

The smaller girl looked back at Sara, her eyes wide. 'Where's the other one?'

The taller girl screamed. Sara spun around, but was too late to deflect the fist that thumped into the side of her ribcage with the force of an industrial hammer, lifting her cleanly off the ground and throwing her against the wall. She jabbed out her elbow blindly, causing white needles of pain to stab under her arm. Her strike connected and her attacker reared back. Sara whirled around to face him, clutching her flank. The punch must have broken one of her ribs. The pain was blinding and she felt light-headed. When she pulled her hand away from under her arm, she saw that it was slick with blood.

She cursed silently. Neutralize the threat. She had ignored the first part of the mantra. If her training didn't come back to her, and soon, all three of them would be dead.

He was taller than Joe, heavier-built. Older too. But the family resemblance was clear in his facial features.

She could see that the fist that had punched her was curled around a small knife. He must have plunged it in up to the hilt. The blood was matting her blouse to her bare skin, her entire flank now sticky. She fought the urge to vomit.

He ran at her, head down, a tackle aimed at her chest. She was thrown down hard, the ground knocking the breath out of her. Before she could twist around, he was back on his feet and a leather army boot kicked her side.

She struggled up to all fours, coughing up a ropy trail of blood and saliva. Her throat was burning and each breath felt like it was collapsing her lungs. The assault was coming too hard and fast. She had failed and now she was going to die.

The taller of the two girls shrieked and leapt at him, her nails digging into his face as her other hand clawed at his hair. He batted her away easily, throwing her to the ground.

The distraction gave Sara the chance she needed to stand up. She turned to face him, tucking her elbow tighter to her flank to protect her wound. He smiled and approached her. His eyes said it all: *Unless you're packing a gun, this is over.* He was a foot taller than her and at least twice her weight, although he carried himself lightly, on the balls of his feet. His body was angled towards her, a fighter's stance. When the punch came, there was no telegraphing on his part. No tell in the eyes or pull-back in the fist. His knuckles were suddenly on a forward trajectory to her face, a knock-out punch. An uppercut aimed straight to her chin. Designed to end this and begin whatever grisly interaction he was planning next.

Sara took a breath and held it. Something instinctive, some muscle memory deep within her, was taking over. The world around her seemed to slow down and mute. The only sound was her heartbeat, loud, echoing, as if she had stepped into a bubble that separated her from the rest of the world.

She lifted one leg and positioned it behind her. She noticed her movement was fluid, her limbs and body moving at normal speed. In the outside world, the atmosphere seemed denser, more resistant to pressure. The taller girl's arms lifted in slow motion as she shielded herself from the melee. Sara's attacker moved like he was walking on the moon. His fist ploughed the air, approaching Sara at diminishing speed. She tracked its arrival, easily moving out of the way. By the time it was close to her face, she had flattened her body, so her shoulder was aimed at his chest and her head aligned in the same direction. His fist passed through the air where her head had been, the miscalculation tipping the rest of his body forward. She reached up and grabbed his wrist, even as his centre of gravity was tipping over, and pulled, extending the trajectory. His reaction was just beginning to appear on his face, his eyes widening with surprise, when she placed her shoulder in his sternum.

The pressure in Sara's ears was increasing and she realized she was holding her breath. She exhaled and, in a second, the separation between her and the world collapsed and everything spun forward at normal speed. Her attacker flipped over her shoulder and she dropped down onto him, her knees pinning his elbows, her weight pressed onto his chest. Without thinking, the flat of her hand drew back, heel out, and slammed down into the centre of his face. He let out a scream that ended prematurely when his brain was punctured by his nose bone. But then the scream resumed, higher in pitch. Sara turned in confusion to see the smaller girl staring at them, her mouth wide, her voice rising. Sara's eyes rolled up into her head and everything went black.

2

Waterman sat in a plastic chair in the hospital corridor. He was alone. The entire floor had been cleared, and beyond the exit doors, two military policemen stood guard by the only access lift. He checked his watch. It was four minutes to ten in the morning.

The viewing pane to the operating theatre took up most of the internal wall in front of him. He'd watched the surgical team for the first hour, occasionally catching glimpses of Sara's intubated face as they changed positions around her. But then his bad knee had buckled from tiredness and he'd sat down on one of the plastic chairs.

The lead surgeon had stopped by only once, about an hour ago. He was a short man in his early fifties, with the trim figure and lean look of a competitive cyclist. Thin spectacle lenses magnified bright blue eyes. He told Waterman that the length of the blade had most likely saved Sara's life. A short, stumpy knife, like the one used on her, was typically for close-quarter combat, designed for slicing an artery and bleeding someone out. It wasn't designed for hammer-force blows. But she'd lost a lot of blood, and the next few hours were crucial. He'd then taken Waterman's number and said he would call him with any updates.

But after the surgeon had returned to the theatre, Waterman hadn't moved. He had plenty to keep himself busy. The day shift at GCHQ had started at nine a.m., and his smartphone was emitting a steady stream of pings as emails arrived.

In front of him, the small coffee-table was strewn with newspapers, each one turned inside out, then folded so that the crossword was on the facing page. They were all complete, their white boxes filled with his scratchy handwriting. Waterman sifted through the stack, searching for another.

Puzzles.

His strength had always been puzzles.

As a teenager, he'd been able to do *The Times* crossword in minutes. Since then, the puzzles had increased in complexity, and so had the stakes. Now, the consequences of not solving them gave him nightmares, but he knew of no one better than him at the job.

The puzzle of Sara Eden was picking at his brain now. He felt he couldn't leave her until the riddle of last night was solved. What had happened? One minute, the forensic teams were winding up the operation at the nightclub, the hope of finding Sara slipping away, and the next, one of the abducted girls had run into the club parking lot, soaking wet, babbling about a storm drain. The police had followed her and found the other abducted girl, with Sara, unconscious and bleeding heavily, along with two dead men. Less than an hour had passed since Sara disappeared. It was too remarkable for words. But what did it mean?

Waterman approached puzzles as if they were corridors with a series of open doors, each representing a potential answer. You had to walk down the corridor, closing each door where the answer didn't fit, until there was only one left. However unlikely, this was the door to step through.

In this case, what had made Sara leave with Joe Briggs? If she had identified him as the abductor, why hadn't she pressed the panic alarm? Why had she thrown it away? Those were the questions the puzzle posed.

The first door had a simple answer: that Sara did not know Briggs was the abductor when she left with him. It was blind luck, or bad luck, that she'd happened to exit with him. But if that was the case, her ability did not exist. Salt wouldn't like that answer, although for Waterman it was the most likely.

The second door had another simple answer: that Sara did know Briggs was the abductor because he had given himself away, intentionally or unintentionally, inside the club. There were no mysterious powers behind this door.

And behind the third door was the answer Salt wanted, which was that Sara knew Briggs was the abductor because her psychic ability had identified him as such.

The problem with the second and third answers was that they didn't explain why she had thrown away the remote. The only answer Waterman could think of was that she thought she could deal with Briggs better than

43

Special Branch so had allowed herself to be kidnapped. And that meant Sara was reckless, and of little use to them.

So, she was either a fraud or reckless. Whichever way Waterman looked at the events of the evening, this was the end of the road for the Sara Eden project. And perhaps that was best. Military intelligence worked in deep webs of cooperation, with any single operation supported by multiple agents, handlers, intercept teams and cross-agency support. There was a shared vocabulary they used in their common goal of preventing terror attacks on the realm. It wouldn't work with a maverick whose intel was half-formed hunches.

Despite all of this, Waterman knew that it would not be easy to convince Salt to give up on Sara Eden.

Waterman stood up and walked over to the viewing pane. He tried to read the faces of the surgeons, looking for any clues on Sara's chances. There was always the possibility that she would die, taking with her the answer to tonight's puzzle.

He heard the doors at the end of the corridor flap open and turned to see Salt arriving, clutching a mobile phone.

'There wasn't time to get her to an MoD unit,' said Waterman, turning to face him, 'so I told them to bring her here.'

St Thomas' was the closest hospital to where they'd found Sara.

'It was the right move,' said Salt. 'I've got a military air medic helicopter waiting on the roof.'

'I don't know when we'll be able to move her. She's lost a lot of blood,' said Waterman. 'Is there any family we should call?' When Waterman had signed the hospital papers for Sara's admission, his pen had hovered over most of the boxes. Address? Emergency contact? Blood type? He'd realized he knew nothing about her.

'She's not going to die,' said Salt. He was about to say something else when his phone buzzed. He looked down at the screen. 'I've got to take this.'

Waterman watched him walk to the far end of the corridor, the phone pressed to his ear. He felt a wave of profound fatigue hit him. He stepped over to the outside window and lifted the latch, enjoying the cool draught on his face. Five storeys below, the pavements were quiet, the morning commuter rush having been displaced by mums wheeling pushchairs, tourists and shoppers taking in the sights.

'I've got to go,' said Salt, rejoining Waterman. 'As soon as she's recovered, find the next operation for her.'

'You want to continue?' asked Waterman, incredulous.

'Two found girls. Two dead men. I would say that's a success.'

'Tonight didn't prove anything,' said Waterman. 'You wanted proof and all we have are questions.'

Instead of responding, Salt stared over Waterman's shoulder. Waterman turned, following his line of sight. Through the observation screen, the surgeons had stepped back and were taking off their gloves. One gave a thumbs-up sign to Salt. Salt patted Waterman's shoulder. 'She was trained for this,' he said.

Waterman could feel the frustration building in him. 'Yes, trained twenty years ago. By people I've never met and whose capability I can't now test.'

Salt pulled out a single creased piece of paper from his inside jacket pocket and handed it to Waterman, who unfolded it. The crest of St Thomas' Hospital was on the letterhead and underneath was a table of medical results, with conclusions by a pathologist. It was Joe Briggs's post-mortem report. Waterman scanned the short paragraphs and looked up at Salt. 'She didn't kill Briggs. He died of a drugs overdose,' said Waterman, struggling to process the implications of this fact.

'Look at the time of death,' said Salt.

Waterman searched the report. 'It says at or around four twenty in the morning.'

'Do you get it now?' asked Salt.

Waterman looked back at the report, shaking his head.

'I'm sorry, I . . .'

'You will. Now, get some sleep, Robert. Find me the next operation.'

He had almost reached the far door when Waterman called after him. His attempt to keep an imploring tone out of his voice wasn't entirely unsuccessful. 'What is going on here?'

'What do you mean?' asked Salt, his hand on the door.

Waterman approached him, dropping his voice as two

of the surgical team exited the operating theatre and walked down the corridor in the opposite direction.

'You're keeping me in the dark. Giving me just enough light to see myself trip over.' Waterman couldn't believe he was saying this. Insufficient sleep had removed his filters.

Salt stared at him for a few seconds. 'You think I'm setting you up?'

'I know how damaging it could be if word of her gets out,' Waterman pressed on, surprising himself at each step. He had crossed a line he had not intended to cross, but now he had done so, he might as well say it all. After giving Salt years of fierce loyalty, after being flattered on some level for being taken into the man's confidence with Sara Eden, having information kept from him felt like a betrayal. Under the reserve that filmed over his professional interactions, there was a lake of emotion he preferred not to acknowledge. 'You don't want her linked to you. You need a fall guy. You're running the operation but keeping me close in case it blows up.'

Salt walked back and guided Waterman to the window. He held up the phone in his hand. 'The call just now was from Bregman, director of the NSA. We're signing a new intelligence-sharing agreement with the Americans. Negotiations have been top secret. NSA funding of GCHQ's budget is going to increase tenfold.'

Waterman didn't respond, but the information was seismic enough to derail the train of his emotions. He knew Bregman well. The gravel-voiced former admiral had a way of pushing his buttons, his endless refrain being that GCHQ needed to do more to justify the NSA's financial contributions. A significant increase in funding would mean one thing.

'I'm going to end up working for Bregman,' said Waterman, under his breath.

'Things will change.' Salt nodded. 'The Americans will have full access to our intel. And if they find out we're running an agent like Sara, well, two things could happen.'

Waterman answered for him. 'If they think she's fake, they'll come down on us hard. Stop sharing intel with us. That could put the lives of British agents in the field at risk.'

'And if they think she's real . . .' began Salt.

'. . . they'll want her,' finished Waterman.

'That's the other reason you're handling this personally,' said Salt. 'No one else can know.'

Salt pushed the door open, then stopped, his fingers resting on the handle. He turned back to Waterman. 'The future is changing, Robert. Britain is moving away from Europe and closer to the US. A US allied with Russia. This is more than just pieces moving on a board. The game itself could be changing. We need an asset like Sara now, more than ever before.'

3

Waterman waited until they moved Sara to a private room. After the attending physician had left, he slipped inside.

It was a sterile cube. White walls, white sheets, white cushions on the chair by her bedside, white blackout blinds pulled down to the floor. The only sounds were the soft hum of the ceiling air vents.

Sara lay in the bed. The tubes had been removed and she was breathing freely. Waterman had hoped she would be awake, that she might answer some of his questions, but she was still under sedation. A monitor on wheels was next to her bed, wires running from a pad attached to her arm, an electric-blue shark's fin pulsing out at short intervals on the screen.

Waterman took the seat next to her and stared at the pathologist's report.

What puzzle was hidden inside it? Salt had said that the proof of Sara's power was in the post-mortem. Waterman had read and reread it so many times he had memorized its contents. The state of each organ, the etiology of death. 1.5g of MDMA present in Briggs's bloodstream, over twelve times the recommended maximum dosage. His metabolism was unable to detoxify the drug, leading to a fatal hemorrhagic stroke.

Waterman rubbed his beard. Salt had said that the clue lay in the time of death: 4.20 a.m. He ran through a timeline in his mind. Sara had left the club with Briggs at approximately 3.20 a.m. Minutes later Waterman had run to the fire-escape stairs and found her missing. Briggs had taken Sara. At some point the knockout drug had worn off and Sara had woken up in the storm drain. Then Briggs had died, an hour after she exited the club with him. The timeline yielded nothing of significance to Waterman, certainly nothing that could prove Sara had psychic abilities.

Waterman heard two pings in rapid succession. He pulled his phone out of his jacket pocket and checked his email, then breathed out in exasperation. There was a developing situation at GCHQ, and his absence was causing problems. He should have left the hospital hours ago. Should have arranged a car to take him to Cheltenham at dawn. An entire alternative timeline spread out before him now, one he knew he should have taken. In this parallel world, he would have ensured he had slept – even if it was only two hours on the train – and attended the meetings. He cursed to himself and stood up, holstering his phone back in his pocket. He walked quickly to the door and, after a last glance at Sara, left the room and pulled the door closed behind him.

As he did so, he froze, his hand on the doorknob, his feet rooted to the spot. Instinct told him that the answer to the puzzle of Sara had appeared.

What was it?

He backed up through the last sixty seconds.

Closing the door.

The last glance at Sara.

Reading his emails.

Thinking through the alternative timeline, what he should have done.

The alternative timeline.

He pulled out his phone and jabbed at the keyboard, dialling a number he knew by heart.

'*Did you figure it out?*' Salt's voice echoed slightly. He must be sitting in the back of his private car.

'We were going to take Briggs to Savile Row,' said Waterman. It was the West End central London police station. A grey brick bunker nestled amid the tailors' shops of the iconic street. It had been cleared by Special Branch for Briggs's interrogation. 'That's a half-hour drive, plus we'd need to process him when he arrived. He died of the stroke around four twenty a.m. That means he'd have been dead before we'd got him to an interview room. He would never have told us where the girls were. They would never have been found.'

'*That's right,*' said Salt. '*That's why she ditched the remote. Letting him take her was the only way to find the girls.*'

Waterman was quiet for several seconds, processing the implications of what Salt had just said. He reopened the door of Sara's room and walked back in. Her eyes were still closed. Waterman approached the bed.

'It's not enough,' said Waterman at last, looking down at her. 'It's too tenuous as proof.'

He was standing close to the bed, the phone pressed

to his ear. From there, he had a close-up of her injuries. Her lip was split. The left side of her face was mottled with yellow and magenta bruises. A gash on the bridge of her nose was held together by butterfly stitches.

'*I never said it was enough,*' replied Salt. '*But it's something. Enough for another deployment, at least. Get me proof.*'

Waterman sat down on the chair again. From where he was sitting, he could see the thick bandage covering Sara's flank. It was spotted in the centre with tiny flecks of red where the fresh stitches had pressed against it.

'I have one question,' said Waterman.

'*Yes?*'

'Why is she doing this?'

'*I told you. She came to me.*'

'That's not what I mean. She almost died tonight. Why is she willing to take such huge risks? Any other agent would have called for backup.'

Waterman thought he sensed hesitation in Salt's voice as he said, '*We trained her to take those risks.*'

'I read the file. You trained her in *how* to operate, not *why*. Until we know what's driving her,' pressed Waterman, 'we'll never know if we can trust her.'

Waterman didn't need to mention the recent event at GCHQ. Last month, a young researcher in the Atlantic Intercept Division had clocked up over a hundred hours on the job during her first week. Her line manager had chalked it up as a desire to impress, as did the group supervisor. Waterman was not as convinced. He pulled the records of her security card entries and found a few too many trips to the copying room after midnight. He informed Salt, who referred the situation to MI5. An operation was launched and the researcher was rewarded with a gift for her labours. Waterman wasn't involved, but found out later the gift was a Union flag lapel pin. The bug hidden inside it brought to light a roommate with ties to the Russian Embassy. It reminded him that even the world of SIGINT was not immune from analysis of human motive.

'If we're not vetting her, we need to be doubly sure,' continued Waterman.

'*What are you saying?*'

Waterman considered this. What exactly was he saying? He looked down at Sara's battered body. What would the stakes need to be for someone to risk death? And then to be willing to risk it again? The decision corridor stretched in front of him. Too many doors were open. Too many determinants unknown. It was impossible to make an informed decision of which doors to try and which to dismiss. He needed more data. And the only way to get it was to put Sara, and by extension GCHQ, in the line of fire again.

'*Tick-tock, Robert.*'

Waterman was on the horns of a dilemma. If he benched Sara, he risked losing valuable intel and making an enemy of Salt. And if he deployed her, he was inserting an untested and potentially dangerous asset into an anti-terror operation.

'I need a few days to think about it,' he said, at last.

'*The science will never get you comfortable, Robert,*' said Salt, then hung up.

4

Waterman lay under the thick covers of his bed, asleep. Two days had passed since the evening at the nightclub and he was still paying off the sleep debt he had incurred that night. This morning, however, despite his best efforts to remain asleep, a sound was summoning him back to consciousness. His dormant mind slowly began to work to identify it, and as it did, the sound separated into distinct chopping, triggering an association in his mind. Then he was bursting through the surface, his eyes open, the cream crown moulding of the bedroom ceiling staring down at him anticlimactically. The printer was churning out pages one floor above.

He exhaled slowly, as if to draw a curtain behind him and close off the night, and looked over to the other side of the bed.

Susie was snoring gently. He watched her for a while, envious – she had the placid look of a stone effigy in a country church – then pulled on his dressing gown and climbed the stairs to his private study.

It was just before dawn, and through the windows of the attic room he could see the string of streetlights haloed against the night sky. The room was small and snug, lit only by a lamp that cocooned the desk in a bright glow even as darkness clung to the corners.

Waterman flipped on the standing lamp, banishing the shadows and illuminating the puzzles that filled the space. Stacks of crossword albums, brainteasing books, framed certificates. A celestial map covered the ceiling. This room was his tether to the past. To the big kid in school whom everyone expected to be athletic but had two left feet. Who wanted to be cool but lacked the social vocabulary. Who remained isolated, like the solitary cube on a Rubik's puzzle that can never find its matching colour wall. Until the day he picked up his first puzzle. His study was his way of reaching back, reminding himself that the path was the same.

On the desk, the printer was still humming in the aftermath of disgorging its contents. Waterman sat down and lifted the first page, still warm from the guts of the machine.

This was his morning routine.

Each slip of paper contained a fresh catastrophe that would befall the country.

Waterman had started this. Computer forecasting was the newest tool at GCHQ. Data-mining was the traditional activity of the eavesdropper. It sifted through the world's telecommunications looking for potential threats. Billions of phone calls, emails, social-media posts each day, all connected and correlated by supercomputers housed deep underground, hunting for traces of conspiracies being hatched. The results were screened by hundreds of analysts, working as a human filter to prioritize results. Until now, they'd never used the data to try to forecast probable events in the future. Waterman greenlit the covert project, under the codename Cassandra, and now each day the lurid forecasts arrived just before dawn. The software took data points that could have correlations and predicted a range of potential future scenarios.

Waterman pulled the last piece of paper from the pile. The data points were intercepts between Black Dawn, a Serbian terror group relatively new on the scene, and several terror groups in Europe. The substance was the same in each. Black Dawn needed C-4 explosives. A lot of them. The data-forecasting software spun out myriad projections, from the likelihood of them procuring the C-4 to the potential targets. But the data was too thin to support any reliable forecast with anything more than a single-digit likelihood of it occurring. The table of results was several pages long, filled with possible alternative scenarios. There was a separate page of potential 'persons of interest'. Waterman ran a finger down the list. They were mostly men, some women. Anyone who had visited chatrooms or social-media accounts linked to Black Dawn. Almost forty in total. The likelihood of a connection between any of them and the terror group was too slim to justify the court order he'd need to put a tap on any phones.

Waterman switched on his computer and searched his emails for the spreadsheet of underlying calculations. He knew they needed more intelligence, but the underlying assumptions to the algorithm might need to be tightened as well. Sometimes a couple of data points could be recoded, sufficient to pull the forecast onto a new course, bumping up some of the likelihoods to double digits. It should have been checked already, but Waterman never assumed anything.

His eyes drifted off the screen to the wall in front of him. A framed certificate hung at eye level. His first national crossword competition win. Aged thirteen. He'd stayed up the night before, working his way through past crosswords, getting match fit. He'd given everything he'd had – in that case, his time and effort – with the same shaky hope that a poker player experiences when he pushes his whole pot into the centre of the baize. Waterman had discovered puzzles when he was ten, a year after his father died. What began as a distraction quickly became an obsession. An attempt to fill an unfillable void.

Now he had a lot more than just his own time and effort. It was no longer just him solving the puzzles. He ran the largest eavesdropping facility in Europe. Had almost eight thousand staff. Access to the deepest intelligence reports. The most powerful supercomputers in the world. And Cassandra was meant to be the next step. An analytical way to predict the future. Waterman had allocated millions of pounds from his budget to develop her.

But it was becoming clear to him that Cassandra was an exercise in hubris. Even with GCHQ's access to data, its quantum computing power and the most sophisticated AI software on the planet, Cassandra could not simulate intuition. And without intuition, forecasting of human behaviour was next to impossible. The possibilities were so endless that probabilities of any outcome rarely went into double-digit percentages of likelihood.

Salt was right. The data was never enough.

He opened the spreadsheet of calculations and stared at the thousands of rivers of code that ran down the page. Somewhere in there might be the cell to recode. A needle hidden in a countryside of haystacks.

For the first time, he understood Salt's interest in Sara Eden. Yes, Waterman could trust data. It would never betray him or let him down. But it wasn't enough. If Sara's ability was real, it could be the deciding factor in the life-and-death decisions Waterman faced every day. Results were the issue. Trust was secondary.

A shrill sound sliced through the silence. His mobile phone was vibrating on the desk. He twisted the screen so it faced him.

UNKNOWN CALLER.

Only key staff had this number. He picked it up, but before he could answer, another sound layered onto the mobile phone's.

A house phone was also ringing. House phone? He didn't even know he had a house phone. No one he knew had the number. Susie and the girls always called his mobile. He began to hunt around the room, looking for a base or handset.

As he did, another sound emerged, higher in pitch, rising in urgency, knitting itself into the existing two sounds.

It was coming from his laptop screen.

His Skype window was open and the sound of crickets, the default alert of choice, chirruped from the speakers.

Choosing from the options available, Waterman picked up the mobile and answered the call.

Two minutes later he was in the shower, and a few minutes thereafter, hastily throwing an overnight bag together. From what he had just heard, he might not be home again for a few days.

Before he left, he sat on the edge of the bed and placed his hand over Susie's. She was still fast asleep. He watched her chest rise and fall. He wanted to say goodbye – she always hated it when he left without a word – but she looked so peaceful. After giving her hand a gentle squeeze, he quietly headed downstairs.

As he stepped out through the front door, the pre-dawn air stung his cheeks and brought tears to his eyes. In front of the garden gate, a black Mercedes was already waiting, floating on a cloud of exhaust fumes.

The call from Salt had been short and informed him of only two things.

First, a helicopter was waiting at a private airfield a mile away. It would have no other passengers and would depart immediately upon his arrival, taking him directly to GCHQ.

Second, the latest round of intercepts confirmed

Black Dawn had procured their C-4. An attack was imminent, and finding the Black Dawn terrorist from the forty suspects was GCHQ's top priority.

Waterman waited until he was sitting in the back of the car before telephoning Salt. He'd made up his mind.

'Call Sara Eden. This will be her first deployment.'

PART TWO

5

Lying in her hospital bed, Sara's eyes rolled underneath her closed lids. Her breathing became ragged. Her fingertips twitched. The sonar-ping of the EKG machine picked up pace, the silence between the pulses becoming shorter. It would not be surprising for the victim of a savage attack to re-imagine the violent episode during her sleep. The subconscious's main remedial measure for trauma is to re-stage.

But Sara was not dreaming about her recent kidnap and near murder.

She was experiencing a recurring nightmare, which had plagued her since her teenage years.

In her dream, Sara was sprinting. But her quarry had too much of a head start. Sara caught only fleeting glimpses as the runner rounded corners. Wisps of brown hair, a disappearing heel. She was becoming increasingly desperate, knowing what was at stake if she could not catch up. Tonight, as Sara lay in the hospital, it seemed she was closing the gap. For the first time, she saw patches of clothing as she rounded corners. The legs of a tracksuit, a swishing ponytail.

The EKG spiked again, the LED display jumping wildly. One of Sara's hands rose from the bed, fingers extending, reaching for thin air.

Now in her dream someone was calling Sara's name. The voice seemed to be coming simultaneously from above and behind her, distracting her from the chase. She ignored it, but the voice became louder, more insistent.

Then the world flashed white and her eyes were opening onto a new one. She looked around the hospital room. The only colour was on the opposite wall, a framed abstract print of a slash of red on a cream canvas. Grey dawn light peeped around the edges of the blinds. She took it all in.

'Sara . . . Sara.'

He was perched on the edge of the chair by her bed. He was in his fifties. Solidly built, filling his lab coat so it bunched up slightly under his arms. Clean-shaven head. She could tell from his glazed eyes that he hadn't slept yet.

'Sorry to wake you. Seemed like you were having a pretty intense dream. I'm Dr Anders.'

She had seen him before. He'd measured her pulse yesterday, during a brief period when she had been awake, in her hospital gown on a trolley. When his fingers pressed to her wrist, something flashed into her mind for the briefest of seconds. Anders crouched in a street, in his shirtsleeves, pushing his bunched-up jacket under a woman's neck as she lay prone on the concrete. He tilted her head and pressed his lips to hers. His hands were shaking and spittle sprayed onto the woman's cheek when his cheeks inflated. Pedestrians stopped and watched silently, aware of the gravity of what was happening. Sara didn't know if this was the past or the future, or who the woman was to Anders, but she could tell from the rising panic on his face that the woman meant something to him. Possibly everything.

Sara had never known where the flashes came from. At various points in her life she had thought they were signs of madness, or the product of an active imagination recycling images she'd subconsciously seen somewhere. Most of the time they were impossible to verify, and she had learnt the hard way that sharing them with another person rarely achieved anything other than disbelief and anger. But she couldn't dismiss them as easily. The flashes stayed with her, imbuing her with a constant sense of dread.

'I wanted to check in on you. My shift just ended.' He paused, but when she didn't respond, continued: 'You've made a remarkable recovery, all things considered. Your vital signs have stabilized. We'd like to move you to outpatient care soon. Probably in two or three days.'

He reached for her wrist to take her pulse, but this time she pulled it away, slipping both hands under the covers. He nodded stoically and patted the top of the covers.

'Sorry, you just woke up.'

The memory of her dream returned to Sara. Not the flash from contact with Anders but her own dream. She had been so close. Close enough that her hands had begun to reach out, fingertips extended. Closer than ever before. A few more steps might have done it, might have closed the gap for good this time. And as the futility of this realization settled on her, the tight-chested feeling of urgency that survived the dream now melted into an all-consuming ache in her heart.

'Is she a friend of yours?'

The doctor was looking at her inquisitively.

'Who?'

'Gemma,' he said. 'You said her name in your sleep a few times.'

Sara twisted in her bed so he couldn't see her face crumple.

6

After he'd left, she listened to his shoes squeaking down the corridor until the only sound in the room was the solitary hum of the air vents above her.

Her emotions were coming in waves. The gnawing sadness was ebbing away and, in its place, an over-powering guilt was rising. No matter how fast she ran, it was never enough to save Gemma.

She lifted her chest, attempting to roll herself into a seated position. Pain lanced her side, intense enough that she gasped. Her head collapsed back onto the starched pillowcase. She could feel the stitches in the skin under her arm stressing with pressure.

She gritted her teeth and lifted her head again, rolling forward to compensate for the pain in her side. There was only one way she knew to alleviate the guilt. Find someone new. Protect another innocent.

This time, she managed to pull herself upright. Her bare feet dangled over the side of the bed. Above the sheets, her skin felt cold under the hospital gown, goosebumps clacking up her back. She slowly slipped off the bed, her bare toes touching the linoleum floor.

Her clothes lay in a neat pile on a chair by the window. She tested her weight on her feet, but almost immediately her knees began to buckle. The IV-drip stand was within reach and she gripped it as a support, lifting herself until her body weight was resting on the stand, then using it as a crutch to cross the room. As she moved, she conducted a quick audit of her physical health. Her mouth was desert-dry and a migraine split her head in two. She wouldn't get far unless she could replenish her energy.

When she reached the chair, she sank down on it to get her breath. Her clothes smelt freshly laundered and someone had ironed and folded them neatly. The only evidence of the attack was a six-inch repair running down one side of her blouse, as neat as the needlework in her own skin.

She pulled her clothes on and made an attempt at grooming her hair in the small mirror above the sink on the other side of the window. She never wore make-up and spent little time primping, but she didn't want to attract unnecessary attention. There wasn't much she could do about the cut on her nose or the bruised left side of her face. Most likely, people would assume she had a jealous boyfriend. She gripped the IV stand again and stood up, then let go and took an exploratory step forward. Her knees held this time. She took another.

The corridor was empty, but for a snack vending machine. Sara pulled some coins from her jacket and rolled them into the slot. A protein bar and a Diet Coke shunted forward on their respective shelves and clattered into the hatch. She drank the Coke in three greedy gulps, feeling the jolt of caffeine like a battery spark.

'Where are you going?'

He was standing at the far end of the corridor, by the lifts. She turned in the opposite direction, casing for another exit, but could see the only other way out went directly through the nurses' station. There were too many staff milling around to make a viable escape.

She turned back to him, taking a decent bite of her malty protein bar. Her strength was returning. She sized him up. He was large, a block of muscle and bone in a black suit that looked two sizes too small for him. One finger pressed an earphone deeper into his ear. The other hand held back the flap of his jacket, exposing the holstered Glock 17.

Energy was flowing back through her limbs. She knew, if she wanted to, she could cover the ground between them in two long strides. A downward jab of her heel to the top of his patella would drive the knee-cap several inches down his shin. Then, as his head plunged down in reaction to the leg injury, a forearm slam to the back of the skull. It would all happen quicker than it would take for him to reach for his holster. But that wasn't the plan today.

'Call Waterman. Tell him I'm ready.'

He looked confused and bemused. She didn't blame him. The face she had seen in the mirror looked anything but ready, and she was leaning to one side to protect her injured flank. He held up the index finger of one hand. 'Don't move.'

He raised his hand and spoke into his sleeve. 'This is Barrett. She's on the move. Says she wants to come in.'

His eyes never left hers as he listened to the response. The guard ended the call without any sign-off and dialled another number immediately.

'I need a car and escort in front of Thomas' right away.'

The guard motioned her towards the lift. Sara finished her protein bar and followed his direction.

The doors opened on the ground floor and they walked down a short corridor and into a huge, vaulted atrium, the guard tight at her side. The hospital was a hollowed-out shell, with exposed lift shafts and pedestrian gangways that criss-crossed the airspace. Ahead, medics in scrubs sat around tables in a café, the faint smell of disinfectant battling with the burnt-almond aroma of brewing coffee. On her left was the waiting room for Accident and Emergency, an area of the ground floor sectioned off by rows of brown plastic chairs arranged in front of a check-in desk. Pockets of people were spread across the waiting area, sitting on chairs, staring at the floor or checking the screens to see if they had been called.

Out of nowhere, a body rounded the corner and collided with Sara. Hands grabbed her wrists as a woman attempted to stop herself falling, skin pressing to skin. In the moment of contact, Sara's world powered down. Sara could see her as if she was staring through the wrong end of a telescope. It was a woman in her thirties in a hospital gown. Dark sunken eyes stared out from the rim of a floral chemo beanie. Her grip was so insubstantial that Sara could barely feel it. Then the physics of the collision tipped the woman backwards and the skin contact was broken. The lights powered on again and the guard was suddenly sandwiching himself between them, forcing Sara back, his arms wide to protect her. Sara looked at the woman in the bright lights. She was now expensively dressed and at least forty pounds heavier. The beanie was gone and long blonde hair fell in a mane on one shoulder. For the first time, Sara noticed two young children standing beside her.

'Sorry, my head's in the clouds,' said the woman, getting up and giving Sara an apologetic smile. One of the children reached out and held her mother's hand.

'You all right?' The protection officer was looking into Sara's face. She nodded.

She'd been so focused on leaving the hospital that she'd forgotten to put on her gloves. She reached into the pockets of her jacket now with trembling hands and removed them, pulling them on and walking towards the front entrance, leaving them all behind.

You can't save them, Sara. There's no point trying.

Those were her mother's watchwords.

Sara hadn't heard her mother's voice since her mother had hidden her in the care system, twenty years ago. But that voice was still perfectly preserved in her mind. Sara took a deep breath. Maybe she couldn't save them. Maybe her mother was right. She had never believed in change. Life trajectories were immutable. Set by character, genetics or dumb luck. They couldn't be steered. Just because foresight brought guilt didn't mean there was anything Sara could do about it.

A black Mercedes G-Class SUV was waiting by the kerb in front of the entrance. Blacked-out windows. The guard materialized at her elbow as she stepped up to it. He was slightly out of breath from running after her.

'Farrar will take you to Director Waterman,' he said, as he pulled open the rear door. She caught a side glimpse of the driver as she sank into the leather seat. Square jaw, regulation haircut, he could have been the other officer's twin.

Thirty minutes later they were on the elevated section of the M40. Sara laid her head against the window and stared out at the city spread below them. What she had been telling herself since leaving the hospital was beginning to sound less and less compelling. Because sometimes foresight did bring responsibility. It had with Gemma. She was the prime mover. The first casualty of Sara's ability.

7

The room exploded with light. Sara lifted her head, her eyes screwed tight to shield against the glare.

'Three minutes.'

It was her mother's voice.

Sara knew from the pressure on her eyes that it was the middle of the night. And yet, when she prised them open, her mother was fully dressed, standing at the connecting door of their hotel rooms, her hand on the light switch, two packed bags by her feet.

Sara looked at the other bed, where her brother was sitting up in his pyjamas, staring in confusion into the middle distance, his hair standing on end, like waves about to crash. His eyes were open but she could tell he was not yet fully awake.

They knew better than to argue. Sara rolled out of bed, her movements automatic. She climbed into a pair of jeans, her foggy mind allowing her body to lead. Then, like a sleep-walker, she began stripping her bed, folding the sheets and pillowcases. Christian opened the door of the wooden wardrobe. Their clothes took up one shelf only: he scooped them up and placed them

75

on his bed. Sara pulled their athletics bag from under her bed and began stuffing the clothes into it.

There was nothing else in the hotel room to collect. No toys. No photographs. No mementos. They travelled as cleanly as monks who'd taken a vow of poverty.

Three minutes later she and Christian stood at the door. Their mother walked into the room carrying a bucket and a bottle of antiseptic. They watched as she sprayed the surfaces, then wiped them down, her hand moving in slow, methodical circles.

A few minutes later, they walked down the hotel corridor. Through the windows on one side they could see the poorly lit car park and the tail of their truck, parked behind a skip at the far end. When they stepped outside, the air was freezing and assaulted their bare skin.

Sara held the back door of the truck open for Christian. He ignored her and walked past, getting into the front passenger seat.

'I didn't like the look of that receptionist. Hotels aren't safe any more,' said her mother, to no one in particular as she buckled her seat belt.

And with that, they drove off. Sara looked through the back window at the hotel in which, five minutes ago, she had been fast asleep.

She made no complaint. They had been on the run for as long as she could remember from a pursuer neither she nor her brother had ever met.

*

This time they drove for hours, avoiding main roads, along empty back streets lit by diffuse cones of light from streetlamps. She must have drifted off again because she was jarred awake by the interior lights of the truck flipping on and the tolling clang of the open door. She was lying curled up on the seat, her head tucked down. Her mother crouched in front of the open door, holding a pizza slice in one hand and a can of Coke in the other.

'You have to share it. We're almost out of money.'

Sara rubbed her eyes. They were in the floodlit forecourt of a petrol station, puffy-eyed drivers leaning on their cars, fuel pipes snaking from the pumps like black umbilical cords. Sara took the offerings, tore the pizza slice in half and gave one piece to Christian, who took it without looking at her.

They continued driving, the sky dawning orange on the horizon. The landscape downshifted. Flat land and green countryside spread in every direction. The occasional farm was the only relief in the expanse of fields and clumps of scrub. They were driving through a tiny village when her mother spoke. 'This looks good.'

The truck took a few turnings at random until they were driving along a cul-de-sac, council houses on either side. They stopped in front of one house, a boxy structure that looked too narrow for its floor space, front door and living-room window bunched almost together. A battered and faded 'For Sale' sign was stuck into the lawn. Her mother left the truck and walked up to the house, staring through the front window.

'Looks like it's been vacant for a while,' she said, her face pressed to the glass. Then she kicked the 'For Sale' sign a few times, grasped it and shook it, wresting it from the ground. She threw it into the back of the truck.

Sara walked down the garden path and looked through the front window. The grime was so thick she could barely make out the tiny living room. Discarded black cable lay on the floor amid dust balls. 'Why are we running?' said Sara to herself, her voice barely above a whisper.

'Because they're not going to stop searching for us.'

She hadn't realized her mother was standing next to her.

Phoebe walked towards the truck.

'Wait, where are you going?' asked Sara.

'Into town, to get supplies.'

'What should I say if someone sees me?' asked Sara.

'No one's going to notice a ten-year-old,' said her mother.

Christian, standing next to her, was staring at Sara, a vague smile on his face. 'And they're not coming for us. They're coming for you,' he said, with a sneer.

'C'mon, Christian!' Hearing his mother's shout, he turned and followed her to the truck.

There wasn't much to explore while they were gone. The house was locked. The front lawn was a patch of worn grass barely larger than a family car. A path by the side of the house led to the back garden, which looked like the dumping ground for the rest of the estate. Broken furniture, white plastic bags crammed with refuse, a mattress spring and an old fridge covered the ground between the two neighbours' fences.

'Who was that charming creature?'

Sara turned to see a girl her age peering over the fence. Large, wide-set, feline eyes. An Afro pulled into two twisted braids. 'He's usually not that bad,' said Sara.

'Usually much worse, then?' asked the girl.

Sara walked over towards the fence. 'Yes, how did you know?'

A smacking sound heralded a scuffed trainer appearing on top of the fence. Two hands gripped the slats and the girl vaulted over with surprising grace. She was dressed in a blue tracksuit, a school logo emblazoned across the chest and arms.

'I've got one of the little shits myself. Three years younger. I'm Gemma.'

She was holding out her hand. Sara eyed it warily. Gemma took a step closer. 'I don't bite.'

Sara made a decision and put her own hand into Gemma's. And in that moment, she saw everything that was to come. Damp palms pressed together on walks around the estate. Whispered secrets in crawl-spaces, heads so close they could see the palimpsest of their own faces written across bright irises. Gemma would become her best friend. She would teach Sara that she wasn't alone in the world. She would give her hope. And in the end, she would take it all away.

8

'We're less than a mile away.'

Sara snapped awake, suddenly aware of the pain radiating up her neck. She'd slept with her head at an awkward angle, her temple pressed to the window.

She looked closely at Farrar for the first time in the journey. She presumed he worked for Waterman. Or Salt. GCHQ had a security force of at least a hundred and fifty, each licensed to carry firearms. He would have been told nothing about his passenger other than to get her there safely.

The dual carriageway twisted around a corner and she caught a first glimpse of the main GCHQ building through a line of thinning birches. The huge steel circular structure looked surreal in the picturesque Cotswolds, like the discarded hubcap of a vast interplanetary vehicle.

Farrar flipped his indicator and turned off onto a side road, away from the main entrance.

She guessed that it was Waterman's idea to bring her in by the heavy goods bay. Guests who arrived at the front of GCHQ were subject not only to ID checks but were also surreptitiously photographed and scanned in the vaulted lobby with facial-recognition software in the black orbs that studded the ceiling.

The sentry waved the SUV through, lifting the barricade so it could pass. The road tipped down at an incline and, ahead, Sara could see the entrance to a huge tunnel, tall enough to provide access to even the largest HGV.

A feeling of disquiet fluttered in her stomach. The secretive organization several hundred feet above her head held its fingers to the world's pulse. It listened to the undersea cables that carried the world's web traffic and phone calls. It accessed emails and social-media accounts across the globe. It flipped switches on laptops and mobile phones, surreptitiously activating built-in cameras. It tapped into CCTV and police body cams. While others slept, GCHQ listened and watched. It brooked no secrets. She had come in from the cold but, if this project did not work, it would be difficult to return to hiding.

They drove for a quarter-mile before turning into a cavernous chamber the size of several indoor stadia.

'Director Waterman said he'll meet you in the lift.'

When she opened her door, the space was a cacophonous echo chamber of beeping reversing lorries, the rumble of heavy machinery and barked orders. A musty smell hung in the air and condensation clung to bare rock walls. Directly in front of her was a loading bay with a lift door set into the far wall. An illuminated panel above it showed an ascending sequence of numbers – 5, 6, 7 – as a car descended from ground level. When it reached 9, the doors opened.

Waterman was the only occupant. The sight of him

was always jarring to Sara. He looked more like a professional wrestler than a spy, albeit a wrestler in a custom-made suit. An expensive tie emerged from the undergrowth of his thick black beard. She stepped in. When the doors closed, they sliced off the din of the loading bay as deftly as scissors cutting string. They were instantly standing in snug silence.

'So, you decided to discharge yourself?'

Waterman's strong Yorkshire accent lent everything he said an ironic twang.

'I'm fine,' said Sara.

Waterman held her eyes for a few seconds, his face sceptical. He pressed the button for the eighth, one floor above them. They stood awkwardly together. She had met him only a handful of times. Since she'd reached out to Salt, Waterman had been her main point of contact. She knew Salt had charged him with the job of clearing her for deployment. Waterman oversaw the project with the same level of scepticism she would have expected had he been informed that Sara's family power was invisibility. Their interactions were brief, and most of the time his head was buried in the screen of his iPhone.

The lift doors opened onto a corridor that was in direct contrast to the rough-hewn aesthetic of the loading bay one storey below. The passageway had smooth slate walls, poured-concrete floors and recessed lighting. Waterman led the way to the first door and ran his security card through a wall-mounted swipe box. There was the sound of a heavy rod dropping and he pushed the door open. The room resembled a bunker, with a low ceiling and a polished wooden table so large it must have been assembled where it stood. Plasma screens ran around the outer perimeter wall, playing terrestrial and satellite news channels.

'They switched on the TVs but not the heating. Sorry,' muttered Waterman, walking to a wall heater and searching for the control panel. 'We use this room for off-book meetings.' He opened a flap and pressed a button. 'There. Give it a few minutes.' He sat down on the far side of the table, his hands folded.

'So, can I tell you about a friend of mine?' He started without preamble.

Sara looked at him in surprise. Waterman never talked *to* her. He talked *at* her, relaying various orders of Salt's, she presumed, but there was never anything personal in the interactions. He went through the motions, most often slightly resentfully, like a middle manager forced to give an office tour to the boss's kid. But now he was looking straight at her. There was no iPhone in sight. No distractions at all. She had his attention.

'Is that a rhetorical question, Director Waterman?'

Waterman smiled. 'I suppose so. My friend is a behaviour-detection officer. Works for a major airline. She's a second line of defence to the scanning machines. Sits at a desk all day and looks at monitors of CCTV cams stationed above Heathrow's screening halls. Pretty good at her job. Flagged something recently. Family of five flying together. Do you know why she flagged them?'

'I'm guessing that's another rhetorical question.'

'Yes, it is. My friend couldn't put her finger on it, but said it had something to do with the wife's manicure. She thought it was too perfect for a mother of three. So, they pulled the mother in. Found out the kids weren't hers. The couple were running drugs. Borrowed the kids as decoys.'

'You want to know how your friend knew?'

Waterman nodded. 'Of course. Most of the world's communications flow through this building. I have more computer-processing power by square foot than anywhere else on the planet. We see pretty much everything. But a person's manicure is not a data point I would ever flag. So, I became a bit obsessed with that story after she told me. And, without my friend knowing, I pulled her employer files. Found something pretty interesting. In the last twelve months, there were nine drug busts on *arriving* flights on my friend's employer's airline. That means nine times in the last year passengers on her airline were only caught when the plane *landed*. So, she caught one but missed nine. Interesting, isn't it?'

'Almost as interesting as the fact that you snoop on your friends,' said Sara. She was getting to know more about Waterman in these last few minutes than she had in the whole time she had known him.

'I snoop on everyone,' said Waterman, the smile fading from his face. 'My point is, I wanted to believe. We all want to believe in things like intuition. We remember the one time the hunch was right, not the nine times it was wrong.'

Sara lifted up her hands and took off her gloves. She stretched out her arms towards him, palms up. 'If it's so bogus, you won't mind holding my hands then.'

Waterman looked warily at her. He pulled back his hands from the table. 'Did you know Joe Briggs was going to die that night?'

Sara didn't blame him for not having the courage of his doubts. As the keeper of the nation's secrets, he had more to lose than most. Anyway, she didn't need to touch him to know what lay behind this conversation. He was looking for some ledge to stand on before taking a leap of faith into the void.

'After Salt assigned me,' he continued, 'I looked into some of the literature on psychic power. There's a lot of speculative analysis. Scientists trying to put a non-science into their own vocabulary. It's not very helpful. The problem is, no literature on the subject has been written by psychics.'

Sara wanted to help him. She could see he was struggling to make the jump. But how do you describe something irrational in a rational way? She had spent her entire life trying to create some sense of where her flashes came from and had come up empty. Only one person had ever described it to her in a way that resonated.

'My mother described it best,' she said. 'The future and the present are connected, like links in a chain. The butterfly beats its wings and the tsunami arrives days later. If I had connected to the butterfly, I'd have seen the tsunami coming. But I couldn't tell you how

86

they were connected. One or two links in the chain is all I get to see. To answer your question, I knew he was going to die. I just didn't know how.'

Waterman breathed out slowly through pursed lips. 'The problem is that it makes it difficult for me to prove.' He looked sceptical, but she could tell her mother's description had landed with him. There was a subtle shift in the energy in the room. He leant forward, his hands back on the table.

'There's only one sort of proof I can give you,' said Sara. 'Find me a new project.'

Waterman reached into a pocket and pulled out his iPhone. 'I have something for you. But before that I have one last question.'

'Go on,' said Sara. She could tell he'd saved the best for last. His mind moved methodically, testing everything to collapse before moving on. Whatever the next question was, it was the last obstacle to clear before he became invested in their process.

'You were almost killed the night before last. I would have thought a near-deadly attack was a pretty important link in the chain. You didn't see that one coming?'

Sara knew the answer to this question because it, too, was part of her mother's credo. Although it was the one part that Sara wasn't sure she believed. 'I don't get to choose what I see.'

9

'Who was that girl I saw you talking to?'

Her mother walked around the kitchen, lighting candles. She and Christian had returned two hours after they'd left, lugging boxes from a local home-supply shop. The flap of one now covered the broken windowpane in the back door. Upstairs, blankets taken from the hotel lay on the floor of the main bedroom in two-dimensional simulacra of beds.

'No one,' said Sara. The kitchen was still bare, but now gleaming from the antiseptic scrubbing her mother had administered.

'She's the next-door neighbour,' said Christian. He stood by the door, watching them. 'I saw her.'

Her mother froze in the act of striking a match. 'You touched her?'

'No,' said Sara. She didn't look away as her mother locked eyes with her, staring her down.

'Here,' said her mother to Christian, passing him a fistful of candles. 'Light them and put them around the house. Nothing in the front rooms overlooking the street. Sara, with me.'

Her mother opened the back door and led Sara into

89

the garden. At dusk, the half-light softened the sharper edges of the ruined garden, making it seem less like a refuse tip.

'What did you see?'

'Nothing,' said Sara, struggling to keep her face neutral. The images she had seen when Gemma's hand had pressed into hers were seared into her mind. Terrible things Sara had never imagined were part of this world. She wanted desperately to share what she had seen with her mother, to co-opt her into some plan to save Gemma. But she knew what she would say: 'You can't save them, Sara. You know that.'

Her mother crouched so she was at eye-level with her daughter. Sara could see her face clearly now. There was no anger, just the hunted look of a fugitive who'd spent so long evading capture that running was now first nature.

'I don't know whether you really understand all this yet, Sara, but when they find us, they'll take you from me. It's the end of us. Just because I know it's going to happen doesn't mean I won't stop running for as long as I can.'

Sara looked at the dismal garden and the row of tiny identical houses on either side of the fences. There was nothing distinguishing about this neighbourhood, nothing significant upon which an eye could get purchase. It felt like they had fallen off the face of the world into an anonymous netherland. 'Maybe they won't find us here.'

Her mother sighed and sat cross-legged on the stone step jutting out from the lip of the door. She brushed the skirt over her knees. 'I see things too. Maybe not like you. But I do see things. You've shown them to me,

90

whenever I've touched you. I've seen how they catch us. We give ourselves away.'

The light had almost gone and her mother's face was lit by the faint glow from the candle seeping through the kitchen window. With her thick brown hair, narrow shoulders and long limbs poking through her summer dress, Sara experienced a dislocating sense that she was looking at the future version of herself. Would she become like her mother, choosing a life that was just about survival, just trying to get to the next day?

'Can we change the way we are?' she asked.

'No,' her mother said at last. 'No one can change the past. Or the future.' She looked away, over the tops of the fences that surrounded their home, to the identical plots that spread out as far as the eye could see. Sara could tell her mother was experiencing the same strange randomness she was feeling.

'What can you see when you connect?' asked Sara.

'They called it second sight in my day,' said her mother. 'But that's wrong. You can *control* sight. But we can't control what comes to us when we connect. If we could, we'd never choose to see the things we do.'

Something about the subject snapped her mother out of her reverie. She stood up, brushing the dust from her skirt. When she looked back at Sara, her face had returned to an implacable mask. 'Telling that girl anything is like setting off a flare into the sky.'

10

Waterman pulled a remote control from a drawer in the table and began changing the channels on the screens around them. One by one, the rolling images of TV news were replaced by static head shots. Mostly men but some women. Some photos were mug-shots, with serial numbers running along the bottom; others were blown-up surveillance photos, the detail grainy and pixilated.

'So, this is the next project?' asked Sara, twisting around to look at them all. It was as if she and Waterman were being scrutinized by a silent gallery.

Waterman nodded. 'Yes. These are "persons of interest" in connection with a terror cell. Some are family members, others friends. For some we don't know the connection, just that they've been named in intercepts. We don't have the manpower to put surveillance on them all. Nor do we have enough on most of them to get a judge to sign off on it. Normally, at this point, we'd need one to make a mistake, to give us more intel. And we don't have time to arrange for you to connect physically with each of them. Our intel suggests the strike is imminent.'

Sara stood up and walked to the nearest monitor. A woman in her twenties, her hair in a ponytail, stared at the camera with blank black eyes. Her neck and shoulder-blades were covered with tiny print tattoos in a language Sara didn't understand.

'Can you get anything from a photo?' asked Waterman. Sara noticed that the habitual irony was now missing from his tone. He appeared to be genuinely engaged.

'It's not the same as touching someone. But photographs and intimate possessions of people, even those who are dead . . .' Her voice trailed off. What did she want to say? She'd never had to explain this to anyone before. Any words she chose felt inadequate: too much was lost in the translation from the intuitive to the rational. 'Touching a photograph isn't as visceral as connecting to someone with physical touch. There isn't the cascade of images I get with skin to skin . . .' She trailed off again.

When she had touched a photo or keepsake, there were one or two flashes, like Polaroid bulbs going off in quick succession in a dark room. It could be shocking, faces staring back at her, strange objects in the periphery that were impossible to define. She had to be ready to glean everything she could in a fraction of a second.

She could feel Waterman's need to map her ability, to produce a schematic he could use for the future. She had never tried to articulate why her power worked in different ways. It had always seemed obvious to her that an inanimate object would betray less about its owner or subject than physical contact with the person. But why? Snatched memories of half-remembered conversations with her mother replayed indistinctly in her head, whispers about 'energy' and the attenuating relationship between a subject and the medium of connection, but any deeper understanding remained stubbornly outside her reach. She realized that Waterman was looking at her expectantly.

'Sorry, still trying to find a vocabulary for this,' said Sara.

Waterman nodded stoically. 'Don't worry, it will come.'

She reached out for the screen, laying the tips of her right index and middle finger on the surface. After a minute, she broke contact, looking up at Waterman and giving a minute shake of her head. 'Not her.'

'OK. Why?' asked Waterman, patiently.

There was something else she hadn't mentioned to Waterman. Each connection created an intimacy between Sara and the subject. The power to make someone unwillingly disclose their secrets needed, in her mind, a check and balance, and the bargain she had made with herself when she'd decided to come in was that she would always receive the secrets as a faithful trustee, and only breach the confidence if the need felt overpowering.

'I . . . She's not involved.'

Waterman lifted his iPhone from his jacket pocket and swiped his finger several times across the surface. 'That's Jana Bojic. She's got at least one prior for being a mule for a Serb money-laundering gang.'

'You said you're looking for a connection to missing explosives. She doesn't have one.'

'If you have *any* valuable information on Bojic, I want it.'

Sara shook her head.

'Why do you think you're here?' asked Waterman.

The answer to his question was becoming increasingly clear: the overpowering appeal of having her was to see into people's minds, to the moment when the plan was hatched, before any incriminating words or actions began.

'I'm here to stop innocent people getting killed,' she said.

'Supplying information on suspects will protect people against being killed.'

'That woman, Jana Bojic, has four younger brothers in a one-room apartment in Belgrade who depend on her wire transfers. She is not a terrorist.'

'It's a quick step from money-laundering to terror-financing.'

'And I'm telling you she never takes that step.'

Waterman was quiet for some time.

'That's the way it's going to be?' he said at last. 'Intel I can never verify. Conclusions I can never validate.'

'It's right or it's not. If it's right, it's going to have value to you. If it's not, I'm a fraud or a fool and of no use to you.'

Waterman took a deep breath. After a few seconds, he picked up the phone sitting on the table and dialled a number. 'Email me the background file on Jana Bojic.'

He put the phone down and walked over to his iPhone, which he'd left on the desk. Shielding it from

Sara's sight, he flicked his finger through several pages. After a few moments, he looked up at her. His face registered surprise and confusion. 'You've never seen or heard of Jana Bojic before just now?'

Sara nodded.

'Would you be willing to take a polygraph to confirm that?'

Sara allowed herself a smile. 'I suppose that means you've received some corroboration.'

'Bojic is one of five siblings. Four brothers and her.' Waterman's expression was shifting, surprise and engagement slowly emerging from his habitual look of bemused scepticism.

'Shall I keep going?' asked Sara.

He nodded blankly. She laid her fingertips on the surface of the next mug-shot. After a few seconds, she shook her head. This time, Waterman didn't press her. She repeated the process, going from screen to screen, slowly moving clockwise around the room. After she had completed one wall, she stood for a moment, breathing hard, her hands pressed under her armpits. The things she had seen were jangling through her.

'Can I have a glass of water?'

Waterman stood up and opened a cupboard, tilting his head to look inside. He pulled out a bottle of water and poured her a glass. Sara noticed him staring at her shaking hand as she drank it in one.

'Is it always bad things?' he asked.

Once again, Sara struggled to put the experience into words. It wasn't about good or bad. Some memories just had more power than others. The more traumatic or joyful they were, the deeper they seemed to stamp themselves into a person's psyche. Even when those memories hadn't happened yet.

'Not always,' she eventually replied.

She was standing next to Waterman now. The next photo was of a man with dreadlocks pulled into a pony-tail, dressed in a baggy T-shirt, jeans and a pair of Jordan Courtside 23 sneakers. A blurred surveillance photo had snapped him stepping off a pavement, one hand cupped around his mouth while the other pressed a lighter to the tip of the cigarette he was holding between puckered lips.

'Darius Maric,' said Waterman, rolling the next name off the list. 'Freelance audio engineer.'

Sara let her fingers rest on the glossy surface. She closed her eyes. After a few seconds, her breath became ragged and she pulled her fingers away as if she had been burnt.

'Bodies. Everywhere. Women. Children.'

11

Waterman stood up abruptly.

'Where?'

Sara had taken a step back from the screen. The images were still shuddering through her. What looked like sandbags, several deep, covering a street, were in fact mutilated bodies. A ruined mountain of flesh.

'Sara.'

She snapped back to the present, looking at Waterman in surprise. 'It's him. Maric.'

Waterman seemed doubtful, staring at his iPhone, sliding his finger down the screen. 'Are you sure? Maric is a supplier. Mostly drugs to bands. There's some evidence he skims money for terror groups. But nothing to suggest he's been radicalized.'

Sara stared back at Maric's photo. 'It's him. And you're wrong. It's personal for him.'

'Is he alone?'

Sara shook her head. 'There's someone else with him. The other person has the bomb strapped to them.'

Waterman indicated the screens that surrounded them. 'Do you see the person here?'

'No,' said Sara. 'It's not anyone here.'

Waterman didn't speak for some time. When he did,

it was as if he'd come out of a daze. 'Where does this happen?'

She looked back at the screen, suddenly reticent about reconnecting. Her feet seemed frozen too. There was something obscene about the carcasses in that junction. People rearranged into meat. Seeing them again was the last thing she wanted.

'Sara?' Waterman was staring at her expectantly.

She took a deep breath and forced herself to approach the monitor, reaching out and pressing her fingers to the screen. In her mind's eye, a fireball rolled upwards over a crowded intersection, while the blast and shock waves lifted cars like they were tin cans and flipped them into shop windows. A thick black cloud filled the air. Then, after a throb of shocked silence, isolated cries of panic quickly became a chorus. She winced involuntarily, but forced herself to look up from the carnage at the surrounding area.

'It's a wide junction. Multiple pedestrian crossings. The cross-street is heaving with crowds.' She broke contact with the screen, then let her fingers reconnect, the scene replaying. She looked around to glean more detail. This time, she forced herself to look at the bodies. Could she tell anything from ethnicity, from their clothing? What remained of them looked European, their clothing Western. But the street could have been in any town or city in Europe.

'There's so many people,' said Sara, her eyes searching Maric's impassive features. She was so close to his face now that it had become a pixilated blur. 'It's not just a busy shopping day. There are . . . hundreds of people crowding the streets and the pavement. It looks like some sort of protest or march.'

She was sailing right into the heart of the storm, where her mother had told her never to go. She was trying to save them all. And now, unless she could stop it, it would feel like their blood was on her hands. She needed more detail, but getting it was almost impossible. The image was elusive, shaking and juddering at the edges, melting into different perspectives. She broke contact with her fingers and pressed them to the surface again to make the scene reboot.

'Start with the basics, Sara.'

Sara nodded. He was right.

'It's daylight,' she said. 'The sky is bright. It feels like midday. No clouds.'

'What else?'

'There are shops lining both sides of the street.'

'What else?'

'The shop signs. They're in a language I don't understand.'

The images were vibrating so violently it was difficult to get a fix on them. Her eyes kept sliding off them, the writing twisting and fishtailing. Close to the edge of the frame, a green awning was torn apart by a concussion wave, sailing up into the sky, revealing white signage running along the top of the shop. Sara focused on it and began reading it out loud.

'I see a few letters . . . A . . . P . . . O . . .'

The front window of the shop suddenly buckled in

slow motion, then blasted outwards, a million glass fragments spraying into the street, simultaneously turning the inside into a swirling maelstrom of debris. She saw the interior for a fraction of a second. Plastic bottles on shelves. Stacks of nappies. A recessed office at the rear packed with what looked like medicine packets and bottles. A cardboard stand of two beaming models, all white tank tops and perfect teeth, was positioned near the back of the shop.

'It looks like a chemist . . .'

'Chemist is *"Apotheker"* in German,' said Waterman, hesitantly. 'That could be the APO you saw . . .' He stopped himself, unwilling to prompt her any further.

Sara dropped her hands and turned to face him. 'Is there a way to check what protests are scheduled in the next twenty-four hours in Germany?'

'Germany's Ministry of the Interior might know,' said Waterman, 'but each German state's laws are different. Some might not require advance notice, so there would be no record. If, indeed, it's Germany. Dutch, Danish, Swedish and Norwegian languages all have Germanic roots. Could it be in one of those countries?'

Sara could feel the sweat pricking on her back. She needed detail. Something that could reclaim this street from anonymity.

She turned back to the monitor and raised her fingers, pressing them again to the glass. She'd felt as if she'd picked the scene clean of detail and it was still not enough. The burst of light and heat from the bomb flashed again in her mind. It had such a terrible magnetic power that it was difficult to look anywhere else. Then a thought occurred to her. The blast radius was pulling all her attention, obscuring everything else. This time, she let her vision relax, allowing her peripheral sight to engage in the hope that some other detail might emerge.

Close to her, once again, the awning ripped free and whipped up into the air. She saw something as it was torn away. The barest glimpse, appearing as the green cover rolled in and out of the frame.

'There's something . . .' she said.

She couldn't decipher what she had seen. It looked bizarre, anomalous. Like something transposed from a totally different cityscape.

'There's a series of buildings,' she said quietly, 'at the far end of the street. They're in their own compound. Concrete security barriers ring the pavements around it.'

She broke away from the photo and looked back at Waterman. 'There's six buildings. The façades have a mosaic pattern. Black and white. Like a chessboard.'

Waterman frantically typed details into his iPhone. 'Seems like Europe's full of buildings with chessboard façades,' he said. He tilted the phone towards her, showing her the results of a search page with a collage of thumbnail photos. 'Mostly public buildings . . .' His voice trailed off.

'What?' asked Sara.

'Black Dawn is a Serbian terror group,' he said, under his breath. He quickly picked up the TV remote control from the table and pointed it at a nearby screen, banishing Jana Bojic's picture and returning to cable news. He rolled over channels until he found what he was looking for. It was EuroNews 24. Footage played of a stocky man in his sixties with a shock of white hair, sitting in the dock of an airy courtroom. He was listening intently through earphones attached to the desk in front of him.

'That's Vlado Bagas,' said Waterman. 'A Serbian general on trial for war crimes against Bosnian civilians. The verdict is due tomorrow. There've been protests by Bosnian survivor groups outside pretty much every day.'

Waterman flicked through his phone again, then tilted it towards Sara.

'Recognize this?'

She was looking at a photo of the building she'd seen in her vision: one large monolith surrounded by five smaller units, all with the same chequered façade.

'What is it?' asked Sara.

'The International Criminal Court,' said Waterman.

12

Soon afterwards, Waterman left Sara in the conference room to brief the various authorities involved. Having Maric's identity would create a focus for the investigation. All sea and airports would be alerted, but as the attack was to take place tomorrow, he was likely in the Netherlands already. The one missing piece was the identity of the other bomber. Without a face and a name, the authorities would still be missing half the equation.

While he was away, Sara walked slowly around the edge of the room, her fingers grazing each screen again, trying to see if there was anything she had missed. She had just finished her circuit when the door opened again and Waterman stepped in.

'I just spoke to Salt,' he said, without preamble. 'We need to know the other bomber's identity. It sounds like he, or she, is the frontline troop.'

'You'll need to do more research, then,' said Sara. 'Find me more pictures. Because it's no one in here.'

'Salt had a better idea.'

'What's that?'

'You're going to The Hague.'

13

The Hague, Netherlands

Sara watched as the bomb exploded with a brilliant flash. Three blocks away, the ground shook beneath her, jolting the car in which she was sitting, setting off alarms up and down the street.

She lifted her fingertips, breaking contact with the surface of the photograph lying in her lap, then looked out through the windscreen again.

The scene had been scrubbed, as if the needle of time had skipped backwards. Outside, hundreds of protesters once more crowded the intersection in front of the International Criminal Court. Where there had been a smoke-filled graveyard, there was once again a raucous carnival, with young and old beating drums, blowing whistles, or carrying placards with slogans in slanted Bosnian Muslim script.

The explosion was coming. She could feel it. Each time she connected with the photo, the vision became more intense, the sights and sounds more harrowing. The bomb was large. Enough to carve out a crater on the main street. Shrapnel – nails, glass and steel balls – packed into a lining around the device would create a second killing zone outside the blast radius. She knew this because she kept seeing it make mincemeat of pedestrians milling outside the police cordon. Kept seeing children's body parts lying, like doll's limbs, on the pavement. In the blink of an eye, scores of bodies would be torn apart, hundreds more injured.

She looked through the tinted windows of the BMW 7 Series in which she sat. Faces of the soon-to-be-dead-and-injured materialized in the crowd in front of her. A smiling mother crouching to wipe the chin of a toddler. In minutes, she would be lying face down, covering her child, in a vain attempt to shield him. Two teenagers held hands, leaning against a shop front, licking ice-cream cones. The blast would toss them, like ragdolls, down the street. A little girl, about seven years old, carried a cluster of tiny Bosnian Muslim flags as if they were a bouquet of flowers. Sara had just seen her lifeless body lying under rubble, her long brown hair covered with ash and blood.

All the details from her first connection to Maric's photo were around her. The cross-street, wide enough to accommodate multiple pedestrian crossings. The shops that lined each side of the street. The compound in the north corner, where the chessboard façades of six glass buildings winked in the sunlight.

Waterman had soon found the link to Maric. Both his older brothers had been killed in action while fighting for Bagas. Today was the day for him to turn any celebration of Bagas' conviction into a massacre. The judges were due to convene at eleven a.m. to deliver their verdict.

In eighteen minutes.

Since she had confirmed the location yesterday, Waterman had followed the book. He had informed MI5, saying only that the intel was from a reliable source. MI5 had passed the information on to the Dutch authorities. The Dutch had taken the tip seriously, and moved to ban any public assembly in front of the ICC. But a judge insisted the source be named before ruling. Waterman refused and, as of this morning, the protests were going ahead. A ring of steel was in place a half-mile radius around the ICC. Homes had been evacuated, bag and body searches conducted at the only two access points into the area. Sniffer dogs moved through the crowd.

And yet when she'd touched the photograph again this morning, she could still see the bomb burst open, like an angry black flower, time-lapsing towards the sky. She informed Waterman, who had advised the Dutch to do more. And they did. Although she couldn't see them from where she sat, Sara knew there were unmarked vans parked on side streets carrying armed units from the DSI, the Dutch counterterrorism squad. And on rooftops, snipers with the UEOO, the Dutch marksmen unit, stared through the scopes of their Mauser SR93 rifles. And, high above, stealth aircraft with listening equipment circled the skies, monitoring mobile-phone calls and seeking matching voiceprints for known terror suspects.

The authorities had done everything they could conceivably have been expected to do. Every precaution had been taken. Every counter-terrorism move had been played. Today represented a monumental act of trust placed by the Dutch authorities in a foreign intelligence agency that wouldn't give up its source. But Sara could still see the detonation, still see the concussion waves laying waste to the people milling around her. There was something they were missing.

A slap on her window made Sara jump. The little girl with the flags was tapping her fingers on the glass, a broad grin on her face. Sara lowered her window.

'Would you like one?' the little girl asked in accented English.

Sara reached out and took one.

'What is your name?' asked the girl.

'Sara. What's yours?'

The mother came over to the girl. 'Sorry,' she said, grabbing her daughter's hand.

'No, it's fine, but you need to . . .' The mother was already dragging the child back to the edge of the heaving crowd. Sara watched her as she followed her mother, slipping between bodies, pushing deeper into the heart of the assembly gathered in the cross-streets. Soon she was lost from Sara's sight, pressed among the other bodies in what would soon become ground zero.

'Tell them.'

She was alone in the car and spoke quietly, her eyes still riveted to the street ahead of her.

'*You know I can't.*'

Waterman's voice came through her earpiece, as if he was whispering directly into her ear, although he was, in fact, almost three hundred miles away, watching events unfold on myriad screens in the vault deep beneath GCHQ.

'They need to clear the area. It's our only chance now to . . .'

'We're not giving you up.'

'Do it.'

'How would I explain you?'

Sara took a breath. It was the same question that kept returning. They'd agreed the rules when she'd started. And it was simple because there was only one. She had to remain a secret.

14

'So, is there a reason why you're living in a house without electricity?' asked Gemma.

Sara, her mother and Christian had been there for almost a month and Sara had spent most of each day in Gemma's garden, in a bolthole Gemma had created in the space between the hedge and the back fence. A rug covered the earth below them and the branches supported track medals hanging from ribbons. Gemma bent over a writing pad, practising her signature.

'Olympic golds are worth more than they used to be,' continued Gemma, oblivious to the fact that Sara had not answered her last question. 'They're gateways to endorsement deals. You can make a lot of money now. Become a brand.'

The pen waggled like a baton as she added flourishes in different places. 'What do you think of that one?' Gemma lifted the paper to show Sara a theatrical spider's crawl at the top of the page. 'Looks more mysterious if you can't decipher it.'

Sara hesitated, twisting uncomfortably. She knew she needed to plug the gap in her credibility created by Gemma's question about their strange candlelight arrangements, but didn't want to lie or betray her family.

'Don't worry,' said Gemma, as if reading her thoughts. 'You're not the first squatters in the neighbourhood.'

Sara had received the usual invitation to Gemma's makeshift grotto that morning and Gemma had scarcely drawn breath since Sara had sat down. Sara already thought she had gathered a full biographical history of her new friend just from shaking her hand, from her domination of her school track team, to her mother's string of abusive boyfriends, to the feeling of low-ceilinged claustrophobia that came with living in the tiny village, to Gemma's determination to keep improving her sprint times until the tiny village and everything in it was left in her dust. And yet Gemma had more to tell. Her new friend's garrulousness was a relief for Sara, bringing with it companionship without the attendant need for disclosure.

'Do you know who holds the under-twelves 200-metres record? Usain Bolt. Broke it back in 1986 – 20.58 seconds. Then he broke his own record. Three more times that year. Shaved it down to 19.93.' Gemma lay on her stomach, her feet kicking up behind her. 'I'm at 22.38. If I can get down to 22.00 I go to national trials.'

From where they were sitting, Sara could just about see the kitchen window of Gemma's house through the branches of the hedge. The glare of the sun turned it into a vertical puddle of light, the interior gloomy and camouflaged, murky shapes moving inside. One loomed large, staring at them across the length of the garden. Sara could feel her discomfort growing under the gaze. She shifted so her back was to the house, then realized Gemma was quiet, for the first time since she had invited Sara over that day.

'How come you've never asked me?' asked Gemma.

'Asked you what?' replied Sara.

'Why we're sitting in a hedge at the bottom of my garden, and not in my room.'

Sara resisted the urge to look back to the silhouette in the kitchen. She could still feel his stare. Green eyes in a cannonball head resting on meaty shoulders. She didn't need to ask why they were sitting at the furthest point of the property from where he was standing. Sara had seen it all in that first handshake with Gemma. There was only one thing she was missing: the link that would tip everything into the abyss.

'Has he begun to sleep over?' asked Sara, her mouth dry.

'Who?' Gemma looked at Sara in confusion, then a look of distaste consumed her face. 'Oh, him. No, he just started dating my mum.' Gemma gave a grudging nod. 'And, yeah, you're right. That's the reason we're out here. Gives me the creeps. Tried to get me to sit on his lap a couple of days ago. I told him I'd rather die.'

Sara's heart clutched as the images she'd seen attacked her mind again. 'You can come over to ours, if you need to.'

Gemma laughed. 'And sleep on the floor of an empty house?' She looked up at Sara and saw the intensity on her face.

'Don't worry about me.' Gemma smiled. 'I can take care of myself.'

15

Sara lowered her fingertips towards the photo of Maric, letting them rest on the surface. At the moment of contact, the world's heartbeat slowed, then, for a split second, stopped completely. She was suspended in a void. As she touched the photo of Maric's face again, she steeled herself as the angry red blast flashed across her retinas. She had scrubbed every detail of the premonition, and there still wasn't enough to stop it happening. She needed more information. She needed another link.

In the rear of an unmarked van two blocks away, Luuk Janssen sat staring at his laptop, watching data tumble in a never-ending cascade down his screen. He rubbed his palms against the top of his trousers periodically to wipe off the sweat that was causing his hands to slip off the keyboard.

He was struggling to keep up. The crowds were growing and the rate of intercepts had spiked fifteen minutes ago: they were now coming in at the rate of ten a second. As each text or call was captured, it was swiftly converted into text containing the content of the communication, the origin, and whether the communication was an SMS or audio call.

Although he had completed hundreds of drills at the Academy, he was still learning. Luuk had kept on top of the data this morning by imagining his instructor, the great Bram De Vries, was standing behind him, arms folded behind his back, barrel-chest thrust forward, the very embodiment of quiet authority.

'Don't read, Luuk. That's impossible. There's not enough time. Scan. Keep your eyes light. Imagine them dancing across the screen.'

For the first hour, this had worked, but the volume had never been so high at the Academy. At this rate, even with scanning, Luuk soon found it impossible to keep his eyes anywhere close to the top of the screen.

'Catch up, Luuk. If your eyes reach the bottom, you'll start missing calls. And calls could mean lives saved.'

Luuk took a deep breath and took a slurp of his coffee. His eyes were halfway down the screen and dropping further each second.

'Victor One, all clear.'

'Yankee One, all clear.'

'Zulu One, all clear.'

The voices were continuous in his ear, chatter as surveillance units gave updates on visual reconnaissance. They were part of the same team as Luuk. Visual and intercept teams were just different ways of sieving information in operations like this.

He saw it subconsciously first. A line of comms that dropped into the top of his screen. A line with a single word. A deeply troubling word. By the time his conscious mind registered it, the flow of new calls had

118

shunted it to the bottom. It was just about to disappear when he pressed the space button, pausing the flow.

He had one or two seconds now to check it before he needed to return to the new calls, otherwise he would never catch up. He looked first at the right-hand column, where the originating number should be. It was blank. No assigned user name. What was called a 'drop' phone. The second red flag.

Luuk pressed the geo-location search button, which used mobile-phone towers to triangulate the user's position to within fifty feet. The search showed the phone was no longer operative. It had been switched off shortly after sending the text. Another red flag.

Luuk marked the text as suspect before returning to the flow.

'There's been an intercept. Still only a possible. They're checking. Stand by.'

Sara's eyes flicked to the clock on the dashboard.

Thirteen minutes.

'What was the intercept?'

'You can't leave the car, Sara. That was our deal.'

'What was it?' repeated Sara. 'It might be important.'

Waterman took a breath before responding.

'The text was: GO.'

Immediately, Sara was unfastening her seat belt, her fingers slipping into the door clasp, her other hand twisting the keys and pulling them out of the ignition. She was not going to have any blood on her hands today.

16

1991

Sara listened to the breathing of her brother and mother. When she was sure that they were sound asleep, she rolled off the blanket and crept out of the bedroom. She crossed the hall and entered the empty room on the other side. It was a bare box, dust balls gathered on the carpet. Gemma's bedroom was directly facing her, across the path that separated the two houses. The curtains were drawn and there was no light on in the room. Sara craned her neck until she could see the driveway of Gemma's house. She always knew when the boyfriend was there as his bright red car was parked outside. She let out a quiet sigh of relief as she saw only Gemma's mother's car in front, a midnight blue Golf. Sooner or later, his car would be parked in front at night. It would be the point of no return.

Sara's mind had been spinning through different possibilities since that first connection with Gemma. She had dismissed calling the police – Sara had promised her mother she would protect the family, and calling the police or social services would shine a spotlight on the squatters next door. And warning Gemma or her mother of something that hadn't yet happened would just elicit anger or ridicule and, anyway, who would believe a ten-year-old until it was already too late? So, instead, Sara kept a vigil each night. She had decided that the moment she saw the red Vauxhall parked outside, she would run downstairs and try to find a way into Gemma's house. Gemma's mother smoked all day and often left the kitchen windows open to aerate the ground floor. Sara would use one of the open windows to get in, then would try to extract Gemma before he reached her door. Or, at worst, if Sara was too late to stop him getting to Gemma's room, she would be a witness and, hopefully, shame him into retreat.

Sara yawned and stretched her arms. She had kept up this nocturnal vigil for a week now and her energy levels were wilting. The good news was that his car wasn't there. At least for tonight Gemma would be safe.

The following morning, the first sight that greeted her was a pale blue racing bike leaning against the wall of Gemma's house, next to the side door to the kitchen. She'd never seen it there before. It was a man's bike. She racked her brain to remember whether she had seen it when she was at the window last night, but realized she had been looking in the opposite direction.

Sara opened the connecting garden gate and walked quickly to the kitchen door of Gemma's house, rapping it several times with her knuckles. A blur approached through the crenulated glass window, the door opened and Gemma's mother was standing there in a dressing gown, cigarette in hand. Gemma's younger brother stood by one of her legs. Sara was going to ask if Gemma could come out, but she stood there, mouth open, frozen. Through the open doorway, she could see him sitting at the breakfast table. He was in his underwear, crouched over a plate of toast. He was staring at Sara with a faint smile.

'Her Majesty says she's not feeling well today,' said her mother. 'Won't come out of her room. You'd better leave her.'

After the door was closed, Sara walked down the side path of the house and knelt down, scooping up a handful of pebbles. She threw one up at the bedroom window. It glanced off the glass with a crack. Sara waited, but the curtains didn't move. She kept lancing the pebbles up until her palm was empty. The curtains never moved.

Gemma didn't come out the next day, or the day after. The blue racing bike was there each morning. Just the sight of it filled her with so much grief and guilt it made her chest feel as if it was filled with broken glass. A painful jigsaw was assembling slowly in her mind, the puzzle pieces being pub sessions, a boyfriend too far over-the-limit to drive, and a bicycle as alternative transport.

In the short time since Gemma had burst into her life, she had given Sara her first genuine friendship, and in the end Sara had failed her. On the third day, Sara's heart clutched when she noticed Gemma's curtains were open. Sara rushed downstairs and was about to

knock on the side door when she found herself looking at the hedge at the bottom of the garden and,
through its branches, their little grotto. There was
something white pinned to the branches.

She ran to the crawlspace and saw it was a folded
piece of paper. Sara lifted it and opened it, recognizing
the ornate, swirling handwriting immediately. It was a
letter. Addressed to her. As her finger pressed to the
page, she smudged some of the writing. The ink was
still wet.

As Sara read the letter, each word mashed the air
from her lungs until there was no breath left in her
body.

17

'Where did it come from?'

'It was sent from an apartment a few blocks from you. Burner phone that was switched off immediately afterwards. Armed units are dealing with it. Stay put, Sara. Do you understand?'

'I can't help you sitting in here.'

Sara pushed open the door. She stepped out and immediately flattened herself against her car as two unmarked vans flew past her, their high sides inches away from Sara's face, accelerating as they approached the intersection.

She began running in the same direction, ignoring the pain that stabbed into her side from her injury, flipping out the earpiece so she could no longer hear Waterman's shouting.

The crowded pavements and streets meant it was impossible to take a straight line to her destination so she dodged and wove through pedestrians. As she ran, groups of celebrating men wolf-whistled at her, trying to get her attention.

Ahead of her, she saw the vans parked at right angles at the corner of two residential streets, flashing lights behind their windscreens washing the front lawn in neon white and blue.

She checked her watch again.

Ten minutes.

Already, a knot of curious bystanders had gathered on the pavement, held back by a DSI officer wearing a balaclava, a Heckler & Koch MP5 submachine-gun hanging from a shoulder strap. At the end of a short path, a splintered front door hung on its hinges.

Sara slipped the earpiece back in and spoke low into the mic planted into the collar of her jacket. Her breathing was ragged and she gulped deeply between words.

'The text. Where was it going?'

Waterman was still shouting. '*Sara, it's not just you. You'll put others at risk too.*'

'You need to tell me everything.'

She could hear him take a deep, steadying breath.

'*It was another drop phone. Last location before it was burnt was at the south end of the intersection. Could be anywhere now.*'

Sara knew there was no point in running to the intersection. The recipient wasn't Maric: he would have been spotted by the surveillance teams. And there was no time to comb through CCTV footage to see who had received the text. That exercise would take far longer than the time they had left. She looked around, panicked, her heart rate spiking. She needed access to the apartment. That was the only place where any clues might be. But the chances of her passing the DSI officer were zero.

An ambulance was parked behind one of the police vans. Its rear doors were open. Sara ran over and swiped one of the EMT kits sitting on a ledge inside. She had taken a step away when she stopped and returned to the open rear door, lifting a black hat emblazoned with a medical logo that was hanging on a hook and pulling it down low on her head.

She pushed through the onlookers, holding up the kit to the officer, who waved her through.

She ran down the path and inside the front entrance. Above her, she could hear voices shouting, overlaying another sound, a hissing and spluttering that was human and inhuman at the same time.

She took the steps two at a time. When she reached the top of the stairs, the shouting voices had stopped, as well as the spluttering. All she could hear now was whispering and a rapid thumping noise, like a manic drumbeat.

Two armed officers standing on the landing saw her EMT cap and kit bag and immediately pointed upwards to the next floor. Sara nodded and ran up the second flight of stairs.

The landing was crowded with armed officers. The entire units from the vans downstairs must have been there. For some reason, they were not in the apartment but were standing silently, clustered around its threshold. She felt their eyes on her as she turned the corner. She walked past them quickly and in through the caved-down door at the end of the hall.

She recognized him immediately. Maric was lying on his back on the floor, arms and legs shuddering, the heels of his heavy boots beating the wooden floor frenetically. Two male EMT workers knelt over him, one wedging Maric's mouth open with a rubber block while the other probed with a gloved hand. Sara walked closer. He was having a fit, his limbs thrashing, as if an electrical current was passing through them. His face was contorted and dense gobs of spittle foamed down his chin.

The EMT pulled something from inside Maric's mouth and threw it on the floor next to the body. It was a broken husk of plastic.

The EMTs muttered to each other as they carried out their duties.

'Strychnine?'

'*Nee*, cyanide.'

Maric's convulsions were slowing down, his limbs lying limp between spasms, his toes tilting listlessly to the floor. Sara could tell he would be gone in seconds. She looked at her watch.

Eight minutes.

She knelt by the body, picking up Maric's hand and gripping it in hers.

One of the paramedics looked at her in confusion. Her eyes were closed, her breathing becoming deep and arrhythmic. Before he could say anything, his attention was drawn back to Maric, who was sucking air through gritted teeth.

She didn't have long. Once Maric's brain activity stopped, the possibility of a personal connection would be lost for ever.

She held his hand, could feel his pulse, faint and irregular, as the world slowed, the beat becoming fainter as sounds around her dulled, then became an active silence. Suddenly chaos erupted. An angry back-beat thrashed somewhere, dark and crashing. Lightning flashed, like white spider webs, piercing the darkness. No sooner did one image appear than another took its place. She knew the maelstrom of chaotic images was the by-product of Maric's dying mind, which was crumbling even as she probed it. It was impossible to make sense of anything she saw, impossible to look for the links in the chain. Then something flashed near her. For just a fraction of a second, like a subliminal still embedded in a film. A mushroom cloud reaching towards a blue sky. It was the explosion, tearing through the junction, laying waste to the cheering crowds. It segued to the image of a man walking away. He was wearing a leather jacket. He pivoted on one heel and turned to face her, and for the briefest of moments she was staring right at him. Behind him, a set of painted bars appeared, white on black, filling her field of vision. Suddenly, he and every other sound and image disappeared and Sara found herself back in the void. The entire connection was over in a couple of seconds.

She dropped Maric's hand and opened her eyes.

One of the EMTs was closing the eyes of the motionless body.

Sara jumped up and ran through the front door, pushing her way through the crowd on the landing.

As soon as she was clear of the house, she was speaking into the mic between ragged breaths.

'The other one. I saw him. Male. Late twenties. Shaven head. Somehow there are stripes involved. It could be a

129

pattern on something. Maybe on his clothes. Maybe in a backpack. But the bomb is close to the stripes.'

She could hear a muffled murmur at the other end of the line. Waterman was giving an instruction to someone.

'*OK. We've got eyes on the intersection now. Sara. Listen to me. Get to safety. Now. We can handle it from here.*'

She looked back in the direction of her car. There was enough time for her to drive safely outside the danger zone. Three or four blocks was all it would take. Then she thought of the little girl, in the middle of the crowd, holding her mother's hand. How could she find safety before they did?

Sara checked her watch.

Six minutes.

The crowds had swollen again.

'Can you see him?'

In her earpiece, she could hear whispering, then a raised voice, then a heavy thump. Waterman had closed a fist around his mic to muffle what he was saying.

'Do you have eyes on him?'

Sara's voice was frantic. She was still one block from the intersection, but had reached the police barriers erected to stop traffic. Beyond them the roads heaved with what resembled a street party, families and children of all ages bashing out tuneless rhythms on makeshift instruments. She did her best not to remember the images of slaughter she had seen, how in a few seconds the party would become a slaughterhouse.

'Where is he?'

The bodies were becoming more and more tightly packed as she worked her way to the centre of the junction. Finally, she was forced to stop as she hit a solid wall of bodies that wouldn't yield.

Four minutes.

She looked to her left and right, desperate for some pocket of space that could let her through.

Then the crowd shifted, a ripple of something moving through them. Like the group was taking a collective breath. In the ebb, the drums stopped. Something had gripped their attention. They were watching, waiting. Seeing something she couldn't. Then she heard a voice raised – loud, authoritative – followed by a loud crack.

A gunshot.

The rank of people in front of her surged, and then the line broke and people were running, screaming. A herd stampeding. Charging towards her. Sara battled forwards, shielding her head and pushing through the melee of bodies, until she found herself standing in open space on the other side of the charge.

He was by the far pavement. Arms up in surrender, smiling at the armed DSI officers screaming at him. Shaven head and a strange lopsided smile. Raising his arms had caused his leather jacket to swing open, revealing a makeshift vest, eight plastic cylinders ducttaped to a harness, bound together by wires. Sara could see the leather jacket clearly. On it were emblazoned multiple swastikas. White stripes at perpendicular angles.

Police were shouting at the crowds, screaming at them to move back. The wide radius of space around the man was growing, creeping back, putting more and more distance between him and everyone else. No matter how much it grew, it never seemed enough.

Sara could hear Waterman talking on a phone, giving instructions to the DSI, telling them the size of the suspected bomb and likely blast radius.

Two minutes.

No time to call negotiators. Or a bomb-disposal team. It was all going down now. On cue, four marksmen appeared from the police ranks, standing with their guns raised, pressed into shoulders, right foot forward. Waiting for the order.

Her eyes were trained to the same spot the police were all staring at: the man's right fist, which was clenched around something. A wire snaked from his wrist into the sleeve of his jacket.

An order must have been given, because she saw a marksman's gun jerk back, then a sound, like dry wood snapping, echoed around the quiet square. The skinhead's hand jerked upwards and he cried out, his legs buckling.

She watched as the police inched forward towards him. A pocket battery connected to a wire rolled away from his fist. A puddle of red-black blood sat glistening on the road next to him. The injured man lay prone, rocking forward, clutching his hand.

Sara reached into her jacket pocket and tugged out the photograph of Maric. The photo still had his energy, while a personal connection couldn't be achieved after someone died, she touched her fingertips to the surface and felt the world slow down. She needed to see it. Needed proof. Of the carnival continuing. Of that little girl still with her mother, handing out her flags. Of all these families around her safe. Alive.

But she watched in horror as the bomb again ripped through the junction. But this time, somehow, it was worse. The number of dead and injured had increased. When the smoke cleared, there was a carpet of bodies, stacked two or three deep in places.

Her focus was interrupted by cries of pain behind her. She turned to the protesters standing behind the police line. The effect of clearing the square was that everyone had been shunted to tight pavement spaces, pressed up against shop fronts, where the overcrowding was almost unbearable. Men shouted desperately to the police to lift children over the barrier to save them from being crushed.

A terrible realization was dawning on Sara. This wasn't over. They were being played. The bomber was a diversion. Planted there to be discovered. The police response, to evacuate the crowds, was what Black Dawn wanted. The protesters were now herded onto pavements, packed tight against the outside walls of the shops. The plan was always to jam them tighter together to inflict the maximum damage.

'He's a decoy. To concentrate the crowds. The bomb must be near the shops. Waterman?'

There was no sound at the other end.

She looked at her watch.

One minute.

The stripes were connected to the bomb. The future could not be cheated. It was implacable, immovable. She had seen it when she had touched the Serbian's hand. She thought she'd seen the stripes on the skin-head's leather jacket. But she was wrong. She needed to find out the real stripes. Find the stripes and find the bomb.

Sara looked around her desperately, suddenly seeing stripes everywhere. The pedestrian crossings that linked all sixteen pavements, eight crossings in all, the chequered façades of the ICC, which looked like vertical stripes from this distance.

And then she saw it.

A school bus was parked a few yards away, on the edge of the intersection. Near where the crowds were now packed. On its side was a logo, a shield with an overlaid portcullis, thick white columns against a black background. The appearance of the columns was unmistakable – they were the white stripes she was looking for.

And then she was running.

18

Sara clenched her fist around the letter and squeezed out of the bolthole. She ran to Gemma's back gate and lifted the latch with a shaking hand. Everything she had seen in that moment of first connection with Gemma had come true, despite her best efforts. Sara's mother was right. Even with all her powers, she couldn't save anyone, no matter how hard she tried.

There was only one image left from the vision still to manifest. The most terrible one of all. Sara tried to banish it from her mind as she ran down the street towards the canal. The ink on the letter was wet, which meant that Gemma couldn't have left long before Sara found it. If Sara was fast enough, she might catch up with her, might be able to stop her before it was too late.

When Sara reached the towpath by the canal, it was empty in both directions. Sara turned right instinctively, running towards the canal's terminus, which was half a mile ahead. She rounded a tight corner and could see it, far ahead. The lattice structure bridging the canal brought the water to an abrupt stop, creating a wall of froth raging high up the sluice gates.

A hundred yards ahead of her, a blue spot on the

towpath, faintly distinguishable as a tracksuit and a large bob of bushy hair, was moving fast. Gemma was running for all she was worth. Sara tried to increase her speed but she was no match. By the time she reached the weir, the footpath's dead-end was empty.

Sara's eyes raked the churning waters but she could see nothing other than a series of seething suck-holes that churned angrily.

She took a step towards the edge and gritted her teeth, her legs braced for the jump. She was not going to let it end this way, even if it meant risking her own life. If there was a chance Gemma was still alive, that she might save her, it was worth it.

'I wouldn't,' said a voice behind her. 'You know she's dead. No one could survive down there.'

Sara turned to see her brother walking towards her along the towpath. With his furrowed brow and serious walk, he looked more like a tiny adult than a nine-year-old child.

Sara looked back at the water and knew he was right. The white foam surged several feet higher than the water, and anything that fell in would be consumed and dragged violently down by the powerful currents. She also knew Christian was right because she had seen it all weeks ago, the moment she had pressed her hand to Gemma's. In a searing flash, her friend's body had pin-wheeled and spun through the water, dragged down to the riverbed. Sara took a step back, the tears flowing freely now. 'You knew?' Her voice was cracking as she spoke.

Christian nodded. 'I knew you were lying about not touching her. So I went to that little nest she made in the hedge.' His face was inscrutable. 'There were enough of her things there to connect with. I could see what was coming.'

'And you did nothing about it?'

'Neither did you,' he shot back. 'Until it was too late,' he added.

'The difference was, I tried,' said Sara.

Christian shrugged and turned to leave. After walking for a few steps, he looked back over his shoulder and pulled something out of his pocket. It was a handful of Gemma's track ribbons, the medallions winking in the morning sun.

'Mum's right,' said Christian. 'You can't save them. The only choice is how you want to use what you learn when you connect with them. These are probably worth something.'

'That's the difference between you and me,' shouted Sara.

But he walked on, never turning.

19

The front door of the bus was open and the driver was on the step, talking on the phone, his eyes rooted to the drama playing out in the street. She pulled him out onto the pavement in one fluid movement, closed the door and sat in his seat.

Forty seconds.

Sara put the bus into gear and drove, shunting through the packed street like an ice-breaker, parting panicked crowds before her. A few DSI officers saw her and ran over, pointing their submachine-guns at the driving seat, screaming at her in Dutch.

She ignored them, pressing down on the accelerator, speeding up, twisting the steering wheel, bringing the bus straight into the centre of the intersection. On the other side was the fence surrounding the ICC, and beyond it an area of grass that ran around the perimeter of the building.

Windows cracked around her as bullets studded the side of the vehicle. Sara ducked below the steering wheel, swapping her foot for her hand and pressing down with all her might on the accelerator, charging the bus forward.

She couldn't see outside, but felt the jolts as each of the bus's wheels mounted the pavement. A second later, she was thrown forward as the bus hit something that shattered the front window, shearing it off completely.

It must have been the fence around the ICC compound.

Ten seconds.

Sara yanked the front door open.

Five seconds.

She glanced back to check the bus was far enough from the crowds.

Two seconds.

Stretching her hands out, she leapt as far as she could.

Zero.

The explosion was deafening as the bomb detonated. A surging shock wave tossed her, like a leaf in a hurricane, spinning her to the side, then up into the air so she was facing upwards, her eyes struggling to remain open even as the world went dark around her.

She heard sounds first.

She opened her eyes, slowing, wincing from pressure on her forehead. The world was still spinning.

A voice was saying something to her, distant and robotic in her ear, but she couldn't make out the words.

Two masked men ran towards her, scooping her up, lifting her.

'*MI6, Sara. They'll take you . . .*'

She threw her arms around their shoulders.

On her left, she saw a cluster of DSI officers standing in a circle. On the pavement, at their feet, the man wearing the suicide vest was shuddering, his limbs slapping the pavement, his knuckles bloody from the impact. Foam erupted from his mouth. A wall of bodies blocked her view as several DSI officers ran up to her, pistols raised, screaming orders at her and her companions.

The MI6 officers lifted up their warrant badges. One of the DSI officers holstered his pistol and approached, his hand held out to inspect them. Through the gap between the DSI men, Sara saw the skinhead shudder, then twist his head in her direction. He smiled his lopsided smile again, his teeth streaked with blood, then grimaced as a spasm of pain passed through him, before his body went slack.

20

Waterman walked out of the front doors of GCHQ and stood for a moment. He glanced around him and took a deep lungful of air. The world looked the same. The same rows of parked cars he had seen that morning. The same cloud wisps floating through the pale blue sky. Behind him, people milled around the sundrenched concourse of the building, each consumed by their routines. Heading to meetings, coffees in hand. Checking their phones. It was just another day. Yet everything seemed totally, utterly different.

Based on nothing other than touching a photograph, Sara had found a bomb almost three hundred miles away, and one day in the future, and prevented a massacre. Waterman's logical mind struggled to find a context for what he had just experienced. No part of it fitted into his orderly world of cause and effect.

'How is she?' Salt was standing behind him, staring out at the Malvern Hills in the distance.

'Concussion. Scrapes and bruises. Nothing broken,' replied Waterman, astounded. 'I don't understand what just happened.'

Salt looked around him, then motioned towards the car park. They walked along the asphalt until they came to his car. One of the perks of being chairman of the

JIC was a driver, but the car was empty. They opened the rear doors and both sat in the back seat.

'I've never known for sure how she does it,' resumed Salt, after settling into his seat and closing the door. 'The best guess we have is it has to do with frequencies. The subconscious receives data on a different frequency, the receiver for that information is somewhere in the limbic system. When you and I shake someone's hand, what we feel is texture, pressure, warmth. But when Sara shakes hands, she gets an entire other set of data from that connection. Her hypothalamic region is genetically developed to pick up data we never perceive.'

Waterman stared out of the window, processing. He couldn't deny Sara's ability any more. He was now trying to understand it, to find as many nexuses as he could with his scientific world so he could explain it to others when necessary. If Sara was going to work for them, others would need to be briefed. Even if her existence was classified STRAP-3, there were still twenty or so people in the country who would have to know she existed, and to trust the intelligence she provided, even though it was through a highly unusual source. The heads of MI5 and MI6. Key politicians. It seemed the Americans would need to be briefed too. None of them would be able to rely on sensory proof, like Waterman had just witnessed. He'd have to prepare a briefing note, to frame Sara in a way that her deployment wouldn't be perceived as an insane step into the supernatural.

'Is that how she beat Joe Briggs's brother?' he asked,

144

at last. He had read the police report on the injuries to Steven Briggs. He was a bruiser, six foot four and almost twenty stone. He ran a boxing gym on the Old Kent Road and had a fat file of prior convictions, cautions and reprimands. Waterman couldn't imagine how Sara had inflicted the damage she had on him. It couldn't have been a function of brute strength.

Salt nodded. 'In fight-or-flight situations, the traditional cascade of epinephrine, dopamine and serotonin into the brain takes her mental state to a whole other level. Her overdeveloped intuition goes into hyperdrive. During her training as a child, she described the entire world slowing down around her. It means she's one step ahead in any combat situation.'

'I suppose this is the end of Cassandra and computer forecasting,' said Waterman, at last. He thought unhappily of the thousands of man-hours he and his team had invested in the project. Until a few days ago, he was convinced it would become the catalyst to change the face of intelligence. But with Sara in the picture, there wasn't much point in having a forecasting program that, at best, assigned only percentage forecasts to the future.

'Actually, let's keep Cassandra going,' said Salt. 'And for now, Sara will continue to be our secret. At least until we deploy her successfully in a domestic UK operation.'

Waterman shifted uncomfortably. 'What do you mean by "deploy"?'

Salt blinked once, slowly, and turned his steel-grey eyes towards Waterman. 'Is there a problem?'

'Well, I'm already trying to contain the fallout from the ICC operation. We shut down any enquiries from the MI6 officers on the scene. Told them her identity was confidential. But that's not sustainable if she's going to be interacting with a fair amount of UK personnel.'

The scale of subterfuge required to keep Sara's identity anonymous in a domestic operation made Waterman intensely uneasy. Creating a non-official cover for use against his own intelligence community was fraught with peril. They all had access to the same resources, and given the competition and rivalries between the divisions, keeping mutual secrets could be a difficult task.

'She's an asset,' said Salt. 'That's all you need to tell people.'

His tone was final, shutting down any response. He pulled out a pen from his pocket and opened the hatch in the arm rest, then reached in, pulled out a blank piece of paper and wrote down a mobile phone number. 'This is how you can contact her.'

'I should be able to track her through the IMEI,' said Waterman, rallying. Even if he was going to have to learn to conceal Sara's identity, at least she wouldn't be concealed from him. The IMEI number was the DNA of every mobile phone, allowing cell towers to identify who was calling.

Salt shook his head. 'I've seen the phone. It's a stealth model, military-level security and encryption techniques. Randomized IMEI number-generator. We won't be able to track her.' He looked directly at Waterman and held his eye. 'She wants to get involved on her terms.'

Waterman's apprehension was increasing. Regardless of his admiration for his mentor and the perceived value of Sara, this was drifting further and further away from Waterman's expertise. He was a SIGINT expert. His world involved the uncomplicated beauty of algorithms and data forecasting. It was a people-less landscape. He had none of the training in HUMINT and field craft this operation required. And he could see how much of a liability he might be to both the operation and Sara. He suddenly grasped how far he'd let his ego be stroked by Salt's confidences. Now Sara's ability seemed proven, it was time to pass her on to a suitable agent to handle her. Someone with field experience. Anyone in MI5 would do. Just not him.

Waterman was about to tell this to Salt when he found himself staring at Salt's shirt and realizing his brain had stalled.

'Anything else?' asked Salt, looking at Waterman closely. 'Are you all right?'

Waterman nodded quickly but didn't respond.

'Fine, I'll call you,' said Salt, signalling the meeting was over by reaching across Waterman and opening his door.

Waterman stepped out into the fresh air and began to walk to the gates. The jolt of adrenalin he'd just experienced was ebbing away, leaving a queasy feeling. His mind was uneasy, pacing down corridors, testing doors again. It was possible that he had imagined what he had just seen. Or he might be leaping to conclusions. But even the possibility that it was what it appeared to be was making his head spin.

He walked through the lobby and scanned his ID card through the turnstiles. Someone said hello to him but he was too distracted to notice who. He increased his pace, making a beeline for the lifts. The image kept returning as he walked. Salt's jacket falling open. The crisp white linen, the tie buckling as it followed the contours of the shirt.

A lift door opened and Waterman stepped inside, jabbing his finger on the button repeatedly to prevent anyone else entering. He didn't want them to see him so unsettled.

Bob Swift was sitting at his customary chair in the Arena when Waterman entered. Barely twenty-two, looking, like most analysts at GCHQ, as if he was on his way to a college class. Baggy short-sleeved T-shirt over a long-sleeved one, jeans, trainers. With a PhD from Cambridge in hand last year, Swift was on the same fast track as Waterman had been, and Waterman had taken him under his wing.

Waterman pulled a chair over from another desk and kept his voice just above a whisper. 'I need you to check something for me,' he said, glancing surreptitiously around. 'Look up all the radio and digital frequencies transmitted from the north-east corner of the car park in the last ten minutes.'

'Is this a mobile phone call?' asked Swift.

Waterman shook his head.

Swift waited, eyebrows raised. Then, when it was clear no further information was forthcoming, he turned back to his computer. His fingers played the keyboard causing rivers of code to flow down the screen. He turned back to Waterman. 'Nothing.'

Waterman leant back in his chair, deep in thought.

'You're asking about a transmitter,' said Swift. 'Why would anyone bug the car park?' When Waterman said nothing, Swift continued, realization spreading across his face. 'There was a meeting in the car park. And you think it was bugged.'

Before Waterman could stop him, Swift was calling up the security cameras from the north-east corner of the car park. Serried rows of vehicles appeared on the monitor, with one car parked on its own. Footage replayed of Waterman and Salt stepping into it.

'You think someone might have bugged Commander Salt's car?' asked Swift, incredulously.

Waterman shook his head.

The image appeared again in his mind. It was clipped to Salt's shirt pocket.

A Union flag pin.

It looked identical to the bug used last month on the GCHQ mole, whose roommate had had ties to the Russian Embassy. Same size. Same colour. Same decorative flourishes on the flag.

Maybe it was just a decorative pin, thought Waterman. That was the most likely explanation.

But if that was the case, why would Salt slip a

decorative pin into a shirt pocket? He was a fastidious and conservative dresser, and decorative pins were worn by men on lapels. Unless they wished to hide them from plain sight.

Again, Waterman dismissed his doubts. Swift had just confirmed that there were no transmissions from the car park, which discounted the possibility of a radio bug.

But Waterman couldn't help himself. The sight had been so jarring that he kept trying the other doors, testing every possibility. Waterman had seen the details of the MI5 operation on the mole quite by chance, which meant that he wasn't intended to know that the bug was in a lapel pin.

After examining all the other doors in his mental corridor, he was standing in front of the one door he didn't want to open. Because if the pin was a bug, it meant one of two things. Either Salt was ignorant of the device's purpose, in which case someone was bugging the most powerful person in British military intelligence. Or he was wearing a bug on purpose, in which case Waterman was in a lot of trouble.

21

Few of the terraced houses of Great Russell Street in Bloomsbury functioned as residences. The four-storey, cream-coloured structures were too large for anyone but the wealthiest families, who preferred their mansions to be in more fashionable neighbourhoods. In the absence of any takers, businesses had colonized the area shortly after the Second World War.

Number 27 was different from the other houses, distinguished by its filthy exterior and shreds of torn plastic sheeting hanging from the rusty scaffolding that wrapped around the front. It stood out in the street, as incongruous as a vagrant in a line of catwalk models.

Sara lifted one of the plastic flaps and ducked into the building site. Although it was the middle of the day, she had no concern about running into any contractors. It had been decades since a builder had set foot in the property.

She picked her way through the rubble and discarded wiring to reach the back wall of the house. The front half of the ground floor, closest to the street, had been renovated, but the building work stopped abruptly near the fireplace and chimney flue. From there, the stripped-back plaster had exposed something completely new, the ornate domed ceiling of another building, the bulk of whose mass was underground and on whose foundations the current grand house had been built. Discarded plans, left to gather dust on workmen's benches on the upper floors, contained detailed blueprints of the older building, buried in earth and discovered only halfway through the renovation work. It took only a few searches in a local planning office for Sara to discover that planning permission had been suspended when the seventeenth-century ruin had been discovered, and the site had been mired in litigation ever since.

She moved a large cardboard siding resting against the back wall, revealing a cavity and a flight of stone stairs. She walked down them slowly, a hand trailing on the wall for balance. They were steep and plunged into pitch darkness. When she reached the bottom, she felt her way to an old writing desk, scavenged from one of the upper floors, then reached for the matchbox resting near the edge.

The space burst into light on the first strike of a match, illuminating the blanket on the floor that marked out her bed and the candles that covered most of the floor space. The legal owners had no idea she lived there, but she was not, technically, a squatter. Her family had a connection to the house. The last occupant had been her great-grandmother, Helen Duncan.

Sara lit a few candles around her makeshift bed, her mind still turning over the events of the last twenty-four hours. A theme was developing from her operations with GCHQ. A deeply unsettling theme. For some reason, her foresight was hiding key things from her, or misleading her completely. When she had connected with Joe Briggs in the nightclub, she had not seen the brother waiting for her in the dark of the drain. And when she had connected with Maric's photo, then his hand, she had seen the suicide bomber but not the bomb on the bus. Both had almost cost her her life. Once again, she struggled to understand the rules of her own abilities. Her mother had said they didn't get to choose what they saw in the moment of connection. But Sara also knew that the most dramatic, most emotion-laden events always pushed themselves to the front. So, she *should* have seen them.

Fatigue was overpowering her. She had barely slept since discharging herself from hospital. When she had returned from The Hague, Waterman had given her a simple instruction. Get some rest and wait for his call.

She stifled a yawn and stretched her arms, wincing with pain. She took off her shirt and peeled back the bandage covering the stitches. Blood had seeped through. She needed to change the dressing. She walked to the far wall and knelt down. The floorboards were buckled with age. She gripped the end of one and lifted it, exposing a hollow. Her grab-and-go bag – a constant companion since her childhood – lay in it. Sara unzipped the top, pushing through a bundle of passports and a stack of credit cards wrapped in rubber bands, before finding her first-aid kit.

After she'd attended to the wound, she lay down and tried to surrender to sleep. But the same thoughts kept churning through her brain. Maybe it was exhaustion, but the thoughts seemed tangled in knots and impossible to separate. She needed to talk to someone, to help separate her thoughts into some sense of understanding. Unfortunately, there was only one person to go to.

She took a deep breath on reaching the landing of the fourth floor. His door was closed, as usual. She banged on it hard, with the palm of her hand.

'What's dragged you from your crypt?' said a voice nearby. Christian sat in a recess that housed a window seat of bare wood panelling with enough room for two people. He was stretched across it, taking up the space, long legs crossed and tipped up at an incline, feet resting halfway up the panelling. It had been a while since they'd last seen each other, but his thick, floppy hair had been shaved off and the beginnings of a beard now sprouted from his chin.

She walked over to him. The bench on which he was sitting was covered with photos of dogs. They were all lean, long legs bookending skeletal ribcages. Sara picked up one of the photos.

'You must be in trouble with track owners?'

Christian furrowed his brow as if to dismiss the thought as ridiculous.

'Hair's gone,' she continued. 'Beard on the way. Reading racing dogs from their photos.'

Christian was quiet for a while before responding. 'Had a couple of rough bets last week. Turns out dogs aren't as easy to read as people.'

Sara wondered where to start. Conversations with her brother were never easy. He had never needed other people, least of all his sister.

'Injured in the line of duty?' He sounded sarcastic, but when she looked at him, she saw he wasn't smiling. He was staring at the side of her blouse. The blood from her wound had seeped through the bandage again and stained the material.

'Two operations,' she said. 'Back to back.'

'And you were injured both times?'

Sara hesitated, then nodded.

'And you're probably wondering why you never saw it coming each time,' he prompted gently.

She turned to face him. She had been hoping that, if she caught him in the right mood, Christian might be a sounding board, someone to listen as she talked through what had happened. She never imagined he might have answers, or if he did, that he'd be willing to share them.

'Both times there was a surprise,' she said, still not sure if she could trust him. 'Something I should have seen when I connected. I don't know why I didn't.'

'It's pretty obvious.' His expression never changed. The same haughty, blank stare. He was just a physically larger version of the child he'd been.

'And what is it?' asked Sara, struggling for patience. He was making her beg for it.

'You should never have offered to help in the first place,' said Christian.

She tried, unsuccessfully, to keep the anger out of

her voice. 'I should have expected you wouldn't understand. You've never cared for anyone but yourself.'

'Caring never made a difference,' said Christian.

'I've got to try.'

'Why? Because of her?'

She looked up at him sharply. Gemma's memory was a painful bed of thorns that she wanted Christian nowhere near. 'Don't mention her,' she said slowly. 'You could see what was coming just as well as I could. I, at least, tried to do something. You did nothing.'

'Yes, I did.'

'You kept quiet.'

'I know. That was what I chose to do.'

She shook her head in disgust. His arrogance was unbelievable. And yet, at some level, she could feel this was going somewhere. Somewhere she didn't want it to go.

'I knew the spies wanted you, not me,' he continued. 'The girl, not the boy. Girls have the stronger ability. And that suited me.'

Christian's destination was becoming clearer now, and a sense of horror was slowly rising in Sara.

'The police were called after Gemma drowned,' he continued. 'And what happened the day after that?'

'You knew she was going to die,' said Sara, under her breath. 'And when she did, the police would come. And that would lead MI5 to us. Her dying was the instigator for the spies finding me. That was your endgame, to get rid of me.'

'It was always about you when we were younger,'

said Christian. 'Save Sara. Protect Sara. You were always her first priority. Do you blame me for wanting her to myself?'

'I knew you hated me as a child. I just never realized how much.' Sara stood up and began to walk down the stairs. Her sense of betrayal and isolation felt absolute.

She had almost disappeared from his sight before he spoke. She turned back at the sound of his voice and saw he was standing now, leaning against the wooden balcony that looked down on the stairwell. His face had softened.

'Look,' he said, running his hand over his scalp. 'Do you know why I don't try to change the future?' He sounded contrite so she stopped mid-step. When he continued, his voice was almost gentle. 'Because when you get personally involved, you change *that* version of the future. That's what's happening to you.'

Sara just stared, processing the implications of what he'd said.

Christian turned and walked towards his door. Before he opened it, he turned back one last time. 'The next might be fatal.'

22

Waterman stood at the maître d's lectern, taking in his surroundings. Balthazar in Covent Garden was an unapologetic hymn to the French dining experience. Plush red leather booths hugged the perimeter of the restaurant; wooden tables and chairs stood in the centre on terracotta marble tiles; two-storey-high mirrors caught and reflected the brassy light under vaulted ceilings. Voluble conversations competed with the sounds of food service.

After checking in, Waterman followed the maître d', weaving through the tables towards the back of the room. The maître d' and the serving staff were all French, a requirement of employment at the storied restaurant. It pleased Waterman when he reminded himself that Balthazar was American, the original in New York. And if he was inclined to draw any conclusions about the talent of Americans for self-creation, he just had to remind himself further that the original owner had been born in Bethnal Green.

He'd never met his dining partner there before, but the choice of venue felt fitting. Much like his companion, its nature was enigmatic, leaving you wondering about its true identity.

Salt was sitting at the back of the restaurant, in a

small private area separated from the main dining room by heavy velvet curtains. On the wall above the table hung a landscape painting, black mountains made more solid through the chiaroscuro effect of light streams from the heavens.

'I thought it was just the two of us,' said Waterman, looking at the table. It was set for three.

'Vincent Shaw is joining us for coffee.'

Waterman was familiar with the name. Shaw was MI5. A journeyman rather than a high-flyer who, by dint of tenure, was now in the managerial class. Waterman had seen his name on emails but they'd never met.

He nodded, doing his best not to feel slighted. He'd never had lunch with Salt before and had been flattered when Salt's secretary had contacted him. As he sat down, he reminded himself to keep his emotions in check. He was liable to become a cliché: the fatherless boy on an endless search for a mentor.

Waterman glanced at the other man's shirt, trying to get a glimpse of his pocket, but Salt's jacket was buttoned, effectively masking all but a thin triangle of white shirt from view.

Sitting on the table next to Salt's bread plate was his mobile phone.

'I know, I know,' said Salt, noticing Waterman's gaze. 'I look like a businessman at a street café in Tel Aviv. I'm waiting for a call. Now, do you know what you want to eat?'

Waterman followed Salt's lead, ordering the salad frisée followed by the entrecôte. Salt chose a Margaux

Ségla 2012 to accompany the food. Once the waiter had departed, Waterman allowed Salt to steer the conversation. He knew the man followed an unspoken protocol at meals, more *Debrett's* than Secret Service, that no business was spoken before coffee was served. It never felt uncomfortable for Waterman, this waiting for business to start. Salt was unlike most alpha males, who set the conversational agenda to the safer harbours where they could talk of their own accomplishments. He was a polyglot who consumed fiction and non-fiction with prodigious appetite and stayed on top of contemporary culture. He was as comfortable talking about contemporary music as he was discussing the impact taxation had on key turning points in history. Even with Waterman's growing suspicions about him, the following hour passed quickly.

The waiter returned with the dessert menu. Salt responded in flawless French, which Waterman didn't follow, but the gist of which seemed to be a compliment to the chef and an order of coffee.

'So, why are we meeting Shaw?' asked Waterman, folding his napkin and placing it on the table.

'When I ran GCHQ, Shaw was one of the few elite agents with whom we didn't have a good relationship. He's old-school. No higher education. Joined the Service from the armed forces. Something of a Luddite. Doesn't go to the right dinner parties. Keeps himself to himself. But he's one of a handful of top MI5 men who can now lead a high-level investigation. Here he comes.'

Waterman followed Salt's gaze to see a short, power-fully built man in his fifties in a tight-fitting grey suit moving through the tables towards them. There was a swagger in his walk, his shoulders subtly rowing the air as he moved. He didn't smile as he approached them.

'Before he arrives, I'm going to freshen up,' said Waterman.

Salt nodded and pointed behind him. 'At the top of the stairs.'

Waterman left the table, turned the corner and climbed the stairs. He pushed open the door and looked around. Three stalls lined one side of the room. The washbasins were on the far wall and, on his right, the urinals. The place seemed empty, but he bent down to look under the raised doors of the cubicles. There were no occupants.

His heart was hammering in his chest as he stepped into the nearest cubicle and wiped the sweat from his palms on his trousers. He reached inside his jacket and took out the slim tablet that had been resting in his jacket pocket. The Pro-DC9 bug detector looked just like an Android phone, but was able to carry out an advanced analysis of a programmed radio-frequency environment. His journey into the world of spycraft was showing him every day how deeply unsuited he was to it. This was the last thing he wanted to be doing, not least because it involved spying on Charles Salt.

He flicked the smooth screen and looked at the read-out. He had set the DC9 for a tight sphere of three feet, to avoid picking up any other devices: anything with an active radio link would register on the device. To his profound relief, a string of green lights ran down the front of the screen.

He breathed out slowly and wiped the perspiration that had pricked his hairline. He stood up and took another deep breath to steady himself. He already felt as if the spell he'd been under the past few days had broken. In hindsight, his paranoia was most likely a side-effect of his involuntary immersion into frontline espionage. Waterman couldn't help feeling a little giddy as he put the device back in his pocket and exited the cubicle, washing his hands before he left. He suddenly realized how painful it had been to contemplate Salt's betrayal, and how ridiculous he had been to let his own anxieties get this far. He left the cloakroom and descended the stairs, feeling lighter with each step. Even Vincent Shaw's joining them now felt like a good thing. Salt didn't need to curry favour with mid-level agents at MI5: he was too senior for that. Which meant that Shaw's presence was for Waterman, to help him make a new contact. He felt a little surge of pride as he walked back into the dining room. It was good to have a powerful person in your corner.

As he sat down, he saw that Salt's jacket was now open. Waterman had a clear view of his shirt pocket. There was no pin.

The atmosphere at the table seemed cordial but strained, although Waterman sensed Salt was too polished to acknowledge it. Shaw was hunched over in his seat, the fingers of both hands plaited together.

'Vincent was just telling me about his last operation,' said Salt.

'Cell in Bradford,' said Shaw. His voice was deep and sliced with ease through the background noise of the restaurant. Waterman could tell that Shaw was not interested in retelling the story for him: he didn't make eye contact with him as he spoke. 'Splinter from IS. Planning co-ordinated knife attacks. Turned one of them into an asset. Arrested the others as they boarded the train to London.'

'When was this?' asked Waterman.

'Six months ago,' said Shaw, looking at him for the first time.

Waterman knew of no operation similar to the one Shaw described. For an MI5 operation not to come up on GCHQ's radar required some effort. It would mean restricting intel to HUMINT, essentially informants and tip-offs, and dispensing with any use of intercepts, whether of phone calls, emails, messaging apps or social media. It was highly unusual and Waterman could tell from Shaw's look that he had chosen to tell them about this particular operation for a reason.

'I hope GCHQ can be a support on the next operation,' said Waterman.

'If there's a need,' said Shaw.

'GCHQ, MI5 and MI6 are three legs of the same stool,' said Salt, an edge creeping into his voice. 'Without one of the legs, the stool falls over.'

'When I hear metaphors like that, I always assume the person saying it wants something.'

Waterman did his best to mask his surprise. It was unusual for someone of Shaw's rank to address the chairman of the JIC in that way. But Shaw's entire persona was unusual. His body language was both defensive and hostile, shoulders hunched and torso bent forward, a human facsimile of a bunker.

Salt caught the waiter's eye and signalled for the bill.

'We don't want anything from you,' responded Salt, 'other than for me to introduce Robert so you have a channel to the top when you next need it.'

Shaw gave a curt nod and pushed his chair back. 'Well, nice to meet you. Excuse me, but I've got a meeting at Vauxhall Cross in half an hour.'

They watched him walk back through the tables and out through the front door.

'Well, he hasn't changed much,' said Salt.

The waiter laid a hardback leather folder on the table containing the bill. Salt took out his wallet, pulled out a sheaf of notes and tucked them into it. He then picked up his mobile phone. Before he slipped it back into his inside jacket pocket, Waterman had a clear view of the hardware casing for the first time. A tiny red light was on in the top right-hand corner. Waterman had the same phone and knew the function of that light. As a frequent dictator of notes, the light on his phone was often switched on. Waterman felt nauseous: the phone was in use as a recording device.

Salt looked around the restaurant wistfully. 'I love this place. The future is Europe, Robert. I hope our leaders have the sense to see that.' They parted ways on the pavement in front of the restaurant, and Waterman watched Salt's retreating figure until it was lost in the crowds of Covent Garden.

A feeling of weary resignation was seeping into his bones.

He pulled out his phone and called Swift.

PART THREE

23

PC Sam White watched the top of the stairs that descended to Victoria tube station. Every few minutes the tunnel disgorged commuters, their appearance as predictable as a tidal flow. The mass moved through the main station, breaking up into clusters, some to the exits, some to the ticket booths, others to particular platforms. The clusters then broke into smaller pods, as life trajectories tugged each person on their own course.

This morning, something about that sight filled Sam with pathos, although he couldn't quite put his finger on why. He turned his mind away from the emotion and took a breath, closing his eyes, conjuring the scene again in his imagination. He had begun doing this in recent months. Testing the extent of his knowledge of the station that had accreted from ten years on the beat. He could still see everything in his mind's eye: the wan light slanting from the vaulted roof, the grubby concourse floor, the ticket sellers in their booths. The confirmation of his familiarity with his environment never ceased to please him. It made him feel like he and the station were one, like it had given birth to a sentinel to walk its grounds and protect its transient visitors.

He moved his focus to his hearing, enjoying the

feeling of that sense sharpening, hidden sounds making themselves known. The rattle of a truck stopping at a red light just outside the station. The announcer over the tannoy, a tinny voice competing with background static, echoing across the hall.

Sam opened his eyes and watched a new wave of commuters flow out of the tube entrance and wash over the concourse. A father in a business suit, holding hands with his school-blazered son, emerged from the mass and walked towards Sam. He watched them as they passed in front of him, the father brushing crumbs from the lapels of his boy's jacket.

Sam's mind was still churning with Fran's news last night. His key had still been in the lock, the door half open, when she told him, crowding the front entrance before he'd crossed the threshold. She was breathless, saying she'd wanted to wait, to show him in person. He looked down to see three plastic sticks in her hand. The evening had been a whirlwind. Tears and laughter for both of them. They'd gone to bed emotionally spent. Within minutes, Sam could hear Fran's breathing become deeper, her body shifting unconsciously to find the most comfortable position. Sam had rolled onto his side, staring at the wall. The euphoria of the last few hours had receded, leaving him reflective. Thoughts tumbled around in his head. About the man he used to be. And the man he was today. If they'd conceived right after they'd married, their kid would be twelve now. Sam had done a lot of growing up in those years, a process he was glad a child hadn't witnessed.

He and the kid would probably have fought like cat and dog, just like Sam and his own father had. But now there was a better chance he could get to know his son. Be a support. Maybe even a friend.

Some of the stardust feeling of last night still clung to Sam that morning. As he watched the father and son round the corner and disappear from view, his mind turned to practical things. Finding the right school. And babies weren't cheap. Plus, they'd outgrow their one-bed flat pretty soon. It was going to be tight for a bit. He'd need to ask the station about overtime.

Maybe that was why the sight of the commuters had made him mournful. The idea that the new fragile life coming to join them, whose safekeeping was in his charge, would one day be an anonymous face in a station, battling crowds, made his heart heavy.

Something in Sam's line of sight snapped the thread of his thoughts, crashing him back to the present. The next wave of commuters was emerging from the tunnel. But this time something was different – wrong. Sam was running before he knew it, his elbows bent, arms pumping like pistons, torso inclined, legs launching him into a sprint towards the tube entrance. Around him, people stopped and stared, faces downshifting from curiosity to surprise to fear as he swerved around them, keeping as straight a course as he could, never letting his eyes leave his target. Even though it was moving at speed, he was catching up, the space between the two of them closing. Almost there.

What happened next at the station would be

remembered by the survivors for the rest of their lives. The moments would come back to each of them most clearly in their nightmares, sights and sounds that would haunt them for ever.

First, an enormous eruption, as if the fist of God had punched through the station floor, flinging commuters, dirt and masonry into the air. Bodies shooting up like corks released from deep water. Then a deafening crack, echoing around the vast space. Screams. Everywhere screaming. People scattering for cover, luggage and bags dropped to the floor, the febrile crackle of fear, adrenalin, like static, in the air. And then a cloud of dust, mushrooming up to the ceiling and spreading out wide, like an angel's wings unfurling.

24

Two hours after the explosion the COBRA meeting was convened.

Waterman's car moved up Whitehall from Parliament Square as emergency vehicles flew past in the opposite direction, sirens screaming. His driver stopped a short distance away from the entrance to Downing Street. Waterman stepped out and walked briskly towards the heavy oak doors of 70 Whitehall. He pressed the buzzer and announced himself, then took out his keys and other pocket paraphernalia in anticipation of the airport-type screening process in the lobby. Once he had cleared security, he walked down the flight of stairs to the basement and headed to a door at the far end of the hall, entering without knocking.

The room was the nerve centre for the UK government's times of extreme crisis management. Like most similar rooms in nation states around the world, it had the feel of a bunker: a low ceiling dominated by a long recessed strip light, wood-panelling, eight large monitors mounted on the far wall, and a large conference table with twenty-five leather chairs around its perimeter.

Waterman took in the room at a glance. Around the table were ten men and two women, a scattering of police uniforms, as well as military and civilian attire.

The room smelt of coffee and, faintly, aftershave. The prime minister sat on the far side of the table, in the middle, towards the screens. The faces around him wore the same grim expression: a professional mask of determination clamped onto whatever feelings were lurking beneath. Charles Salt sat next to the PM and motioned Waterman to the empty seat next to him.

Most of the screens were showing different news channels, both terrestrial and satellite. The indigenous-language versions of Russia Today and Al-Jazeera played next to the main English channels. It seemed that the eyes of the world's press were on Victoria station. Helicopters' cams with juddering views of the station's roof showed the ring of fire engines and police cars around the entrance. Ashen-faced presenters stood behind the police line, beyond the fire engines, talking to camera.

Every few minutes, all the channels broke away to play the same two pieces of footage. The first was a ten-second clip taken on a mobile phone. A female backpacker in her late teens stood on the concourse, waving brightly at the camera as commuters moved in the background, then the audio picked up a deafening crack and peal of thunder, and the girl ducked instinctively into a crouch as debris flew across the station behind her. The second clip, played immediately afterwards, was of a female commuter, whose formal business attire stood out in contrast to her dust-caked hair and bandaged forehead. She held on to a paramedic in the station forecourt, pausing to speak to a press pack that thrust a thicket of microphones at her. 'I saw him. Running. Full-pelt. He . . .' her face contorted for a second, a spasm holding back tears '. . . he was Asian. Or Arab. I couldn't be . . .' Her sentence choked off and she was led away.

The PM broke the spell that the footage seemed to have cast over those in the room. 'Let's start.'

Waterman walked around the room and sat between Salt and the stenographer taking minutes. The public's perception of the quietly spoken PM was of a grey bureaucrat, due mainly to the thinning hair that resembled a monk's tonsure and the boxy thick black-framed glasses. Waterman knew the perception couldn't have been further from the truth. The PM's ascent through the party had evidenced a man with an aptitude for ruthlessness, and what he lacked in public-speaking skills he made up for in cunning.

They each said their names and positions for the record, moving clockwise around the room, speaking with the flat authority of those at the head of their respective professional pyramids. Two senior officers from Scotland Yard. Two weapons experts from the Ministry of Defence. A senior officer from the army. As they spoke, Waterman realized there was no representative from the Security Service.

At that precise moment, the door opened and Vincent Shaw stepped into the room.

'Sorry I'm late,' he said, addressing the PM. 'Just got the call that I'm leading for the Agency.'

The PM pointed Shaw towards an empty seat, then

pushed a set of printed briefing notes along the table towards him.

Shaw made eye contact with Waterman and Salt, his expression devoid of emotion, picked up the notes and pulled a pen out of his pocket.

'Deputy Commissioner Bale,' said the PM, tipping his head to a heavy-set man in his fifties with thinning red hair sitting on Shaw's left, 'why don't you start us off?'

Bale nodded. There was a tremor in his hand as he reached for his water glass.

'The device detonated at eight sixteen a.m. Initial evidence suggests that it was a suicide bomb.'

A woman at the end of the table lifted a pen. It was Marion Bridges, the home secretary. She was a rising star in her party, a former barrister with a steel-trap mind, famous for tearing into opponents on the opposite benches.

'I hope we're not relying on eye-witness testimony. That woman was clearly in shock. What is this "initial evidence" you mentioned? What about CCTV footage? There must be multiple lines of sight on the detonation. It's a public building so we don't need the owner's permission.'

Bale looked uncomfortable. 'The station's cameras are all connected to the same server. When the memory is full, the system goes into reboot, clearing the memory and sending the footage to offsite storage. The reboot started a few minutes before the explosion. The cameras were all down.'

'The explosion happens minutes after the cameras

go down?' asked Bridges, eyebrows raised, playing to an invisible jury. 'Who had access to the reboot schedule?'

Bale shook his head. 'The reboot is self-programmed to happen whenever memory capacity is approached. We're reviewing the server log, but there appears to be no pattern to the reboots. The next step is for us to wait for the CSI team to produce their results.'

There was quiet around the table. For the last few years, CCTV footage had been the first resort in all terror investigations. In its absence, information would need to be painstakingly collected and sifted by hand to find any clues as to the attacker's identity.

Waterman thought he noticed the glimmer of a smile appear on Shaw's face for the briefest of seconds.

'Make sure they are expedited,' said the PM. 'I agree with the home secretary. Eye-witness testimony is notoriously unreliable in situations like these. But now the media have played that interview, the public is going to react. Fear and prejudice may fill the vacuum of information. We need tangible evidence as quickly as we can find it.'

'The National Front has already requested permission for a march at noon,' said Bridges. 'Other anti-immigration bodies may join.'

Salt raised his eyebrows. 'National Front? No one's claimed responsibility yet.'

'Their assumption is that it was orchestrated by jihadists,' replied Bridges.

'If we deny the Front's application, it won't stop

them marching and there'll be more likelihood of violence,' said the PM. 'Let's approve it. Two hundred yards from all public buildings and any other marches. Heightened police presence. The nationwide minute's silence is happening at one. No marches before two, and all must end an hour before sunset.'

Waterman stared at the TV screens. A vigil had already assembled near Buckingham Palace Road. 'Love Not Hate' banners speckled the crowd.

'What about the terror threat?' asked Bridges.

The threat level in the UK had been at 'severe' since 2017, which meant that a terror attack was highly likely. There was only one higher level, which was 'critical'. Bridges' question was a loaded one. An increase in the threat level not only meant that an attack was imminent, it also meant that maximum protective security measures could be taken, including the deployment of British Army troops to support armed police officers at all locations designated as key sites across the UK. The deployment was controversial for many reasons, not least that there were no clear parameters for when to end the operation. It would also give Marion Bridges a wide extension of her current powers as home secretary.

'It's premature to consider that,' said Salt.

It was too soon to see British troops on English high streets. And definitely too soon to hand the reins of power to Marion Bridges.

'And when the time's right, it's a decision for JTAC, not us,' added the PM.

The Joint Terrorism Analysis Centre was responsible for setting the threat level and was under MI5's purview.

'Let's move on,' continued the PM. 'Deputy Commissioner Bale, let's go through the timeline.'

The slip of paper that Bale handed to each person ran through each step of the emergency response to the bombing. It would become key evidence in the public inquests of those killed.

8.16 a.m.	Bomb detonates near the Victoria line tube entrance of Victoria station.
	Two ambulances parked at the station provide immediate assistance to the injured.
8.30 a.m.	Armed response vehicles are on the scene.
8.35 a.m.	Appointed Force Duty Officer notes in her log that she considered withdrawing all emergency responders as she feared a second device. She decides against it and explosive-searching dogs are deployed.
8.45 a.m.	Paramedics using improvised stretchers carry away the injured.
	A temporary storage facility is onsite in Victoria to house the bodies.

9.15 a.m.	The Greater London Authority's Children and Adults Social Care services arrive at the site, joined by the British Red Cross psychosocial team.
	Fifteen ambulances are now at the scene as well as ten ARVs.
9.30 a.m.	Shops and offices within a half-mile radius of the station are evacuated.
9.45 a.m.	Three hundred Authorized Firearms Officers (AFOs) are deployed in Central London.
	Paramedics treat walking wounded at the scene. Seriously injured are taken to St Mary's and St Thomas' hospitals.
10 a.m.	All casualties now evacuated.

'Is the area secure now?' asked Salt.

Bale nodded. 'The duty officer declared it so and handed over control to the Scotland Yard crime-scene manager fifteen minutes ago.'

Waterman was annotating his copy of the timeline when Salt slid a folded piece of paper across the table towards him. Waterman unfolded it and read it under his cupped hand: *This could be a project for our mutual friend.*

'If that's all, let's reconvene this afternoon,' said the PM, standing up.

As Waterman exited the room with the others, he noticed that Salt was waiting for him at the door.

'So, what do you think?' asked Salt, under his breath.

'She'll need front-line access,' said Waterman. 'That means embedding in the MI5 task force. And that means . . .'

'. . . getting Vincent Shaw to agree,' finished Salt.

'And what do you think are the chances of that?'

'You're resourceful, Robert. You'll think of something.'

25

An hour later the helicopter picked Sara up. She'd watched as it dropped in a vertical line to the middle of Russell Square. She'd given Waterman the location at which to collect her when he'd called. The park in the square was only a few hundred yards from where she slept, but the density of houses in the area made identifying hers impossible.

Christian's words were still playing in her head. She had plenty of reason to doubt him, but intuitively knew that what he'd said was true. *When you get involved, you change the future.* It fitted the pattern of events since she had volunteered, tasking herself with putting her abilities to good use. It made sense to her now. The future was like a sealed environment that no one had ever stepped into. By exploring it, she was contaminating it. She had always thought of Christian's choices as being driven by selfishness, but now she saw them for what they were: self-preservation. By handling the future, she was making it unstable.

The helicopter's landing gear rested on the grass, the bulk of the vehicle settling, pressing the skids akimbo, the spinning blades battering the trees. The side door popped open, beckoning her.

It was too late to back out now. She knew she was

making some difference – the girls in the drain had been rescued, and only the bombers had died at The Hague – but it was clear now the level of personal risk that came with it. For her, the future could be booby-trapped.

She ran, her body bent double, the blades roaring and blending the air above her. A few minutes later, the skyline of London spread out across the horizon.

'The problem is the absence of information,' said Waterman. He was sitting in the back, next to her. 'Without CCTV, we're reliant on witness testimony and physical evidence left at the scene of the crime. The process has begun, but it could take days. Salt secured permission for us to fly over the site on our way to Thames House. There's a no-fly zone in place over London.'

They were both wearing noise-cancelling head-phones and speakers to communicate over the sound of the engine and rotors. The effect was to pipe his voice straight into her ears, just like the operation in the Netherlands.

Waterman was her main point of contact but the description was beginning to feel ironic. He remained always one step away from her, a voice whispering in her ear but rarely by her side. When she had climbed into the helicopter, their fingers had accidentally touched as she sat down. There was a gelatinous feeling to his skin, a soft give when her little finger pressed on his. She had looked quickly down and seen his hand was covered with a shiny substance, almost like a

184

membrane. She recognized the transparent glove instantly. The spies had all worn them when they had trained her twenty years ago. They were the barrier that protected them from Sara: it made sure that they were in Sara's head but she never got inside theirs.

They were flying at a low altitude, barely a few hundred feet above the tops of the buildings. The packed grid of properties above Oxford Street gave way to the green expanse of Hyde Park and the steel-glint of the Serpentine lake. For a few seconds, the helicopter was reflected below, a tiny metallic fly skimming over the surface. The traffic beneath them was snarled, lines of cars pressed bumper to bumper all along the edges of Buckingham Palace. Up ahead, she could see why. Police had cordoned off the approach roads to Victoria station, backing up traffic for miles.

Four helicopters hung suspended at points around the airspace above the station, at different altitudes, like toys on a child's mobile. As they approached, Sara could see the police markings on their shells. The helicopter closest to them was directly in their flight path and, after some communication from the pilot that was too crackly for Sara to make out, peeled away to the side to allow them access.

'I can stay here a couple of minutes only.' The pilot's voice was suddenly loud in her ears. 'Scotland Yard is worried the downwash might disturb the crime scene.'

Sara looked through the window onto the station. All she could see was its roof, slatted in different shades of grey, covering the entire structure. The front fore-court was packed with emergency vehicles, parked at abrupt angles, and beyond them a temporary barrier had been erected, screening off the station from the outside world.

'We can't see much,' said Waterman. 'Just there.' He pointed to a section of the roof near the junction of Buckingham Palace Road and the front of the station. A part was missing and, through the gap, Sara saw, for a dizzying second, down into the station below. White square tiles of the concourse floor. A black crater of earth, debris piled around its sides. As the helicopter drifted, red smear marks on the concourse came into view, puddle deep in places. It was like an aerial view into an abattoir.

'I can't tell much from up here,' said Sara.

'Where do we start?' asked Waterman.

Sara stared down through the jagged hole in the station ceiling. Someone had done this. Someone had walked into the station this morning at rush hour. They'd sought out the crowds. Got close enough to see their faces. Mingled with them. Near enough to notice them and be noticed.

'With a personal item from someone in the kill zone,' she said.

'Take us to Thames House,' said Waterman, tapping the shoulder of the pilot. He turned back to Sara. 'We've got to play this carefully. The only way to get you inside there is to embed you into MI5.'

*

A few minutes later, the landing gear rested on the circular pad in the centre of the roof of the building on the Embankment.

As Sara grasped the door handle, Waterman touched her shoulder. 'You're going to be working in Vincent Shaw's task force. You should know he's not a big fan of GCHQ. We've made the case that the absence of CCTV makes GCHQ's involvement crucial.'

Sara cracked open the door. The wind roared in, and she had to shout to be heard, even with the microphone and speakers. 'And he accepted that?'

Waterman shook his head. 'No, he refused.'

Sara looked at him in surprise. 'So, why are we here?'

Waterman opened the door on his side, doubling the noise level in the compartment. 'I can be very persuasive,' he shouted.

26

Vincent Shaw looked around the briefing room. Most of the five agents at the table knew nothing about the detonation beyond what was being reported on TV. They would need guidance and it was up to him to provide it. Shaw's faith kept him true to his purpose. He would have liked to begin the meeting with a prayer. It would give the men and women in the room comfort, he knew, but the Service forbade it, and in any event, Riz and Simon weren't Christian.

It had been more than a decade since the last tube bombings. They'd had CCTV to identify the attackers then. MI5 had a critical role, but the bulk of the investigation had been done by the data-analysis units of government. They had set their algorithms loose, like search dogs, baying through the dark infinities of the web, sniffing out voiceprint and photo-ID matches for those already in their databases. It offended him that the search had been automated. The blood spilt had been human. There had been no room for nuance or discretion that time. They had ceded control to the machines in the basement at Cheltenham. But not today. Whether you described it as luck or Fate, no machines had witnessed the terror attack today. And the result was that human eyes and ears, and human processes, would sift through the wreckage and find the trail.

Shaw looked to his right. Roger Pembroke, his number two, gave him a tiny nod. Pembroke knew his way of working better than anyone. And was loyal. Would take a bullet for Shaw. That was what he needed now. To have his staff on a war footing.

'OK, let's start.'

The general murmur cut out. Shaw was well versed in the nuance of power and his physicality was a part of it. He'd played rugby all his life since school, even at club level in the early years at Thames House. He liked his suits tight-fitting to accentuate a physique honed by training and activity on the pitch. The legacy of innumerable tackles was written across his face. In an institution where most still worked at a desk, his body projected power. And he knew that his voice had also played a major reason in his advancement. It boomed with little effort, crowding out anyone else who might be speaking. It ensured he was heard, even in crowded rooms, even where those rooms were stacked with higher-ranking officers.

'We have a good group here today.' He looked around the room, introducing them all with a nod. 'Riz Malik, Jenny Grove, Simon Fawzi, Joe Sullivan, Roger Pembroke. One of the strongest teams I've worked with in thirty years at Thames House. As you've probably heard, CCTV isn't available on this attack, so this is back to basics for us.'

A knock at the door interrupted him. A bearded

man in a suit, at least Shaw's size, walked in, trailed by an attractive female assistant. The sight of the man was so unexpected, here in MI5's headquarters, that it threw Shaw for a second. He did his best to mask his anger, but couldn't help the contempt leaking into his voice as he spoke. 'Mr Waterman, to what do we owe this honour?'

Shaw already knew the likely answer. Unwilling to be sidelined, GCHQ had found something to maintain its relevance in the investigation.

'This is Sara Eden,' said Waterman, tipping his head to the woman. Shaw noticed the men in the room staring at her with undisguised interest. Shaw could see why. She had the sort of looks that most men are attracted to, could probably have gone into the beauty business if she'd wanted to. Instead, she'd chosen to trail around with the Wookiee of Cheltenham. He must have something on her.

'She's going to be working with your team,' said Waterman. 'Special liaison with GCHQ.'

'Thanks,' said Shaw, drily, 'but that's not necessary. All information will be shared through the normal channels.' This was performance art by Waterman. Shaw had already said no when Waterman asked him at the COBRA meeting that morning. Waterman was gambling that Shaw would waver in a direct confrontation in front of his team.

'Sara will be a conduit to GCHQ's resources. That's a formidable amount of information,' said Waterman.

Shaw did his best to look unimpressed. 'Embedding one of yours in my team isn't going to happen.'

'I'm not asking you, Vincent.'

Waterman was doing his best to press his buttons, and it was beginning to work. 'And I've already told you, you have no authority –'

'Actually,' said Waterman, interrupting him, 'I'm here to ask your team.'

'And what does that mean?'

'MI5 officers are entitled to recruit agents. That's their discretion. We're here to see whether one of the officers here wishes to work with Sara. As an agent, she'll provide considerable intel.'

Shaw made eye contact with each member of his team. A warning. 'I think you'll find there are no –'

'She can ride with me,' said Riz.

Of course it was Riz Malik who spoke. Shaw should have seen that coming.

'Riz, they're obliged to share everything they have anyway. This is just –' Shaw started.

'It'll be useful having a direct line,' said Riz. He was already pulling up a chair for the girl.

Shaw could tell where this was going. Riz was a legend with women. There were already two internal investigations under way regarding his seductions during deep-cover operations. Shaw gave it forty-eight hours before Riz got her horizontal. He would have been out on his ear years ago, but he was one of the most talented officers in T Branch, which covered domestic Islamic terrorism. His networks were second to none, and he had shown himself time and time again to be a cold-blooded operator.

Waterman must have known all these moves would happen when he brought the girl here. Riz's reputation wasn't a secret in the security services, and given that the most dominant of Shaw's enquiry lines would be Islamic terrorism, it was likely Riz would be in the task force. Waterman had dangled the bait and Riz had bitten as expected. And now Waterman had a ringside seat in the operation.

'That's settled, then,' said Waterman.

'Fine,' conceded Shaw. 'But Ms Eden will need to wait outside. This is an officers-only briefing.'

Thirty minutes later, Shaw watched the officers as they filed out of the room. He was determined not to let Waterman take charge of this operation. Shaw was going to make a stand. He was tired of being outmanoeuvred by GCHQ.

It didn't take a crystal ball to see that MI5's days were numbered. Maybe not in five or ten years, but in thirty or forty, military intelligence would be one division of artificial intelligence. Drones, algorithms, ubiquitous facial-recognition software. The robots were coming. All the insight and spycraft learnt in the crucible of the twentieth century's hot and cold wars would be lost. What had happened just now wasn't an isolated incident. GCHQ was gradually creeping into MI5 and MI6's everyday life, as insidiously as a tide sliding up a beach one inch at a time. But GCHQ wouldn't succeed this time. The CCTV machines had failed today for a reason. Whoever had committed today's bombing would be caught by human cunning. There were certain things that computers were not capable of. Such as loyalty. And sabotage.

Pembroke was the last to leave and waited by the door, looking at Shaw for any final instruction before leaving.

'Roger, that girl . . .'

'Sara Eden,' prompted Pembroke.

'Yes. Find a way to get rid of her.'

27

Sara was waiting in the main lobby of Thames House when Riz exited the lift. He skimmed his ID over the exit barriers separating the security side of the building from the visitors' entrance and pulled car keys from his pocket.

'Let's head to Victoria first. Look at the victim-identification process,' said Riz.

Sara could see him more clearly. He was not much taller than her, but had a wiry physique. He was wearing glasses now, black frames that gave him an air of studied intensity, which contrasted with what he was wearing, a black polo shirt and jeans with what looked like brand new Stan Smith trainers.

She followed him through an exit door that led to an enclosed stairwell. Riz didn't speak as they walked down two flights of stairs, but looked back a few times at her. There was something in his eyes she couldn't quite place, something out of keeping with an MI5 officer's expected demeanour.

He pushed open a door marked with a stencilled 'P2' and stepped into a vast car park. The side lights on a BMW 3 Series flashed yellow once about a hundred yards away. It wasn't until they were seated in his car that she spoke.

'So, why did you volunteer?' asked Sara.

'What do you mean?' said Riz.

He started the car and drove towards the corkscrew exit ramp.

'Your boss doesn't seem to want me anywhere near this investigation.'

They were heading to a dead end. The exit ramp ran right into a thick metal wall. Riz stopped the car and waited. After a few seconds, a tremor shook the wall and it rose slowly, retracting into the ceiling. Daylight flooded in through the widening gap.

'He's not my boss,' replied Riz. 'He's operational lead. It's not the same thing.'

Sara had been trying to decipher his character from the signals he had been giving. The body language in the meeting – his chair turned subtly away from Shaw's direction. The glimpse of a grin when he had exited the elevator. The looks in the stairwell. And now, with his comment on Shaw, the pieces fell into place. Riz was cocksure, but not in an arrogant way. There was something supremely confident about his manner. He seemed unfazed by the events of the morning. If anything, they seemed to energize him. Sara found herself staring at him. It was difficult not to.

The gate retracted into the roof and he pulled out, then almost immediately pumped the brakes. A black Lycra-clad cyclist flew into view. He wore a thick helmet, a tiny cycloptic camera fixed to the front. As he veered around the car, he stuck a middle finger up at Riz.

'Charming,' said Riz. He drove into the stream of traffic.

'He's crafty, by the way,' he continued. Off Sara's confused look, he prompted, 'Vincent Shaw.' He looked at her as if he was sharing a confidence. Like they were pupils plotting in class. 'You'd better keep an eye out for him.'

'I can take care of myself,' said Sara.

They were driving along the outside lane of Parliament Square. A police barrier blocked access to the approach road to Victoria Street. Riz flashed the lights built into the front grille and pulled out his identification card, pressing it against his closed window so that the officer on duty could read it. The officer nodded and lifted the barrier for them to pass.

'You never answered my question,' said Sara.

'The head of one of the UK's three security agencies vouched for you. That's good enough for me.'

'You're lying,' said Sara. She softened the weight of the words with a smile.

'OK,' he replied. 'Why did I take you on, then?'

The answer was obvious to her now. With a better understanding of Riz, it had become clear. He'd agreed to work with her simply because Shaw had told him not to.

When she didn't respond, he looked at her, a cheeky grin now flowering on his face. 'You can read my mind, can you?'

She gave him an enigmatic smile and looked out of the window, surprised at how quickly they'd started flirting with each other – and how much she was enjoying it.

She could sense him about to say more when his eyes registered something ahead. He flicked his indicator and pulled over. An ambulance was approaching on the other side of the road. Its lights were flashing but there was no siren. It moved at a stately pace, barely faster than walking speed. Four police motorcycles, two in front of the ambulance and two in the rear, flanked the vehicle. On the pavements, pedestrians stood still, watching. Next to Sara's window, an elderly man in a grey suit and fedora took off his hat and held it to his chest.

'We're almost there,' Riz said, as he resumed their course. The sight of the motorcade had shifted the energy in the car. He sounded business-like, and when Sara looked at him again, he was staring intently ahead.

A huge crowd of pedestrians was gathered on the street in front of them. Fathers with their children. Older people. They stood still, silently, holding hands.

Riz flashed his lights and uniformed police parted the crowd. As they drove through, Sara read the simple messages on the placards. LOVE NOT HATE. NO FEAR. ONE LOVE.

The car had slowed almost to a stop as it approached newly erected twenty-foot-high white screens that surrounded the station entrance, obscuring the crime scene from the public eye. Riz switched off the ignition and pulled on the handbrake. He had parked the car in a space sheltered from the press area.

'The CSI team has a tent inside with the clothes and belongings of the deceased from the centre of the blast. Stay this side of the barriers. Anonymity is a pre-requisite for an officer. And an agent. We're undercover, by definition. If you get caught on film entering the crime scene, you'll give Shaw his reason to drop you. And remember, the press will do whatever they can to get photos of a crime scene.'

They exited the car and walked towards the towering cloth walls that now screened the interior of the station from the crowds. The wind was picking up and the walls flapped and puffed like sails.

A trail of white-uniformed personnel moved in and out through a gap in the walls. Riz slipped through the gap and Sara followed him.

28

Shaw stood in his office on the seventh floor of Thames House. It wasn't a corner office, but it was river-facing. Well, it was if he stood in the corner and pressed his forehead to the glass. He took a deep breath. Below him, the Thames wound its way like a thick brown rope, drawing everything in its path.

He could have played the game if he'd wanted to. Made the right friends. And the right enemies. He saw peers of his do it well, to their advantage. They were in their corner offices now, with generous car allowances and fat pensions waiting for them on retirement, maybe book careers too. He'd tried for about a year to emulate their scheming. But he'd fooled no one and the exercise had made his skin crawl. He knew he was not a creature of the system, and he also knew that made him vulnerable.

A muted chattering sound came from above and he looked up to see a helicopter fly over, its nose tilting forward as it swooped down to the river. Waterman heading back to his base.

Shaw's thoughts kept turning to GCHQ. Whenever he thought of it, the image of a whale appeared in his mind, a city-sized whale, swimming through oceans of data, sifting everything in its enormous jaws. Sooner or later, everything went through that beast.

Butterflies fluttered uncharacteristically in his stomach. GCHQ hadn't found out yet. He was sure of it. If they had, Waterman wouldn't have flown all the way to London on a personal plea. If Waterman knew, Shaw would have had a private visit by an unsmiling GCHQ operative, who would use the leverage to force Shaw to do whatever they wanted.

He tried to calm himself. He'd used all possible precautions. Different photo, false name and bio. He toyed with the idea of using his own laptop with VPN routers, but GCHQ, no doubt, had ways of slicing through those layers like a hot knife through butter. He signed on from internet cafés, after midnight mostly, a hoodie top pulled over his head to hide from the CCTV.

It was madness to have done it. Pure madness. But he was learning more and more that, in life, not everything was a choice. Who you were began to take over your everyday life, growing like a cancer after middle age, consuming those parts that could at one point have been influenced into rational decision. Identity calcified over time.

The helicopter was a speck in the sky now, about to merge with the jagged horizon.

Shaw had given up promising himself he'd never make the same mistakes. There was little point. If he wanted to do it in the future, he would, and there was nothing his present self could do to stop him.

The phone on his desk rang, breaking the train of his thoughts.

'Shaw,' he announced, after pressing the speaker-phone key.

'We need to discuss crowd control at ground zero.' It was Pembroke.

'Go on,' said Shaw.

'The far-right rally's route runs up Hudson's Place and then up Wilton Road. It means the vigil and the press will be pressed right up against the sterilized area. There's a risk the press are going to have line of sight into the station.'

Shaw was quiet. Pembroke was a good officer, but his obsequiousness had slowed his advancement. He lacked initiative and deferred too much to Shaw for answers. The information he'd provided should have been filtered through the system, to Scotland Yard and community policing liaisons as much as to Shaw. This was just another bone Pembroke was dropping at Shaw's feet.

'What do you want to do?' prompted Pembroke, as the silence stretched on.

A plan was budding in Shaw's mind and, for once, Shaw didn't mind Pembroke's slavish devotion. The information he had just provided could be very useful.

'Where are Riz and Eden now?' he asked.

'At Victoria,' replied Pembroke, after a confused pause.

'Good,' replied Shaw. 'Meet me there just before one.'

29

'Is there anything in particular you'd like to see?' asked Pam Smith, the senior identification officer. She was tall, in her fifties, wearing a police uniform.

Sara, Riz and Smith stood at the entrance to the large temporary tent that had been erected immediately on the other side of the towering screens. It was a simple covering held up between two wooden poles, and Sara could see through it to the station entrance. A line of scene of crime officers, SOCOs, was inching slowly across the station forecourt, their eyes trained to the ground.

Two long trestle tables dominated the interior of the tent. The centre of each was piled high with debris. It was a mixture of scraps of clothing, torn rags and various pocket items: phones, wallets, bags. The debris gave off a sharp sulphurous smell that stung Sara's nose. Officers sat at the tables sifting through it. Next to each was a laptop, and an officer broke away sporadically from sorting to tap out a search on the keyboard.

'We're quite short-staffed at the moment. We have four officers and six bereavement nurses, but we need more.' Smith spoke with the distracted air of someone under an intense deadline.

Riz pointed to the remnants sitting in boxes at the

corner. 'We won't take up much of your time. Can you show us how this works?'

Smith nodded, stepping back to allow them to move further inside the tent. 'This is where all items believed to belong to the victims are kept. Here, we first search for anything that can identify the owner. That's our main purpose: to identify victims from the possessions we found at the scene. Once the deceased has been identified, we put the items in a box on this table.' She pointed to a table in a shadowed corner of the tent Sara hadn't noticed before. It was square and partially filled with cardboard boxes, each containing debris.

Sara found herself staring at the box nearest to her. Sitting on top was a torn, blood-speckled baby carrier.

'When this is complete,' continued Smith, 'we'll have the clothes laundered. All other items are professionally cleaned. They will then be returned to the next-of-kin. Is there anything particular I can help with?'

Riz motioned to Sara then stepped back a few feet. When he spoke, it was in a hushed whisper. 'Look, you were embedded for a reason. Just let me know what you're looking for and how I can help.'

Sara was surprised. For someone as self-assured as Riz seemed to be, he was also intuitive. She found herself wanting to trust him, although she knew it was too soon. 'I need to search the items here.'

Riz nodded, and stepped back towards Smith. 'This is my colleague, Sara. She'd like to lend a hand.'

Smith hesitated, looking doubtfully at Sara, then

back at Riz. 'I've put in a call for additional helpers, but I suppose, until they arrive . . .' Smith looked down at Sara's hands. 'We need to prevent contamination, so we'll need you to wear these.'

Smith reached into her jacket pocket and pulled out a pair of disposable polythene gloves. Sara nodded and took them. As Smith led her to a seat, Sara looked back at Riz, who gave her a nod before stepping away and moving towards the station.

'We're looking for anything identifiable: name tags, wallets, phones,' said Smith. She sat Sara at the end of the closest trestle table, touched Sara's shoulder and moved away. Sara looked at the others, her plan to connect with an item suddenly seeming impossible. She would need to take off her gloves and make direct contact, and Smith seemed everywhere at once, walking among the tables constantly. The tent was also small, and a sense of solemnity maintained an almost perfect silence inside, which heightened awareness. Everyone seemed to be under everyone else's nose. If Smith saw her touching evidence without protective wear, it would likely be the end of Sara's voluntary session.

Her eyes searched the pile of scorched rags in front of her as she wondered where to start. Next to her was a solitary sleeve, dismembered from a jacket, burn marks blasted into the underarm. Close by was a pair of red women's gloves, two fingers missing. None of the items was intact. Everything had been burnt or shredded by the blast. She could only imagine the injuries of the owners. They must have been torn limb from limb.

The indiscriminate nature of the attack was turning her stomach.

A male officer sitting at the next table called to Smith, who approached and sat down next to him. Together they scrutinized a laptop search. Smith's back was almost directly facing Sara. It was the chance she needed. She slipped off her gloves and let her fingers trail along the items in front of her.

The closest to her was a set of keys, attached to a ring on which hung a metal fob with a Jaguar car logo. Dried blood crusted over the fob. She slipped her fingers into the clasp of the ring, squeezing the keys tight in her fingers.

Darkness gathered in her peripheral vision, then swept gradually across her sight until the world around her disappeared. At the same time, ambient background sounds began to recede until she was in insulated silence.

A flash of light sparked in the vacuum. Then another.

She was launched into a shuddering first-person perspective. A pair of men's suit trousers was climbing up steps. Shiny brown brogues. A rush-hour crowd was pressed tightly around her. Her head, one in a sea. Liver-spotted skin hung loosely on the hands. It was a man's memory. An older man. He walked with the trudge of a commuter on a daily migration that was several decades old.

Sara tried to pick up as much detail as she could. The suit was pinstriped and charcoal grey. Decidedly not fashionable. She caught sight of a battered brown leather briefcase, frayed at the edges. The tie looked like it had school colours, thick stripes, and was blotched with barely noticeable stains.

She could feel the weariness in his every step. His head was down and the stairs dominated his view, the crowds around him just a background blur. Everyone seemed to be moving faster than him.

When he reached the penultimate step, he collided with the person ahead of him, a cyclist, still wearing his helmet and carrying the detached front wheel of a bicycle. For some inexplicable reason, the cyclist was standing stock still, despite the fast-moving flow of people. A body bumped into the old businessman from behind, then another, as the crowd ascending the stairs kept surging forward, ignorant of the bottleneck. The businessman tried to reroute, but to his surprise, it now appeared everyone at the top of the stairs was frozen.

As the cyclist shifted, the older man glimpsed what they were all looking at. A shape moving fast across the station concourse. Racing towards them. A blur in black. Those in front seemed to be watching, agog.

The blur reappeared. It was clearer now. It was a policeman, running full pelt, arms pumping by his sides, veering around people. Heading straight towards the tube entrance. The policeman vanished, then re-appeared, only a few yards away now. He was stretching out his arms, reaching for something or someone.

Panic seemed to ripple across those ahead on the steps. The cyclist and all those at the top were in the process of turning, ready to make an escape down the stairs, when there was a blinding flash, then an atomic blast of heat consuming everything. Bodies were being disassembled in front of her eyes as the concussion wave lifted them off their feet, and then Sara found herself back at the trestle table, her ragged breaths and hammering heartbeat seemingly deafening in the deathly quiet of the tent.

She looked around but the officers were all preoccupied with their searches. Pam Smith was at the other end of the tent, laying down a new box on the square table.

Sara sat back, her hands trembling. The explosion had been as powerful as the one she'd seen consume the crowds at The Hague. But she'd been an observer then, watching the devastation happen from afar. This time, she'd witnessed it first-hand, from inside the blast zone, living it from the viewpoint of one of the victims. The horror seemed so much worse. In barely ninety seconds, lives had been yanked out of comfortable grooves and violently ended on the steps of a tube station. The sense of feral panic in that tight, enclosed space still clung to her. And not just that. Something else. A faint sense of guilt that she had been down there with them at the end and had survived. She took a deep, shaky breath, trying to ground herself.

She looked down at the pile of debris in front of her and now recognized the jacket sleeve. It was the same grey pinstripe the older businessman had worn. And on the far side of the pile was one brown brogue, covered with dust.

She laid the keys down and pulled the polythene

gloves back on, then stood up and scoured the entire length of the table, pushing her hands through the scraps to make sure she'd seen everything. When she had finished, she placed all the items she had found together in a separate pile away from the others.

'These belong together?' Pam Smith was standing next to her. She looked at the one brogue, the jacket sleeve, the shred of tie Sara had found and the keyring.

'I think so,' Sara replied. 'I don't have a name, but he's in his sixties. Works in the City.' She knew Smith would press the question, so pre-empted her. 'It's just a hunch.'

Smith laid a hand on her arm. 'Sometimes that's where we have to start.'

Smith was about to leave but Sara reached out to stop her. Something she had just seen was scratching at her mind, a link struggling to be made.

The cyclist on the steps.

He reminded her of something she'd seen that morning when she was in the car with Riz.

'Have you seen a cyclist's helmet here?' asked Sara.

Smith shook her head. 'It wasn't retrieved from the blast zone.'

Sara stood up. 'Excuse me, I've got to go.'

30

Sara was walking towards the tube entrance, looking for Riz, when her phone began to buzz. When she answered, she heard Waterman's unmistakable Yorkshire accent.

'*Any developments?*'

Sara walked towards the middle of the forecourt, until she was out of hearing distance of the SOCOs. 'I'm working on a few leads, but nothing yet.'

'*Be careful of Vincent Shaw. He's not going to roll over that easily. Don't assume you can trust his team either.*'

Sara hung up and walked back to the top of the stairs descending to the tube station.

Riz was standing in a puddle of sunlight, engrossed in something on the floor. She looked up, following the slanting shaft to its source. It was coming through a hole in the ceiling, the one she had looked through that morning when she had hovered several hundred feet above the station on her way to Thames House. The deep scarlet blood spills had been cleaned but she could see ghostly stains, thick swipes that covered the stone steps leading down and splattered the side walls. The only remnants of the people who had stood on the steps just hours before.

Next to Riz, a semicircle of kneeling SOCOs worked

around a deep crater. Over their shoulders, she noticed stress fractures spider-webbing the concrete a further ten feet or so in every direction.

'There was a 360-degree concussion wave,' said Riz, looking up. 'A mortar or suitcase bomb would have a deeper impact crater. This one was a few feet above ground when it detonated. Whoever blew this up wanted to get close. He must have worked his way right into the heart of them before it went off. Here, take these.'

He handed her two tight balls of plastic. In answer to Sara's look, he pointed at her feet. 'They're for your shoes.' He gestured to his own, which were covered with white polythene SOCO sleeves.

She slipped them over her boots and stood next to Riz, who was staring into the mouth of the tube-station entrance. He seemed distracted.

'They're not sociopaths,' he said, finally meeting Sara's eye. 'And they're not all fanatics either. It can start with a seed. Maybe it's revenge, or extreme family loyalty. You plant that seed in an organization whose goal is to create suicide bombers. And then you water it with a community belief in the nobility of the act.' He pointed to the ground at his feet. 'What happened here wasn't done by a loner. And it was a long time in the planning.'

'He didn't work his way into the crowd,' said Sara, keeping one eye on the SOCOs. She hadn't chosen to trust Riz yet. The fewer people who knew what she was doing there, the better. She was standing so close to him she could smell his aftershave, a faint musk of sandalwood.

'How do you know that?' asked Riz, furrowing his brow.

Sara ignored the question. 'He was running. Fast. And there was a policeman chasing him.'

Riz nodded. 'PC Sam White was killed in the explosion.' He turned to face her full-on. 'If you have a source, I need to know it.'

'I can get you something better,' said Sara.

'And what's that?'

'I think I might know where we can find footage of the attack.'

They stood halfway down the stairs, peering into the gloom. The only light came from the low-wattage emergency bulbs that weren't strong enough to illuminate more than a few feet of darkness. Sara could see the silhouette of thick wires swaying from the ceiling, like jungle vines. Occasionally, pockets of darkness were reclaimed by light when broken fixtures sparked and crackled. Sections of the floor seemed to ripple and dance as they stared at it.

'They'd cleared the area for a second device when the drain burst. They've called for a structural surveyor,' said Riz, walking down to the foot of the stairs. Three lines of police tape closed off the entrance. 'Pam Smith said this is the only place that hasn't been swept for victims' possessions. So, what are we looking for?'

Sara didn't answer. She remained standing in the

stairwell, looking around her. Being here was bringing back all the moments from her connection with the older businessman. The bodies pressed around her. The growing crush. She could hear their restive protests, could see them staring at those rooted to the top step.

She recognized more of them now. A willowy girl in her twenties with bright red lipstick, and gloves the matching colour. Those were the gloves with fingers missing that she had seen on Pam Smith's identification table. And on the third step from the top, the diminutive Latin-looking mother with the baby carrier, her arms held around her newborn to protect it from the crowd. Sara was close enough to see the mother's expression as it tipped from concern to fear when she realized she was trapped in the crush. Hands were pushing at the motionless bodies at the top. And then a moment of panic, like a herd of animals spooked, before the surge of movement back down the stairs. Even though she knew it was coming, she flinched as the bomb turned the world upside down.

'You all right?' Riz was staring at her, one eyebrow raised.

The reverberation of the blast was still echoing in Sara's ears as she came slowly out of her trance. 'I'm fine,' she said, taking a deep breath. She walked to the bottom of the stairs, lifted the police tape and ducked under it.

'Keep an eye out for loose wiring,' warned Riz, as he followed her through.

*

They picked their way over the rubble that lay at the foot of the stairs. To their right, they could barely make out the silhouettes of the pedestrian gates to the Victoria line. To their left, they could see a line of ticket machines under the wan light of the emergency strips. It was a twilight world of shadows. Large water spills had collected near the supporting pillars in the main area and there was a powerful smell that Sara couldn't identify. Possibly burning rubber.

She stepped carefully through the darkness, keeping her eyes to the floor.

'When are you going to tell me what we're looking for?' asked Riz.

Before she could respond, a scraping sound from behind one of the pillars made them both jump. Riz motioned to Sara to stay where she was. She shook her head and pointed to the puddle of water that lay at the foot of the pillar. In the bare light, its surface acted like a mirror. The pillar appeared to rise from its depths, a black monolith silhouetted against a fire exit sign. From where they were standing, they could see the shape of a person pressed against it.

Sara and Riz approached from different sides. As the far side of the support came into view, they saw him. His uniform was covered with dirt, and cotton wool was held in place by a plaster stuck to his forehead.

'They discharged me. I had to come back.'

His voice was raspy, as if his throat was caked with dust.

'It's possible to do it. I know it is.' He was talking to them, but his mind appeared elsewhere.

'You shouldn't be here,' said Riz, gently. 'We've got a tent upstairs.'

'You could put the scanners in. Like at airports,' said the guard, blankly. 'Roll them out.'

Riz put an arm around his shoulders. 'C'mon. Let's get you a cup of tea.'

The guard let himself be led away, then stopped after a few steps and turned back to Sara. 'More bombs on the tube lines these past years than all the airlines combined.'

Sara didn't know what to say. Riz made eye contact with her, then guided the man back through the rubble to the stairs.

The sound of their footsteps died away and Sara was left in silence again. She turned back to her search. Nothing appeared to be lying on the open floor. If what she was looking for was down there, it was obscured by something.

There was a small pile of dirt near the ticket machines that appeared to be the result of a cave-in from the roof.

As she approached, she saw what looked like a tiny shred of plastic, no larger than a thumbnail, peeking through the brown silt. She would have dismissed it, had it not been for the colour. It was bright orange. Day-glo orange.

She crouched and brushed away the silt, revealing several ribs of concave orange piping. It was the top of a bicycle helmet. It was impossible to tell whether it was empty. She had seen first-hand the blast separate limbs from torsos. It was not inconceivable that the helmet and the head wearing it remained together.

Her mouth was dry and her heart hammering as she brushed away more of the debris, clearing a space around the perimeter of the crown. Then she hooked her finger around the edge and lifted it experimentally. It came away easily and tipped over.

It was empty.

She excavated the entire helmet from the mound and examined it. What she was looking for was in exactly the same position as the one she'd seen that morning when the cyclist veered around Riz's car.

A helmet cam.

31

Waterman waited by the lifts, ostensibly checking his phone. From where he stood, he had a clear view of both sides of the corridor, all the way to the edges where the circular passageways disappeared around their respective bends.

He was facing the lifts, but the door to Executive Office 1 was in his peripheral vision. It was the office they provided to Salt for his weekly visits to GCHQ. It was larger than the cubbyholes the rest of the executive class had to work in, with a small patio garden accessible through sliding doors.

Waterman knew from Salt's diary that he had a JIC call at 12.40 p.m. That rarely lasted more than a few minutes. Then a lunch at one o'clock with one of the American delegations, most likely to discuss the logistics of the new working relationship. They would eat in the executive dining room, which was a short walk from Salt's office.

It was twelve forty-five now, which meant Salt was in his office and would be leaving soon.

On cue, Salt stepped into the corridor. Waterman inched behind the edge of the wall. Sweat pricked his back, making his shirt stick to him. He waited a few seconds, then tipped his head forward and looked down the corridor again. He could just about see Salt's back disappear around the bend.

Waterman walked quickly towards the executive office. The corridor was becoming packed with crowds of workers heading to lunch, boisterous voices echoing off the walls. Waterman's mouth was dry as his fingers rested on the handle. He was about to break into his boss's office, in broad daylight, in front of hundreds of witnesses, and under the eyes of the black orbs that studded the corridor ceiling.

Waterman tipped the handle. It jammed after a few degrees. The door was locked. He had been expecting that. Keys to the temporary offices could be picked up from the main lobby.

He reached into his pocket and pulled out a spare key. One of the perks of being the director of GCHQ was that no one questioned you when you took keys from the reception desk in the main lobby. He unlocked the door and stepped inside the office, closing the door behind him.

Like the other temporary offices, it was stylistically bare. Grey carpet, large black spotless desk and an Aeron executive chair. Two guest chairs were positioned in front of the desk, slanted towards each other. Through the angled venetian blinds that covered the length of the floor-to-ceiling sliding glass doors, he could see the large manicured circle of grass at the centre of the building.

Waterman had gambled on Salt needing to leave quickly to attend the meeting, and intending to return for the calls in his diary for the afternoon. Since Salt knew he could lock the door, he was more likely to leave the item Waterman sought in the open.

Waterman's gamble had paid off. The laptop was sitting on the desk, its screen inclined at forty-five degrees. An unseen screensaver projected ghostly patterns on the glossy surface of the keyboard. Waterman walked quickly to the desk and tilted the screen upwards. Now came the potential pitfall of his plan. If the desktop was locked at the log-in page, he'd have a problem. He tapped the space key twice, banishing the rotating elliptical patterns. A blank screen appeared with a log-in window.

Voices murmured on the other side of the door and Waterman stared at the handle, waiting for it to turn.

He held his breath, but all he could hear was his heart thumping in his chest.

If someone did enter, there was nowhere to hide. There were no en-suite bathrooms with these offices. The desk didn't even have a front board that he might duck down and hide behind.

He waited, suspended in time.

The voices died away, and he let out a long, steady breath.

The laptop security was an extra hurdle to clear. However, the laptops in these offices were standardized burners for guest use, mostly for browsing the web and document editing. The real firewall protections only came into play when a user wanted to access the GCHQ mainframes.

Accessing the burner laptop had been Swift's suggestion. Although GCHQ had the ability to hack all of Salt's devices, from his iPhone to his secured server at home, it was Waterman and Swift's presumption that such a search would not find anything relevant. Salt knew better than anyone what GCHQ's capabilities were. If he was hiding something, it wouldn't be in any of the obvious places. It was more likely that he would use a burner laptop as a temporary storage place when he was working at GCHQ, knowing he could clear his tracks when he left.

Waterman pressed the power button on the laptop until it switched off, then immediately rebooted it, keeping his finger on F8. After several seconds, the main menu appeared, this time with an additional option entitled safe mode. A new page appeared with username and password boxes. Waterman keyed in 'Administrator' in the username space and left the password blank. When he pressed return, the computer launched in safe mode.

A burst of laughter exploded from the other side of the door, freezing Waterman.

His fists suspended in space as he stared at its handle again.

It was possible that a cleaning crew might come in at lunchtime to empty the bins. Or Salt might have decided to bring his American guests for a private meeting back at the office. Waterman being found there, poised to hack into his computer, would effectively end Waterman's career. And be the beginning of a lengthy investigation by the internal affairs group.

The handle didn't turn and Waterman let out a long breath again.

He needed to speed things up.

He pressed the control panel option on the screen and selected the user accounts on the drop-down menu. There was only one, Temp 1, and he chose it. A change password box appeared and Waterman quickly keyed in a temporary one. He exited the page and logged into the Temp 1 account, which Salt must have been using.

He quickly opened the main files and scanned the desktop and documents folders. He then checked the email outbox. He wasn't expecting to find anything there, but had to look. As expected, there was no recorded activity from this morning, or emails in the 'sent' folder.

Waterman checked the logging and auditing function. This could tell him whether any files had been moved to or from a USB stick.

To his surprise, the function was disabled. Minute hairs began to prickle up the back of Waterman's neck. The default on all these burner computers was for the function to be active. The only reason why it was disabled was that someone must have intentionally accessed the control panel to stop the function. And the only reason to do that was to hide any log of files being transferred to another device.

Spurred on, Waterman typed in a 'HKEY_LOCAL_MACHINE' command. This allowed him to bypass the logging function and see what devices had been used in the laptop since the function was disabled.

Only one came up.

A series of files had been transferred to a USB stick at 12.30 p.m.

The quarry was now in sight: Waterman needed to get his hands on that USB stick.

He was about to log off when he saw something that sent a jolt of adrenalin up his spine.

A leather wallet was sitting on the edge of the desk. It was the same shade of black leather as the desk, effectively camouflaging it from his sight for the past few minutes. It must be Salt's.

Which meant Salt must have forgotten it.

Which meant he could be coming back at any moment.

Would be coming back at any moment.

Waterman knew he should leave right away, but the slight bulge in the folded wallet made him reach for it. He flipped it open.

Nestling inside was a USB stick.

Waterman looked back at the door handle, his heart hammering. He could leave now if he wanted. Walk out and protect a career thirty years in the making. But the sight of that USB stick was mesmerizing. He *had* to know whether Salt, his friend and mentor at GCHQ, was spying on him. And if so, more importantly, why.

Keeping one eye on the door, Waterman snatched the USB stick and thrust it into the laptop. He called up the drop-down menu, selected the control panel, then double-clicked on the external drive icon to display the contents of the USB stick.

A ladder of files dropped down.

Waterman reviewed them with mounting astonishment.

They were all sound files – digitized recordings.

Waterman double-clicked on the first, which was dated four days ago, at 2.04 p.m. The audio player software launched automatically, and a loud din filled the speakers. It was a recording in a public place. A murmur of conversation and the clink of plates could be heard in the background.

'*I just wanted to check on whether you've found her next operation.*'

It was Waterman's own voice.

'*Not yet. We need something with scale. And where she will make a difference. When I find something, I'll let you know.*'

And Salt's reply.

Waterman let his hand rest on the desk, steadying himself. He had suspected that Salt was recording their conversation that day, but it was something else to find out his suspicion was right. A feeling of seasickness rolled through him.

He looked down the list and played the most recent file, recorded that morning at 8.21 a.m.

An instantly recognizable voice burst out of the laptop speakers.

'*Deputy Commissioner Bale, why don't you start us off?*'

It was the prime minister. Waterman's sense of horror was mounting. The COBRA meeting had been under way at 10.21 a.m. Salt and the PM were attending along with the home secretary and others.

Which meant that this was about a lot more than just Waterman. Salt was surreptitiously recording *all* his meetings.

The chairman of the JIC was spying on the heads of his own political and intelligence community.

There was no precedent for this. How would they even open an investigation into the person at the very top of their organization? The moment that MI5 or GCHQ opened up a file, Salt would know.

One step at a time. First, Waterman needed proof. Which meant making a copy of the flash stick.

The best way to do that would be to pull the files to the hard drive and embed them somewhere Salt would never find them, then come back to retrieve them tonight.

He had just selected the files when he heard Salt's voice on the other side of the door.

The handle tipped down and the door opened.

32

'It's a standard GoPro model. It could replay on any device with video playback,' said Riz.

They were standing in the station forecourt, in the shadow of the huge metal awning jutting out from the roof. Riz held the bicycle helmet cam between his index finger and thumb, turning it over in the light.

'All we need is a USB cable,' he said. 'Come on. I've got one in the car.'

Sara followed him as he walked quickly through the forecourt. When they had cleared the line of SOCOs, he knelt down and took off his polythene shoe covers, rolling them into a ball and slipping them into his pocket. She did the same.

'You still haven't told me how you knew what to look for,' said Riz, glancing over his shoulder as they slipped through the gap in the huge screens.

'It was a hunch,' said Sara, trying to sound matter-of-fact.

'That was some hunch,' he said, pulling open the driver's door of the BMW.

Sara paused. She would need to be careful about Riz. MI5 officers were trained to notice everything. Too many 'insights' from her into the case without the necessary breadcrumbs of clues leading up to them and

229

she could soon find herself boxed in. As far as he knew, Sara was just a second pair of eyes and a conduit to processing power. If Riz came even close to guessing her true identity, Sara knew that GCHQ would burn her as an agent without a second thought. She would be out in the cold.

She took a steadying breath, popped open her door and dropped into her seat.

Riz reached over and opened the glove compartment. He was leaning right across her, his face barely a foot from hers, seemingly unaware of their closeness.

'Sorry, this is such a mess,' he said, as he rooted around the interior, sweeping protein bars and half-finished energy drinks to the side in his search.

A day's worth of stubble peppered his jaw. Despite her injunction to take care around him, a tingle of something ran up her spine.

There had been a period of her life, long ago, when she had craved romantic affection. The slow reveal of personality. The delicious incremental steps towards physical intimacy. But her power made these things all but impossible. The very first touch blew down all the doors. Things that should have been kept secret were exposed immediately. Each touch was an assault on her senses. For a while, drugs let her manage the overload of information. Cocktails of pills blunted her power and allowed her to be carried away in the moment. But that was in her twenties. Drugs soon became the end rather than the means. Since she'd cleaned up, there had been nobody in her life.

Riz pulled out the snaky white cable from the glove compartment and sat back in his seat. He plugged one end into his iPhone and the other into the port of the GoPro. An application launched automatically on his iPhone.

'Bugger,' he breathed. 'I've got to download software to see it. Hold on.' He tapped the screen, then laid down the iPhone while a viewing app loaded. 'It's going to take two minutes.' He looked around with what seemed to be rehearsed boredom, then added casually, 'Why don't you tell me your life story?'

'In two minutes?'

'Well, maybe the highlights.' He was leaning towards her, his forearm resting on the handbrake between them. They were so close, she could see his eyes clearly. They were wide, anime character eyes. The whites were bleach-brilliant clear, the irises a mix of chestnut and green.

She reminded herself to be cautious. Riz was charismatic, and a lot of what was going on here was pure theatre. Someone taking out their charm for a spin. Sara did her best not to lose herself in the performance.

'You're an MI5 agent,' said Sara. 'Why don't you tell me about myself?'

Riz nodded, clearly up for the challenge. He tipped his head back and looked her up and down appraisingly. 'Single. Never been married . . .'

Sara laughed. 'And what makes you say that?'

'It was a hunch,' he said, mimicking her comment from earlier.

'OK, keep going. This is good.'

'You've just started at your job. You're clearly a bit of a star.'

'Are these insights, or flattery?'

He paused and his smile faded a little. 'Abandoned by your parents, or an orphan.'

Sara looked back at him with a carefully blank expression, neither agreeing with nor denying what he'd said.

'I grew up in care,' he said. 'I recognize the experience in others. Matures you quickly. But it makes you cautious. And a little isolated.'

'Anything else?' asked Sara. She hadn't realized it, but she was mirroring his body language, her hand resting on the edge of the seat, inches from the brake, her head inclined to his.

The screen of the iPhone lit up as the viewing app launched. Riz and Sara pulled away from each other, suddenly awkward, the spell broken.

'OK, we're up,' said Riz, with a little too much enthusiasm. He placed the iPhone on the dashboard, facing them. A series of thumbnail colour photos filled the screen.

'Looks like the software breaks the footage into clips of ninety seconds each.' Riz flicked his finger down the screen. 'Here's the last one.' He pressed the thumbnail, then looked at Sara in afterthought. 'This could be rough to watch.'

'Don't worry about me,' said Sara. 'I've probably seen worse.'

Riz raised an eyebrow at her comment and was about to say something else when a series of desperate cries burst from the iPhone, startling them.

The audio of the clip preceded the video by a few seconds. It was difficult to make out what was happening. Isolated shouts of alarm could be heard. A voice shouted, 'Get back. Get back.'

Then the video launched: the view from the top of the exit stairs of the tube station. It wobbled as it turned to look down into the mouth of the station. A mass of people crammed the steps. For a shaky second, Sara was gazing at a man in his sixties in a grey pinstripe suit, one hand holding a battered briefcase. Rheumy eyes stared in consternation back at the camera. His mouth moved, his face registering a mixture of complaint and panic, although the words were lost in the din. The camera swivelled back and pointed again at the station concourse. Through a thicket of stationary bodies, a uniformed policeman was running towards the camera, less than ten feet away. And a few feet ahead of him, someone else was running, just out of his reach.

As both sprinters approached the steps, the crowd recoiled, retreating down the stairs, pressing back those already squashed there, eliciting further cries of protest.

The timer at the bottom of the screen indicated there were only three seconds of footage left. The person being pursued by the policeman came back into view again, now only feet from the top of the stairs, his shoulders colliding with commuters as he ploughed through the crowd. As the last second of footage elapsed, he lifted his arms wide, as if he was taking flight. The screen then flashed white and the iPhone went dark before rebooting at the home screen.

'Did you see that?' asked Riz, in surprise. He lifted his finger and pressed the thumbnail again. Once the footage restarted, he used his finger to fast-forward it, causing the figures on screen to jerk about manically. 'Look at that corner,' he said.

Sara kept her eyes fixed on the spot where he was pointing. All she could see was a mass of bodies standing between the camera and the station concourse.

Then, with only one second to go, the crowds parted and she saw the person being pursued by the policeman.

The bomber was a man. Early thirties. He was wearing a grey sweatshirt under a green combat jacket, the hood of the sweatshirt thrown over his head. He was well-built. His mouth was open, pinched in a rictus of fury, as if shouting something.

And, most crucially, he was white.

33

Salt stood at the half-open door of Executive Office 1.

He had been about to step through it when he bumped into Hunter, the head of the computer systems and IT units. Ever keen to ingratiate himself with the chairman of the JIC, Hunter had begun to tell Salt about his new initiative to increase the processing power at the facility.

Salt made little effort to hide his impatience, lifting his jacket sleeve and openly checking his watch. He'd been sitting with the Americans at lunch when he realized he had forgotten his wallet at his desk. He could have waited until the meal was over to pick it up. There was, after all, no requirement for money in the executive dining room. But the wallet contained something more valuable than money. It could put Salt in a lot of hot water if found. It would certainly end his career, if not land him in prison.

'Is this a bad time?' asked Hunter, noticing Salt's discomfort.

'Yes,' said Salt. 'Let's put something in the diary.'

He gave Hunter a tight smile and stepped into the office, closing the door behind him. He walked to the desk and saw his wallet sitting where he had left it.

He picked it up and opened it, experiencing a flood

of relief when he saw the USB stick nestling in the centre. He slipped it into his jacket pocket and turned to leave, then stopped, spying something in the corner of his eye.

He hesitated, then turned back to the desk.

Something wasn't right.

He walked around the desk and placed a finger on the inclined screen of the laptop, tilting it up. Elliptical patterns rotated across the home screen.

Nothing seemed amiss.

A rustling sound behind him made him turn sharply.

It was just the blinds, knocking gently together. Salt approached them and pulled them to one side. One of the sliding doors to the garden was open. Just a few inches. The breeze from outside rattled the blinds.

Salt looked at the sliding door with suspicion. He couldn't remember opening it.

He pulled it wide and half stepped out.

GCHQ's interior garden was an open communal space dominated by a circular lawn. It was empty. To Salt's right there were three interlocking landscaped gardens and he walked towards them. They were designed for stimulating interaction between departments and he could see a few groups of people sitting under arbours. He scanned the faces but didn't recognize anyone. Rank and file having their sandwiches. Or was that a façade? Maybe they were a surveillance team. He stared at each of them, daring them to look back, but they appeared immersed in their own conversations.

Salt had taken every precaution. Had air-gapped the

digital files, so that it was out of reach of the GCHQ crypto-team, should suspicions be raised. Made sure the files were always on his person, hidden inside his wallet, the one item he felt he would never leave behind. He now realized he'd underestimated how much his subterfuge was weighing on him.

For his entire career, he'd always been the hunter. At MI5, then GCHQ, and now at the JIC, he was used to staring at the back of his quarry, flushing them out, causing them to make forced errors, to run.

He wasn't used to being the hunted. He'd thought his unique experience would help him stay one step ahead of the security services, but now he saw that the skills of the hunter were different from those of the hunted.

If one or more of the groups in front of him was a surveillance team, he would never know it. This was what they were trained for.

He turned and walked back to his office, sliding the patio door shut behind him and locking it. Of course, his mind might be playing tricks on him. The explanation for the sliding door being ajar might be as simple as the cleaner having left it open.

He left his office and locked it. As he walked back to the dining room, he came to a decision. He needed to revise his plan. The last few minutes had shown him that he wouldn't survive long as the hunted. Once GCHQ were after him, the chase would be swift. He had given himself a timeline measured in weeks, but that wouldn't work now. He needed to count it in days.

34

The call came less than a minute after Riz had emailed a still capture of the bomber's face to MI5. He listened with the phone pressed to his ear, his eyes blank.

'Fine,' he said, at last. 'When do you want me there? . . . OK.' He thumbed the phone off and slipped it back into his jacket pocket.

'Suicide bomber's name is Simon Lang. British. Home Counties.' He shook his head minutely, struggling to come to terms with the information. 'Ex-army. Father and siblings were in the army too. Did a few tours of duty, in Syria and Afghanistan, but no evidence of radicalization either overseas or since he's been back. Family are dyed-in-the-wool Church of England.'

'Do you think the eye-witness was lying when she said he was Asian or Arab?' asked Sara.

Riz shrugged. 'I doubt it. She was in a moment of high stress, saw a man with a bomb and her mind filled in the rest.'

'What about Lang's motive?'

Riz shook his head. 'He struggled to reintegrate after decom. Couldn't hold a job down, missed sessions with the occupational therapist. Dropped off the map six months ago. Working assumption for motive is PTSD.'

'I don't see PTSD turning someone into a suicide bomber,' said Sara.

'Me neither.' He chewed his lip as he stared out of the window. 'There's a reason my team make quick progress in suicide bombings. We've mapped the phenomenon.' He turned back to Sara. 'It's like how we reversed that footage just now. As soon as we identify a bomber, it's almost as if we can reverse the footage of his life up to that point. Follow him back. They all take similar paths. It's easy to fill in the gaps. It's like a checklist. It's a question of *which* radicalizer, *which* supplier. The playbook is the same. But this . . .' He shrugged.

'So, where does that leave us?' asked Sara.

'Well, for a start, I'm no longer leading the investigation.'

His phone pinged with an incoming text message. He looked down at the screen. 'They just sent the last address for Lang. A squat in north London. There's a CT-SFO team on their way. Shaw wants me to join them.'

Sara nodded. 'Good. I'm coming too.'

There were bound to be possessions of Lang's at the squat. Each one could be packed with information about his life leading up to that morning.

Riz shook his head. 'Pembroke is leading the investigation now. He doesn't want you anywhere near the place.' He looked at her. 'I'm afraid it's goodbye for now.'

She nodded. There wasn't much to say. Without Riz,

she'd be back at square one in the investigation. Possibly further back than that, given the animosity Shaw seemed to have for anyone linked to GCHQ.

As she reached for the door handle, Sara looked down and noticed Riz was holding out his hand.

'Good luck.' He sounded like he meant it.

All she had to do was reach out. In that Trojan shake, a cargo of information could flow through to her, most of what she needed to know about the enigmatic Riz Malik. It was the smart thing to do. It was what Waterman would have wanted too. The more she knew about MI5's task force, the more she could be ahead of the investigation.

She lifted her hand, but let it rest on his jacket and squeezed his shoulder. 'Take care of yourself too.'

It might have been a missed opportunity, but she was enjoying the slow flirtation with Riz too much. For now, she wanted him to keep his secrets. She stepped out of the car and shut the door. She reached into her pockets and pulled on her gloves.

The car lurched forward, then stopped. White reverse lights appeared and the car backed up slowly until the passenger side door was once again alongside Sara. The power window slid down, revealing Riz, bending his head to make eye contact with her.

'Just wondering if I can get your number.' He said it so awkwardly it was difficult not to find it charming. 'You know, in case I need to reach you.'

Sara bent over and rested her elbows on the bottom edge of the open window. 'You could call Director

Waterman,' she said, holding his eye contact. 'He'll get in touch with me.'

It wasn't only Riz who could enjoy the theatre of flirting. After such a cocksure morning with him, she was enjoying seeing him vulnerable.

'It was good to . . . make the connection,' said Riz, apparently unwilling to let the moment go.

Sara smiled at his choice of words. 'I was just thinking the same thing. Give me your phone.'

He pulled it out and handed it to her. She keyed in her number and Riz took it back, giving her a quick nod before driving off.

When his car had disappeared, she turned back to the station forecourt. She pulled out her phone and began dialling Waterman. GCHQ would no doubt have assembled a dossier on Lang that would be useful to read, but she stopped in mid-dial. From where she was standing, she could see televisions being set up on the trestle tables. The minute's silence was about to start.

Sara felt a need to honour those she had seen going about their lives that morning before the bomb had torn them apart. She was walking towards the forecourt to join the others when her attention was snagged.

The media presence on the other side of the huge covering screens had grown substantially. The space was now crammed with broadcasting vans. On-camera reporters primped as they stood before their crews, while others spoke as cameras rolled. The close quarters created a polyphony of voices, overlapping each other, commenting on the morning's events.

On another screen, a helicopter-mounted camera provided an aerial view of the station's outskirts. Metal fences had been erected between the outer edge of the station and Vauxhall Bridge Road. They kept the public out, and hemmed the press into the tight apron of space between the towering white screens and the barriers.

On the other side of the railings, the crowds had been growing and now covered the pavements and most of the street. A carpet of fresh flowers ran around the border of the barricades, hugging the perimeter. Over the chatter of the reporters' voices, Sara could hear the crowd singing, different songs and hymns that combined in a gentle cacophony.

A noise distracted her and she turned to see a car with blacked-out windows approach from Wilton Road and jerk abruptly to a stop nearby. The driver's door opened and Vincent Shaw exited the vehicle. He was only a few feet away from Sara and, to her surprise, was looking at her with a warm smile.

'The minute's silence starts soon, Ms Eden. Let's take our places.'

35

Waterman walked briskly along the corridor running around the circumference of GCHQ, known locally as 'The Street', taking care to avoid the area between Salt's office and the dining room.

The route was a little circuitous due to his detour, with the result that he kept being flagged down by people with urgent questions about on-going projects. Although he was distracted, he made time for each one. This was the nature of his daily life since he'd been elevated to the role of director. The experience of being constantly pulled into new crises had frustrated him for the first month. After ten years as a doctoral and post-doctoral student, he had grown used to seeing projects all the way through, mostly from the seclusion of a dedicated seat in the university lab. But his perspective had shifted eventually. It was just a matter of changing his expectations. He found that if he thought of himself as a triage doctor on twenty-four-hour call, the frustration melted away. As with most things in life, expectation played the larger part in the processing of experience. Don't expect open-ended time frames on decisions. Don't expect eight hours of uninterrupted sleep.

Maybe that was what stung so badly about Salt's

betrayal. He hadn't been expecting it. Waterman was fresh in the director job and continued to rely on Salt for support. In many ways, Waterman was still his pro-tégé. And to find out that Salt was a mole was still painful to contemplate.

He reached the lifts and waited for the first empty one heading down. It was only when the doors closed that he allowed himself his reaction. He swore as loudly as he could, a bellow of rage, anger and sadness that had been stored up for days inside.

The digital screen on the wall flashed the numbers as the lift descended. When there were only two floors left to go, he took a deep breath and quietened.

Surprisingly, he felt the better for it. Now the emo-tion was spent, it was time to focus on strategy. He had had to leave the USB stick behind. Now he had noth-ing. For a second he considered trying to get his hands on it again. He would need tangible proof in making his case. Then he reminded himself that he was now the director of GCHQ. He'd seen the evidence with his own eyes, and there was no higher authority to involve. It was time to take action. As Salt was spying on Waterman and others, it was axiomatic that he was taking the information he acquired to someone else. It was now Waterman's job to follow the trail.

The lift doors opened and he walked along the dark-ened corridor to the bolted door of the situation room, which GCHQ insiders referred to as the 'Agency'. As he lifted his key card to the mounted security box on the wall, he hesitated, a thought occurring to him.

What was Sara's role in this? She was Salt's protégé, his pet project. Could she somehow be a part of whatever was going on? After a few seconds, he dismissed the thought. If Sara was allied with Salt in any subterfuge, Salt would not need audio recordings of his intelligence discussions: he would use Sara instead. She was the perfect tool. No, it was more likely that Salt was grooming her as an asset, and when the time was right to make his trade, he would offer himself and Sara to whatever foreign power he was lining up.

He swiped the key card down and stepped inside the darkened room. He could make out the heads of analysts working at their desks, silhouetted against the light from the surveillance screens on the far wall.

Waterman experienced a sense of nostalgia. The room was his testing ground, where he had honed his field skills, albeit from the safety of an underground bunker in the Cheltenham countryside. It afforded an almost limitless ability to peep into any corner of the planet. Spy satellites could direct their hyper-telescopic lenses sufficiently to read car licence plates in Damascus. Or hijack feeds from internet cafés in Aden. This room, and a similar one inside the NSA headquarters, had made the world much smaller for terrorists, criminals and warlords. There was less and less room to hide. And in a few minutes it would be more difficult for one of their own to hide as well.

Swift was sitting on a raised platform in the centre of the room. Waterman propped himself on the corner of the desk, trying not to show his anxiety. Once he'd said his piece, there would be no going back. If he was wrong, he would end a vaunted career in intelligence and destroy the reputation of a man who had dedicated his professional life to the security of the country.

'We need to open a Code Blue file. Just you and I have eyes on it for now.'

'Who's the target?' asked Swift, his voice barely audible. Blue was the code name for an operation to track a mole within the organization.

Waterman hadn't expected it to hurt as much when he gave the name.

36

Shaw surveyed the crime scene at Victoria. SOCO officers were finishing on the forecourt around the tube
entrance and were moving to the station concourse.
Bereavement personnel were sifting through personal
belongings. In a tent set up near the first platform, officers from his task force were questioning station staff.
It was a human operation, warm bodies avenging the
cold ones. There was no substitute for the human mind,
which was infinitely more complex than any computer
program. Its capacity for empathy lay beyond the cold
calculations of GCHQ.

There was only one interloper. Sara Eden.

The discovery that the bomber was not an Islamic
radical allowed Shaw to take the stripes from Riz, leaving Eden without a primary partner. But he'd need
to proceed very carefully. MI5 and GCHQ worked
closely together on myriad levels, two twisted ladders
wrapped around each other, like a double helix. Men
and women in his agency who were much more powerful than Shaw depended on Cheltenham to get them
results. He couldn't risk alienating them by booting
Eden out on her ear. Waterman may not have jurisdic-
tion over the task force, but he could still make life
difficult for Shaw.

'Ms Eden, there's a few moments to go now. If you could wait over there.'

She had followed him across the main forecourt to a secluded spot in the south of the enclosed area, only a few feet from the towering white screens.

The press was so close to the other side of the screens that they could hear their hushed voices, dropped to whispers in anticipation of the minute's silence. Their silhouettes moved like arabesques on the white surface.

'I'll be back in two seconds.'

Shaw knew the effect that a little sweetness and light could have, especially when people were expecting brusqueness. As he walked off, he glanced over his shoulder. For all her poise, she made a forlorn figure, standing alone by the flapping sails of the privacy screens.

He went to the outer edge of the screen and turned the corner. In fact, there were two screens, a few feet apart, an inner and an outer layer. He walked down the centre of the divide, doubling back towards Eden and the press scrum, but hidden from both.

Eden hadn't moved from where he'd left her, next to one of the screen's supporting poles. Shaw crouched, then gripped the base of the pole, lifting it as gently as he could to minimize rippling. He'd calculated the physics of what was needed on the drive over. Just a few inches, that was all. He took a step back and let the base down with infinite care. He could see through the gap that had been created between the screens now. Eden hadn't noticed, her back still towards him. She was staring ahead, watching the final countdown to the silence on the clock above the station.

Shaw took a quiet breath and walked to the nearest pole on the outer screen and repeated the move, picking up the base weighing down the support pole, this time taking care to stay behind the screen so the press wouldn't see him.

When he was finished, he stood back, surveying the results with satisfaction. The breaks he'd made in the continuity of the outer and inner screens created a line of sight directly into the station forecourt. More importantly, it didn't violate his crime scene, as the angle was oblique, slanting into one corner of the interior station ground only. A corner with only one person standing in it.

Now he just needed to wait until someone in the press corps noticed.

37

Riz stared through the window of the unmarked police van. The abandoned hospital took up an entire city block, its glass-and-brick façade rising above the neighbouring terraced houses, like an ocean liner sitting in a provincial dock.

In the lobby of the building, he could see a young woman, naked but for a pair of panties and worn sneakers, painting a mural on the walls. A few yards away, an old woman in a flimsy dressing gown rested an arm on a broken IV stand, the other hand cupping a cigarette, her hair the colour of ash. A pod of young men, all grimy limbs and dreadlocked hair, were huddled around a small mountain of stuffed plastic bags. A mass of shopping trolleys was parked in a messy cluster by the front doors. Different strains of music pulsed through windows above, colliding to create a din on the ground floor. A trail of people came in and out of the front doors of the squat.

'On your one.'

'Riz, on your one.'

Riz turned. Behind him, Goode, the sergeant of the counter-terrorist specialist firearms officer team, was leaning forward. Like his fifteen-strong unit, he wore a gun-metal grey tactical uniform and helmet. The other

CT-SFOs were packed onto two benches, facing each other. They each carried a SIG 516 semi-automatic carbine and a Glock 9mm sidearm, and wore covert body armour Type II.

'Not yet,' said Riz, distractedly, and looked back through the window.

He was normally more much focused before an operation, but he was having trouble getting his mind off Sara.

He knew what Shaw and the others would think: that he'd volunteered to run her as an asset in order to bed her. His reputation had become fixed after those last two undercover operations. Truth be told, those women weren't even his type. He'd begun relationships with them for one reason only – that it was the only way to get the necessary information from them. He'd been right in both cases: the women had become star witnesses in subsequent trials. But they hadn't forgiven his professional duplicity and had made official complaints. And before he knew it, he was the Johnny Depp of MI5.

It was different with Sara, though – and not because she was good-looking, although that was unquestionable. He'd had only to look at the flustered face of each man they'd encountered that morning to know it. Sure, her looks were part of it. But there was something else beneath. She was hiding something. He knew it because he was hiding the same thing. Damage can always spot damage.

He checked his watch. Five to one. Time to start. 'OK,' said Riz. He spoke quietly but with authority.

'This is the Circus, north-west London's largest squat. First thing to keep in mind is that the land is commercial, not residential, so the squat is not illegal. That means these people are not doing anything wrong.' He stopped and made eye contact with each officer in the van. 'In the last twelve months, there've been no drugs busts, no noise complaints. However, these are the last-known whereabouts of Simon Lang, the Victoria-station bomber. He was the first white suicide bomber, the first British Army soldier to turn suicide bomber, the first British Army soldier to commit a terror act on UK soil. That doesn't happen in a vacuum. Others were involved. There's a good chance this place will supply some leads. Finding them is the best way to stop this happening again.'

Riz could feel the energy in the van. Wired, jumpy. It was almost palpable. Riz knew the dangers these men and women faced. Lang had known he would be identified – this was London, after all, where your picture was captured on CCTV more than three hundred times a day on average. And he had known the atrocity would likely bring a counter-terror squad right here. If Lang had wanted another shot at increasing the death toll from beyond the grave, he would have rigged some part of this place to blow sky high. And the team in here knew it. Type II body armour would protect them against soft-point bullets but not an incendiary blast from an IED.

Goode nodded to him, then addressed the squad. He talked about the objectives of the operation: to find and neutralize any threats, to protect the lives of inno-cents and officers, and to identify and preserve evidence. He talked about how these objectives were likely to be in constant competition with each other. He cautioned them, describing how their nervous systems were flooding their bodies with serotonin and epinephrine, preparing them for battle. They needed to be careful about the effects of those chemicals on their actions. Finally, he said that, as several hundred people lived in the multi-storey space, the common areas had almost constant foot traffic. That made the likelihood of an IED very low in the common areas, but very possible if Lang had had separate living quarters. Finally, he turned to Riz and nodded.

'Ready?' asked Riz.

'Ready,' replied Goode.

Riz cranked open the door and twisted his knees to one side as the officers thundered past him.

As the pack ran to the front doors, Riz held back and walked towards the corner of the building.

The boy couldn't have been more than five years old. He appeared to be alone, which made the sight of him seem surreal. He wasn't unhappy, staring at a plastic toy truck he kept turning over. None of the other squatters seemed to notice him.

'Cool truck,' said Riz, crouching next to him.

The boy looked at him for a second, then returned to examining his toy.

Riz pulled out a scrap of paper and a pen, then pressed the paper to his bent knee, scribbling a note.

He pulled out his wallet and removed a ten-pound note. 'There's a café around the corner. Go and get something to eat. Don't come back for an hour.'

The boy had stopped playing with his toy. He took the money, looking up at Riz for the first time. Riz gave him the handwritten note. 'That's the number of a friend of mine. Her name is Suzie. She's nice. Works for the social services. Got bright red hair. Get someone to call her for you, if you don't ever feel safe. You understand?'

The boy's head tipped to the side, as if weighing the import and consequences of Riz's words. After a few seconds, he nodded.

Riz watched him walk off until he was a safe distance away, then turned to follow the team into the building.

Two CT-SFOs stood by the main door, guns held cross-body, blocking the entrance. The almost-nude painting woman was shouting at them, her shrill voice echoing around the empty lobby. A few yards away, four men lay face down, their hands cuffed behind them, cheeks pressed into the dirt. Their dreadlocked manes gave them an odd, equine look, like mythic creatures, felled and trussed.

Riz slipped through the entrance behind them.

'Ground floor, clear!' Two hooded officers emerged from a doorway on the left of the lobby. The rest of the squad was massed at the foot of the stairs, weapons raised.

'Fire escapes?' Riz asked Goode.

He nodded. 'One on both sides. They're covered.'

'OK,' Riz said, taking a deep breath. 'Let's go.'

They separated into two groups, each flanking one side of the steps, providing less of a target for anyone who might swing around the corner of any stairwell with a weapon.

The CT-SFO team moved up through the building via the central stairs. On the first landing, Goode and an advance party of four officers cleared out everyone they could find on the floor. Once it was clear, two bomb-disposal officers, clad in Kevlar suits, searched for any sign of Simon Lang's possessions.

The operation proceeded without major incident, and twenty minutes after storming the front door, Riz and Goode were climbing the stairs to the third, and last, floor.

'Either we find some evidence of him here,' said Goode, 'or we need to quarantine the place and bring in Forensics.'

Riz nodded stoically. If that happened, they would have to dig in for the long haul. The building was huge and would need to be sealed to avoid contamination. Lang could have been anywhere, either floating around and dossing on other people's beds or in some secret cubbyhole of his own. They would have to do a DNA sweep of each floor, which could take a week.

Together they crested the stairs to the last floor. When the bomb-squad officers pushed through the double fire doors separating the landing from the rest of the area, Riz glimpsed a large open-plan room, scavenged bookshelves and doors carving it into separate living spaces.

A few minutes later, a muffled voice cried out. 'Clear!'

Goode and an advance party pushed through the doors.

Minutes later, Riz heard Goode call his name.

Riz followed them and looked around, getting his bearings. Goode was standing at the far end of the hall, waving him over. As Riz approached, he saw the sergeant was standing by a sleeping pod that was cut off from the rest of the room by two long, low bookshelves arranged perpendicular to each other. Inside was a bed, made with clean sheets wrapped so tightly around the base that they looked almost dry-cleaned.

'You can take the man out of the army but . . .' said Goode, nodding at the stack of clothes folded neatly by the bed.

'It's also the furthest bed from the front door in the whole squat,' commented Riz. 'He wanted exit options, if anything came down.' He pulled a pair of plastic gloves from his pocket. In most investigations, he knew the next steps so well that his muscle memory would have taken over by now. After locating the bomber's last whereabouts, he would expect to find the suicide message. It would be laden with scores of clues, left both consciously and unconsciously by the bomber, whether it was a video or a handwritten letter, which would in turn provide the next set of leads. But with motive still a mystery in the Victoria attack, it was just a blind assumption that a suicide message had been left here. He was flying in the dark, just working by association.

They turned over the entire sleeping area, riffling

through books for hidden notes or revealing marginalia, tipping over the bed, shaking out all the clothes and testing the floorboards.

'We'll need to search the whole building,' said Goode. 'He knew we'd be coming to his bunk.'

Riz pointed to the outline of a wall panel near the ceiling. 'The paint on that doesn't match the rest of the wall.'

He stood on the bed, looking at the wall panel more closely, then pressed a finger experimentally to it. 'Still a bit sticky,' he said, turning to Goode. 'Better get the bomb squad back up here.'

38

Sara listened as the peal of church bells drifted on the breeze, the sounds around her diminishing.

The SOCOs stood up and bowed their heads. Behind the white screens, the bustling silhouettes of the press corps stopped moving, like black stick figures on a white frieze.

The indistinct chants and songs from the crowds died away. As the last chime sounded, silence descended.

It was eerie to be standing in the centre of the city yet for the only sounds to be the faint flapping of flags in the breeze, and the occasional cough from somewhere in the crowd.

To her right, Shaw stepped quietly back from behind the screen and stood with his hands folded in front of him. She hadn't noticed he'd gone until he'd reappeared. His sudden warmth towards her was obviously manufactured, although for what purpose she had no idea.

It would have been easy enough, of course, to brush his hand by accident after the silence was over. To touch her skin to his and plunder his secrets. She would know pretty quickly what Shaw was up to. But to do that was unimaginable. People's secrets would only be divulged without their consent if it would save innocent lives. That had been the promise she'd made herself long ago.

In the silence, she found her mind returning to Riz. There was something childlike about him. The bravado and vulnerability, two sides of the same coin. He had the certainty of a kid who'd been righting wrongs since he could remember. After her mother had hidden her from MI5's clutches in the care system, Sara had seen plenty of kids like Riz. The burning need to right wrongs was their response to their own abandonment. Being placed in care always prompted a reaction. Some retreated inwards, others were angry, and a few behaved as if they'd been given a licence to mirror their parents. But children like Riz had decided to set the world to rights. They had the outward certainty of the zealot. But Sara could also see the uncertainty that often comes when someone has pulled themselves up by their own bootstraps. She and Riz were alike in many ways.

She couldn't put a finger on what she was feeling. Being in this crime scene, standing near SOCOs who had painstakingly picked through every inch of the forecourt, being near Pam Smith and her officers as they carefully reassembled the possessions of lives blown apart, her affinity with and attraction to Riz, even interacting with Shaw, whose fierce protection of his turf was still a form of dedication, it all felt part of the same thing. They were all the same tribe. There were warring divisions within it, but kinship bonded them.

What she was feeling only increased her sense of connection to Riz. He had what she had always wanted. She had never found her tribe. She had thought that the power that made her unique also consigned her to a loner status. But with Riz, she had felt as if she was coming home.

She looked over the tops of the flapping white screens towards Hyde Park. Somewhere to the north Riz and a team were searching a squat for clues as to what had led Simon Lang to do what he had done that morning.

Anxiety began to gnaw at her. An ex-army officer like Lang, with access to explosives, could have left a device in the squat for a final act of brutality. The thought that Riz, so vital and sure of himself, could become one of the day's victims made Sara feel suddenly off-balance. She could have known what was going to happen, had she accepted the hand he offered.

Her heart rate increased. By choosing to keep the mystery, she had also lost the opportunity to protect him. She'd been alone for so long, she'd forgotten what it meant to care for someone. She reached into her back pocket, feeling the outline of her phone. She had his number. She could call him now. But she had nothing concrete to communicate other than her fears.

A ripple of whispers behind her interrupted her thoughts. The silence hadn't ended, but she could hear hushed activity near a press van. Shuffling feet, hissed voices and rapid clicks. She turned, noticing for the first time that a misalignment in the white screens had created a gap of about a foot.

On the other side of the screens, a press photographer was crouching on one knee, his camera trained directly at her, his finger pressed to the shutter release as the camera clicked endlessly.

39

Riz, Goode and the other CT-SFOs stood at the top of the stairs, watching through the window of the fire-exit doors as the two bomb-disposal officers approached Lang's bunk, the thick Kevlar tunics giving them a waddling gait.

'Who's in charge up there?'

The voice came from the stairwell. Young, male, projected with authority. Goode inclined his head towards Riz to check it out. Riz descended the stairs and saw the man standing on the landing below. He was one of those who had been trussed up on the ground floor. His thick dreadlocks were like fraying ropes falling down his back. He didn't seem to have an ounce of fat on him, all stripped muscle and skin. He wore frayed and ripped blue jeans and a paint-splashed forest-green T-shirt. Large, clear-blue eyes were trained on Riz as he made his way down the last stairs and approached him. To Riz's surprise, he held out his hand in greeting.

'I'm Merlin, one of the elders here. We've got some scared people downstairs. What can you tell me?'

He was well-spoken, articulate and neither under- nor over-deferential. Despite the self-title of 'elder', he looked to be in his late twenties. Riz led him down one more flight of stairs before he responded.

'What can you tell me about Simon Lang? He was staying in the bunk on the top floor, north-west corner?'

Lang's name hadn't been released to the media yet, but Riz noticed that its mention in connection with a surprise raid by heavily armed police on his squat didn't surprise Merlin.

'He's been here about a week. We only know him as Simon. We don't usually want people with his background in here.'

'And what background is that?' asked Riz, being careful not to lead.

'Ex-soldiers,' said Merlin. He maintained level eye contact with Riz as he spoke, one equal speaking to another. Riz guessed he sprang from establishment money. He had the sort of comfort with authority that usually came with breeding. 'They're mostly trouble-makers. I know it's not their fault. They see some bad shit in combat, and aren't supported when they come home. But the effect is the same. We're drug-free here. And no physical violence is tolerated. But we've had problems with ex-army in the past – fighting and drugs.'

'So, what was different with Lang?'

'He was honest with us, told us his background up front. We got a good vibe from him. He didn't seem angry or lost. What's this about?'

'We're not going to be here much longer,' said Riz. He needed to head back to Goode's team. Scotland Yard detectives would be here soon enough to inter-view everyone. 'Is there anything else you can tell me about him?'

266

Merlin shrugged. 'We're a close-knit community. We eat together. The showers are communal. But Simon keeps to himself . . .'

Riz nodded, turning to head back upstairs. 'Thanks. There'll be someone around to take your statement.'

'. . . probably because of the burns.'

Riz stopped on the first step and looked back. 'Burns?'

Merlin nodded, his face intent. 'He takes showers late at night. When the shower room's empty. One of the guys saw him once. Said Simon had burns down most of his back.'

'OK, thanks,' said Riz, struggling to find some relevant context for what he'd just been told. The injuries sounded like battle scars. Shaw had mentioned that Lang had served in Helmand for two years. They'd know more when they saw the official MoD report. He headed up the stairs.

'Just in time,' said Goode, seeing Riz ascending. 'They're about to start.'

Riz returned to his place near the window of the double-doors to the main dormitory.

Through it he could see the lead disposal officer pulling out a power tool from a side pocket and fitting it into one of the screws on the panel. He heard a faint whirring sound, then watched as the officer pocketed the screw and moved to the next. When the last was loose, he reached up and, with infinite care, lifted the panel a little away from the wall.

Riz realized he was holding his breath.

The officer tipped his helmet forward, looking for any tripwires. He turned and gave Goode a nod, then pulled the panel away and set it on the floor.

Riz heard a collective breath released around him.

'That's step one,' said Goode.

The disposal officer pulled out a snaky length of telescopic metal from the same pocket and bent it into the shape of a question mark. At the base of the attachment was a camera screen. He pressed the screen, causing a flashlight to illuminate at the tip of the metal, then guided the attachment into the hole.

After almost a minute of searching, he pulled out the keyhole camera and threw it on the bed. He removed his gloves and helmet and shouted to Goode, 'Clear!'

The officer leant in, his head disappearing into the maw of the cubbyhole. A few seconds later he re-appeared with an object that he laid on the bed, then put his head back into the hole to retrieve something else.

Goode and Riz approached Lang's bunk just as the officer stood up, one hand clutching what looked like bricks of bound paper. He put them on the bed too.

Riz crouched to look at them more closely. They were stacks of fifty-pound notes.

'Looks like there's a few thousand here,' said the ordnance officer.

Goode picked one up. 'They still have bank seals on them. What's a dosser in a squat doing with a few grand fresh from the Royal Mint?'

'Almost four and a half grand,' said Riz, finishing his

count. He pulled out an evidence bag from his pocket and began to drop the bundles inside it. Different theories were forming and re-forming in his mind. The brand-new notes pointed to a recent transaction of some sort. Could the bomb have been a professional job? A former soldier becoming a bomber for hire? Riz dismissed the idea. Mercenaries fought for financial reward, but they didn't kill themselves. Profit was their motivation, and money wasn't much good if they weren't around to enjoy it.

'What do you want to do with this?' asked Goode. He had picked up the first object the ordnance officer had removed from the cache in the wall. Riz stood up and took it from him.

It was an iPhone.

The movement of being passed from one hand to another illuminated the lock screen.

The front photo was a beaming selfie of three people, two men and a woman. They were dressed in walking gear, thick jumpers and anoraks. Riz recognized the middle one as Lang, although he looked so different he could have been someone else. He was laughing, perhaps at something one of the others had just said. They all looked happy, carefree. Over their shoulders, a thick mist hung in the air, and in the distance, there was the outline of gentle slopes.

'Better get that to your technical people,' said Goode. 'There's a limited number of attempts at the lock screen, then the system will shut down.'

Riz thought for a moment, then took out his own

phone, held it parallel to Lang's and shook Lang's so that the home screen photo illuminated again. He took a picture of the selfie. 'I might be able to get a quick read on this,' he said, attaching the photo to a text message he was typing.

40

Sara walked quickly away from the spot where she had been standing to safe cover behind the screens.

She saw Shaw watching her, a faint smile on his face. The pieces were quickly falling into place: his affability just now had been intended to throw her off guard, and his disappearance behind the screens had been to open the gap for the press to see her.

'You set me up,' she said, struggling to understand what he'd done. 'I could have helped you.' For some reason, it felt like a betrayal, even though it shouldn't have.

He looked at her enigmatically. 'I don't know what you mean, Ms Eden.'

Before she could say anything further, her phone beeped, the sound booming out in the silence.

She stepped away and slipped it out of her pocket. It was an incoming text.

> We found this in the squat. Think these are the Lang
> siblings. Riz

She opened the jpeg attached to it and stared at the photo.

Although there were three of them, her eyes went immediately to Simon Lang. It was a shock to see him smiling. She had just seen his face in the seconds before his death. She would never forget the look on it: a twisted gargoyle mask of rage. More inhuman than human. But the photo was of someone else entirely, a bubble of joy bursting across his features.

The woman next to him looked to be in her late twenties. Blonde hair in a ponytail. Sara could see the family resemblance. The woman was grinning, too, an arm extended towards the camera, taking the selfie. The other man was older, in his thirties. Of the three, he drew Sara's attention. He was smiling but, unlike the others, the smile didn't reach his eyes, which stared at the camera with detachment.

Sara let her fingertips graze the surface of the phone. When they touched Simon's face, she was launched into the middle of a chaos of bodies. Her perspective was that of someone ploughing through a crowd, elbows windmilling people out of the way, pushing with every ounce of energy to reach the stairs of the tube station. She was back at Victoria, this time seeing the scene from Simon's perspective. A full-throated scream reverberated around her head, drowning the noise of the station. She realized it was Simon's own voice, bellowing. She pulled her finger away. She'd visited and revisited the scene so many times, she felt as if she'd already picked the carcass clean.

She let her finger settle on the sister's smiling face. The world around her immediately rocked with a noise so deafening that she flinched.

It was another bomb.

As big as the first.

The destruction was catastrophic. Bodies blasted into pieces. Shrapnel shredding skin and bone.

She closed her eyes, summoning the image to the back of her eyelids, desperate for some clue as to where it was going to happen and when. The image was so intense it was difficult to focus. She lifted her finger and resettled it on the sister's face, rebooting the images to the beginning. In the split second before the explosion caused a flash fire that consumed everything, she scoured the scene for clues. It was a high street somewhere, with retail outlets at either side: a supermarket, an estate agent, a boutique.

And then she saw it for a fraction of a second.

She squeezed her eyes closed and increased the pressure of her finger on the screen.

One structure rose over the line of high-street shops. Tall, slender, with a peaked top. The steeple of a church. And on the front, a clock.

She stared at the clock for a long moment, the blood throbbing in her temples.

She slid her finger to the side, breaking the connection with the sister and letting the pad of her finger rest on the last sibling.

A few seconds later, she swiped the image away and was dialling a number.

Waterman answered on the first ring.

'Each of the siblings has a bomb.' The words tumbled

out of her. 'There's two more to come. Both during daylight today. The next is the sister. It's going to happen in a few seconds. I don't know where. A town somewhere outside London.'

41

Jack Riley's hands rested lightly on the steering wheel. He'd pulled the bus over with a minute to spare and switched off the engine when the tower bells in Great St Mary's had begun to toll. You never knew how observant people would be during a minute's silence. On Remembrance Day, each year, all Cambridge buses pulled over, but most cars kept driving and many shoppers were oblivious.

Today was different. Every car had pulled over, and the pedestrians stood frozen too. The only movement on the high street was a couple of toddlers tugging at their parents' hands. And it was so quiet in the bus that he could hear the engine ticking over between the sound of the bells.

The shock of what had happened this morning was still palpable. A suicide bomb at one of London's busiest stations. Jack still couldn't believe it. It was London, not Lebanon. He had taken the kids through Victoria only a week ago, on their way to the West End.

The silence was to honour the dead, Jack knew, but it made everyone jumpy too. The media hadn't released any information on the bomber, but they knew it had been a suicide, so it stood to reason it was an Asian or an Arab. People were now on the lookout, keeping eyes on left luggage, on Asian lads with backpacks, on anything that felt suspicious. Things like that happened more often than they should.

Jack kept his eyes fixed on his rear-view. He could see them clearly enough, even with the fish-eye distortion of the mirror.

The two passengers were sitting by the exit door, looking around nervously, avoiding the eyes of those around them, who were staring as intently as Jack was.

The man and woman would have been an odd sight at the best of times, he in Bermuda shorts, sandals and an untucked shirt, she encased head to toe in a black burqa, only dark eyes ringed with eyeliner showing. They might have been two blokes for all Jack knew.

He checked his watch. Ten seconds to go. He could tell the other passengers were jumpy too. They kept looking at the couple. It was impossible to tell what she was hiding under all that material.

''Scuse me. We want to get off.'

Jack looked in his mirror. It was the man who'd spoken. He was standing now, swinging on his backpack, pulling on the straps to relieve the weight. Whatever he was carrying was heavy. Bulky. Jack could see the weight pulled the natural shape out of the bag, tugging it directly down. The wife was up too, standing obediently behind him.

All eyes turned to the driver's cockpit to see what Jack would do.

''Scuse me!'

He was shouting now. In a strong accent. Must be an

Arab or an Asian. But Jack knew that already, even before he'd spoken. It was obvious.

Jack had been on the buses almost thirty years, straight from school, but he'd only felt tension like this once before. Back in 2005, when those four Asian lads had blown up those bombs in London. They'd cancelled his service that day, out of respect, but it was up and running the next, and the fear was evident each time he pulled out into the street. The passengers just sat there, warily appraising each other, searching for any signs of threat.

'Hello! Driver!'

He was shouting again, looking at Jack, pointing to the door. Two female pensioners, sitting in the row in front of the side door, looked at Jack in panic.

'Let them out. Now.'

'We in rush,' said the Arab, in broken English. 'We will take taxi. To hospital.'

Jack twisted in his seat. The couple had moved to the door and were only a few feet away from his cabin. He could see her clearly now, for the first time. There was an unmistakable maternal bump, and she held on to the man as she walked. Through the top flap of the backpack, Jack could see a soft toy and folded clothes for a newborn.

Jack let out a long breath and rubbed his forehead. 'Yes, of course, mate. Here.' He pressed the button to open the middle door and watched them step out, too ashamed of what he'd been thinking to make eye contact with anyone on the bus.

277

The second hand climbed past one on his wristwatch. The minute's silence was over. Jack twisted the key in the ignition and started the bus. He pulled the lever for the front door, and four passengers walked on.

Jack noticed he was breathing deeply, the sweat pricking the back of his T-shirt. These bombs brought out the darkest thoughts in people. He couldn't wait for this shift to be over. Four more hours. He had tickets to the football, but he was tired of the public spaces. Too much paranoia. He pushed the lever, closing the doors, and pulled out into the traffic.

The height of the colleges on the south side of the street kept the road in shadow for about fifty yards, when a single-storey shop on the south side created a break for the sun, flooding the street with bright light.

Jack's mind drifted, as it always did when he drove, contemplating the shadow and the light. How you had to pass through one to get to the other.

When the front of his bus broke through the shadow and into the light, the bright glare lit up the bus, dappling the windscreen with scales of light. Jack stared at it, a smile creeping across his face.

It was the last thought he had.

At that moment, the bus exploded with so much force that the roof was blown clean off, landing almost fifty feet away. The force of the detonation blew out every window in the street, cleanly inwards, leaving precious little glass on the pavement.

42

'A bomb just went off on a bus on Trumpington Street in Cambridge. Too soon for a casualty count, but likely multiple fatalities.'

Waterman was still on the phone. She could hear voices around him. He must be in a situation room at GCHQ.

'Do we know if it was a suicide bomb?'

'Not yet. We're checking to see if there were CCTV cams on the bus.'

She became aware of activity around her. Two suited men were walking briskly over to Shaw, who was reading a text message on his phone. News of the second bomb was filtering through to the teams around her.

Sara walked across the forecourt and through the official exit in the screens.

'Get me up there now,' she told Waterman. 'Send a helicopter to the station.'

The pause at the other end of the line let Sara know that there was something else Waterman was not telling her.

'What?' asked Sara, impatiently.

'It's my fault,' said Waterman, eventually. *'I should have protected you. I knew Shaw was . . .'*

'The photos they took of me.' A cold chill ran through Sara.

279

'A photo just went up, on the Standard's *web page. Someone from the press identified you at the crime scene.'*

Shaw's plan had taken almost no time to complete.

'He set me up,' said Sara in disgust.

'I'm sorry, Sara. I should have known he'd try something.'

The earnestness in Waterman's tone wrong-footed Sara. She'd been expecting a reprimand. She'd certainly earned it. She was so focused on the investigation that she had been blind to the politics. She had grown up outside the system, permanently on the run, and this was the legacy, a total tin ear to the way organizations work. If she was going to survive at this job, she had a lot to learn.

'I run signals intelligence, Sara,' he continued. *'Running human assets is new to me. I guess I'm learning on the job, like you.'*

'Forget it,' she said, her voice softening. 'He was hostile from the start. I should have known he'd try to sabotage me.'

Waterman's reaction took her by surprise. When she had reached out to Salt, she had steeled herself for working in isolation. The mantra she had grown up with was that spies could never be trusted. But there was something strange about her chemistry with Waterman. Maybe it was that they were both bound to keep her identity a secret. Or that he was an intellectual more than an operator. Or that today's stakes were so high. But, whatever was behind it, she seemed to have found something she never expected. An ally.

'You're doing OK, Director Waterman,' she said, allowing herself a smile.

'I'll try to get you back in, but for now, there's no more under-cover work, I'm afraid. Shaw has likely already given orders to exclude you from access to crime scenes and the front line of the investigation. Meet me at our Palmer Street office in an hour.'

Sara hung up. The goodwill on the call had taken away the bitter taste of Shaw's back-stabbing, but she hadn't told Waterman the worst news. She couldn't, because she wasn't sure she believed it. What she had seen when she touched Adrian Lang's face must have been a mistake. Some glitch in her abilities, the nature of which she was still trying to understand. It had taken time to build Waterman's trust in her, to take him from sceptic to believer. And if she told him now what she had seen in that connection with Adrian Lang, all would have been lost. Because the images she saw were only partly involving a bomb. It was the aftermath of the bomb that was the most chilling. Not scores dead, or even hundreds, but thousands. Entire high streets littered with corpses, their faces burnt, their limbs blistered. The bomb wasn't the culprit: it was some greater evil, unseen and unknown, in hiding until now.

43

Riz looked through the window of the helicopter at the high street below. He'd never visited Cambridge before, but he doubted it had ever looked like this. Trumpington Street was about half a mile long, running north–south, twisting through sandstone university buildings. It was lit up now with flashing blue lights from a score of police cars parked at abrupt angles at the intersection of access streets. Flapping police tape blocked their entrances, with curious crowds gathering on the far side of each tape.

'I'm going to put us down in the park there.' The pilot's voice crackled in Riz's headphones. He followed the man's outstretched hand and saw a large plot of green bordered with flowers just beyond the high street.

As the helicopter banked, a sight dipped into view that shocked even Riz.

The detonation had ripped the top of the bus clean off, leaving the shell to resemble a green tin flower, petals peeled back. From his vantage point, he could see directly into the guts of the vehicle. Blue plastic sheeting had been erected inside the interior, covering the bodies that were still there. The interior walls that were left were blood-splattered.

The chopper settled onto the grass and Riz hopped out, ducking his head as the blades roared above him.

He walked quickly across the park. Ahead of him, a uniformed police officer waited, head bent, holding on to his helmet. Next to him, a tall man, short salt-and-pepper hair dancing in the buffeting wind, was dressed in a white sports shirt, scarlet jumper and a pair of avocado-green slacks. The fingers of a pair of slim, white leather gloves peeked out from one trouser pocket. He held out his hand as Riz approached.

'Derek Davies, chief constable of Cambridge. This is PC McBride.'

'I'm guessing you were in the middle of a golf game, sir,' said Riz, not breaking his stride. Davies and McBride turned to follow him, matching his pace.

'Yes. The day went from good to nightmare,' responded Davies, smoothing his hair.

'What do you have so far?' asked Riz.

'Working assumption is it was a suicide bomb,' said Davies. 'An eye-witness says they saw someone running inside the bus just before the explosion.'

'Has the area been cleared?' asked Riz. Cambridge wasn't London. It wouldn't have the terror-response infrastructure of a capital city. Protocols existed for events like this and were uniform nationwide, but it was human nature that, until an event happened, contingency plans were kept in bottom drawers. The plans stressed the dangers of follow-on devices, and that was the first priority in Riz's mind right now.

'We've had the dogs go through,' said Davies.

The three men walked along a short, cobbled lane, the sandstone walls of university colleges rising above them on either side. There was no traffic noise, but Riz could hear helicopters clattering overhead. Media, no doubt. Police tape was strung across the end of the lane. Up ahead, two local police officers stood in the middle of the high street, quietly staring at something Riz couldn't see. He ducked under the tape and walked towards them, following their line of sight.

The street was a war zone. Every window had been blown inwards. Mangled parts of the bus littered the road and both sides of the pavement. A thin column of black smoke rose vertically from the vehicle until, high over the rooftops, it was dispersed by the wind. On the far pavement, teams of paramedics treated injured pedestrians, who lay on the ground with bandages pressed to their faces.

Riz realized he'd stopped in the middle of the street. They were still in the immediate aftermath, with police and paramedics providing triage support. He held at bay the flood of knowledge that usually washed through his mind in the aftermath of a bombing, reminding himself that, at this stage, there was no evidence the bombers had any jihadist links. It made the sight in front of him even more unnerving. Without a context in which to place the slaughter, he found it difficult to manage his rising horror. Why else would someone commit such an atrocity? When he looked at Davies's face, he noticed he was struggling with the same emotions.

'You and your officers have done well,' said Riz. 'ARVs are on their way.'

Before he left Davies, he asked the question that had been turning in his mind during the short flight over. 'Do the buses have CCTV?'

The chief constable nodded. 'All buses are Wi-Fi enabled. There's a live relay of CCTV to the operating company, BusLine.'

'Can you take me to their offices now?'

'PC McBride will,' said Davies. 'I've got to get changed and speak to the media. People in Cambridge need to hear what's going on.'

Riz pulled out a card and scribbled his number on the back. 'A nice lady called Pam Smith is on her way up with a team. That's my mobile. Call me the moment her list is complete.'

Davies took the card, his head shaking minutely. 'List?'

Riz found himself staring at a bizarre arrangement of twisted metal. It was only the four wheels that reminded him it was a bus. He turned back to Davies and held out his hand in parting. 'The list of the dead.'

44

Waterman walked across the asphalt, past the rows of vehicles, to an area of the car park by the far gate. An MoD helicopter was picking him up in fifteen minutes to take him to London to see Sara. He scanned for his visitor.

She was parked in her usual place. The engine was running, and he could just about make out the tinny sounds of Radio 4.

'Sorry I'm late,' he said, as he collapsed into the front passenger seat.

Susie turned off the radio. 'I said we could do it another time. I heard the news. Another bomb, in Cambridge.'

Waterman reached over and took a chicken-salad sandwich from the Tupperware box in her lap. 'I've got to eat sometime,' he said. He'd been in his new role less than a week when the potential toll it could take on his family became clear. GCHQ had a voracious appetite for his time, keeping him at all hours and invading his home time with barrages of calls and emails. After a tense stand-off with Susie last month, an agreement had been reached. They would have one meal together every day, no matter what. He'd called her an hour ago, testing the limits of the bargain they'd reached, to see if it would encompass meals on wheels.

He munched the sandwich, breathing heavily after his march to the car. The windows were fogged with condensation, which gave them a little more cover from any staff interruptions.

'It hasn't been disclosed yet, but it wasn't a jihadist attack. The bomber was white. Ex-army.'

He didn't have to edit too much when he spoke to his wife. All family members who lived with GCHQ senior staff were subject to the same level of vetting. In Waterman's case, this was the very highest level, so-called Enhanced DV. It required completing a 116-page questionnaire on every aspect of one's family, professional and personal backgrounds, which became the basis of an intensive review by the Ministry of Defence. Susie and the girls filled it in patiently, gathered around the kitchen table together. Waterman was grateful to them, although in truth, they all knew they had no option.

He still kept certain things from Susie. But it was mostly to protect her. It was his job to keep secrets, not hers.

'Good God.' Susie stared ahead in shock. After a few seconds of silence, she looked over at Waterman. 'What does that mean?'

He shrugged. 'We don't know yet.'

He had been in the car only a few minutes when a strident melody cut through their conversation: Wagner's 'Ride of the Valkyries'. The ring tone had been programmed by his eldest daughter as a joke, her way of making light of how Waterman jumped each time a call came through the GCHQ switchboard.

'Sorry,' said Waterman. 'I thought I'd switched it off.' He answered the call.

'Hold on, give me a minute,' he said into the phone, as he opened the car door and stepped out. He closed the door and walked ten yards from the car. He didn't have advance notice on what the call was about and didn't want to burden Susie with unknown confidences.

'OK, I'm here.'

'I've got two things for you.' It was Swift.

'Something on Shaw?'

'That's one,' said Swift.

Waterman could almost hear his ear-to-ear grin.

'You're not going to believe this. We found his photo on a gay dating app. He last logged in two days ago. The photo is ten years old. Subtly Photoshopped. Only found it because of the next-gen facial-recognition crawlers that were rolled out on Wednesday. Their algorithms can now pick up a spread of Photoshop attempts.'

'Any supporting evidence?' asked Waterman. He was vaguely aware that Shaw was married. He wasn't confident he had children, but some part of him seemed to remember he did. There were plenty of gay men and women serving their country in the security services. And it was not unheard of for devoted family men to have secret lives, although it was less common for those with wives to have male lovers.

'We tracked log-ins to an internet café in south London,' said Swift. 'Pulled the footage from those times. He's wearing a hoodie, but he forgot about the built-in cams in the desktops. I have a clear shot of him from the last log-in.' Swift hesitated. 'Boss, these lads he's meeting, they're pretty young. Teens mostly.'

Waterman thought for a moment. Evidence of infidelity and the consequent risk to the marriage would be leverage he could use. This was the spy game, where kompromat was always useful, even in intra-national investigations. Evidence that Shaw was consorting with teenage boys would also embarrass him with his peer group. It was no surprise that Swift was so gleeful.

Waterman's mind ticked over. He'd never had to make decisions like these when he was coming up the ranks. Then it had been about accessing and sifting the data. What happened thereafter was always a decision taken by others. Now he was those others.

Swift's discovery was something of a coup for GCHQ. Shaw had been a thorn in their side for many years. It was now up to Waterman whether he wanted to send a couple of officers to London. As long as the teens were of age, no laws were being broken, but Shaw knew better than to develop a habit that could expose him to blackmail by a foreign power. The office visit would have consequences, of course. Others at Thames House would find out. Even though it was only meant as a warning, the visit would be very damaging to his career.

'Send the photo you took to Shaw from an anonymous email address,' said Waterman, at last.

'OK,' said Swift. 'Then what?'

Waterman didn't answer, but his mind was spinning.

Swift's question was the right one. Compromising material gave him leverage. Substantial leverage, in fact. He could probably use it to get all manner of intel and concessions from Shaw. That was what Salt, the master of the game, would do. However, Waterman was developing his own comfort zone for decisions. Shaw's service history kept coming back to him. He had served his country for four decades and been decorated as a soldier. Despite the man's prickly demeanour, he admired Shaw. Waterman needed to do something, though, because if Swift could find the dating site, a Russian cyber-expert might be able to as well. And the Russians would have no hesitation in using the material to squeeze Shaw to the fullest extent. By sending the photo to Shaw, Waterman would spook him from using the app. The strategy would neutralize the threat. That still left the question, though, of whether or not he wanted to use the intel to do some squeezing of his own.

He looked nervously at the car. Susie sat patiently waiting for him.

'What's the second thing?' asked Waterman.

Waterman listened, then hung up. He walked back to the car and opened the door, bending over but not getting in.

'Don't worry,' said Susie, pre-emptively. 'Just go.'

He nodded, leant in and kissed her cheek, then walked quickly back to the main building.

45

Thomas Sanders was a beefy man with a ruddy complexion, thick gin blossom on his cheeks and nose, and grey mutton-chop whiskers.

'Jack Riley was sitting in that chair only two days ago. He was the union rep. Gave his life to the bus service. Thirty-year anniversary was coming up.'

Sanders was in his late fifties and had a thatch of grey hair that rose untamed from his scalp in conflicting directions, the result, Riz noticed, of habitually running his fingers through it.

The offices of BusLine were in a modern building on the far side of the Cam river, overlooking a meadow that McBride had referred to as Midsummer Common. The building was in stark contrast to the sandstone colleges around it. With its long, squat shape and matt black exterior, it looked like a metal filing cabinet that had been tipped onto its side.

McBride had turned out to be a useful resource. In his early twenties, he was too fresh to have become steeped yet in politics or divisional fealties. He also appeared to be in shock, and Riz couldn't blame him. Signing up for the Cambridge force came with an expectation of chasing teenage joyriders, not dealing with bus bombs on the high street. The combination of his youth and agitation had loosened McBride's tongue, and on the drive over he had shared an abundance of information on everything the police had gleaned from the crime scene that afternoon. The SOCOs, when they arrived, would be able to pick more detail from the wreckage, but a few of the local coppers who were ex-forces had guessed the bomb was the same size as the one used in Victoria. McBride had also relayed something they'd said that had stuck in Riz's mind. There was no projectile debris within the bus. Riz would have expected to find nails and ball-bearings in the blast area. This was common with IEDs. An outer casing of lethal metal scraps would create wider collateral damage. The open space of the Victoria station forecourt made for a wide dispersal area, so these projectiles were only found later by the SOCOs. But in the enclosed space of the bus, they should have been immediately visible. To Riz, this was another reminder that the investigation was becoming more different by the hour.

'Can we see the footage from the bus?' Riz asked Sanders.

'Course,' said Sanders. He stood up, revealing a huge convex stomach that hung over his trousers, tipping the front of them forward at an acute angle. 'This way,' he said, puffing his cheeks and letting out a long breath. 'Never thought I'd see this day in Cambridge.'

He led them out of his office and down the central passageway, to the IT room. It was the size of Sanders's office, although it was windowless. Computer servers took up half the room, black blocks with blinking lights encased in white plastic protective covers. A set of free-standing cooling units placed around the edges of the room explained the drop in temperature as they stepped over the threshold.

'We've got a fleet of buses, running around the clock, all with multiple cams running constantly. The amount of data we store here is colossal. I'm not a techie, so I can't give you numbers.' Sanders pointed to two plastic chairs. 'Take a seat, both of you. We found the footage from C-27, which was Jack's bus. It's teed up to play three minutes before the . . .' he searched for the right word, then gave up '. . . it's a cross-sectional feed. There are eight cams on each bus. Four downstairs, four upstairs. None of us have watched it yet.'

It wasn't clear to Riz whether they hadn't done so out of deference to MI5, or because they didn't have the stomach for it.

'Thanks, Mr Sanders,' said Riz. 'We'll take it from here.'

After Sanders had left, Riz leant forward and tapped the space bar. 'Let's see what we have here,' he said, under his breath.

Each of the cross-sectional feeds began playing at once. The screen was divided into smaller screens, each one of a different section of the lower and upper floors. From the rolling diorama of shop windows flashing by through the lower windows, he could tell the bus was moving.

He immediately scanned each passenger's face to see if Adrian or Penny Lang was on board. They weren't.

Riz looked at the people on the top deck. A group of blazered secondary-school kids occupied the back rows, twisting in their seats to huddle in whispered conversation. Solitary passengers sat in other rows, checking their phones or staring blankly out of the window. Long, striped scarves and book-bags suggested they were university students. In the front seat, an elderly couple looked out through the large top windows.

All these lives, oblivious of what was to come. No one had survived from the top deck.

Riz could tell from the view through the windows that the bus was slowing down. It pulled over to the side of the road. McBride pointed to the timer count running in the lower part of the screen. 'This is the beginning of the minute's silence.'

On the lower floor, the cameras showed a woman in a burqa sitting next to a man who looked agitated. There was no audio on the recording, but Riz could see his mouth moving. He appeared to be talking to someone on the bus. Riz watched the drama unfold until the bus driver let the man and his pregnant partner out.

'Ten seconds left,' said McBride, unnecessarily, pointing to the counter.

The minute's silence had elapsed and a faint tremor on the cameras indicated the bus's engine had started. The lower extreme right of the screen contained the camera pointing to the front door. It swung open and a line of waiting passengers began stepping onto the bus.

Eight seconds left.

Riz leant further forward, his face barely a foot from

the screen now. A line formed in front of the driver's booth, as each arrival tapped their card on the reader. A middle-aged couple who looked like tourists. A kid who looked like a student. A mother with a toddler in a pushchair.

Four seconds.

And then he saw her. She looked heavier than she had been in the photo. Her face had filled out and her green cam jacket was tight around her shoulders. Blonde hair in a ponytail. Backpack that looked like it contained something heavy. She stood in front of the bus driver's kiosk and stared down the main aisle.

'Penny Lang,' said Riz, under his breath.

'Seems like she's looking for someone,' said McBride, looking at Riz for confirmation. Riz didn't take his eyes off the screen.

'Pause it,' said Riz. McBride tapped the space bar on the keyboard and the image froze. It was a close-up of Penny Lang, her face turned three-quarters away from the camera.

'What's that?' asked Riz. He pointed his finger at a black shadow that seemed to run down the left side of Penny's face, from her temple to just below her ear. McBride looked closer, then shrugged.

'Some sort of tattoo?'

'On her face?' Riz looked at McBride with surprise. 'Don't think she's the type. Can we tighten the focus?'

McBride leant closer to the keyboard. 'Not sure how.'

Riz rubbed his chin, then tapped the space bar to resume the video.

Two seconds.

Penny's head surged out of one camera frame and reappeared in the next: she was pushing past the passengers who were still standing. She disappeared again and reappeared in the last frame.

One second.

Penny lifted her arms wide, her wingspan spread as far as it would go. For one moment, it looked like she was making the sign of the cross. Then every cam flashed white and the screen went dark.

46

Waterman's feet moved noiselessly along the black carpet. Even by GCHQ's standards, today was a day unlike any other. Not just in the frenetic pace and the scale of the threat they were facing, but also the insidious internal threat known only to Waterman and Swift.

He cuffed the key card through the security swipe and entered the submarine stillness of the Agency.

The screens on the far wall were tuned to public and private communication channels. The terrestrial and satellite TV stations, which took up one corner of the wall, were dominated by street and aerial footage of Victoria station and Trumpington Street. Although there was no CCTV footage from the Victoria attack, Waterman had dedicated an internal task force to support MI5 in the course of their investigations.

Waterman watched as the TV feed cut back to the studio. A collage of official MoD photos of the Lang siblings filled the screen behind the newsreader. Scotland Yard and MI5 had lobbied the press not to use the walking-holiday photo of the Langs that had been leaked after the raid on the squat, the fear being that members of the public might be more reluctant to identify someone beaming at the camera as a member of a suicide bombing cell. From what Waterman could see, the press was toeing the line.

The rest of the screens on the wall were dominated by aerial and satellite footage, as well as street-level CCTV cams that cycled over in fast rotation: the latest generation facial-recognition software was combing through everything to find a match for Adrian Lang.

The Agency was packed, every terminal occupied. All leave had been cancelled and the briny smell of sandwiches soaked the air as people worked through lunch, eating at their desks.

Swift looked over the top of his laptop as Waterman approached.

'OK, what do you have for me?' said Waterman. 'I haven't got long.'

Swift turned his laptop screen towards him, so only he and Waterman could see. He then double-clicked on an icon on his desktop.

A video screen launched.

It was surveillance footage from the dashboard of a car. In the near distance, wipers brushed away rain-drops that pebbled the windscreen.

Over the bonnet of the car, Waterman could see a street somewhere in central London. He checked the header of the box that was opened. The geo-stamp indicated it was taken in Mount Street, Mayfair.

A black Mercedes was parked twenty yards ahead, its orange-red brake lights brilliant in the rain.

A well-dressed man exited the vehicle and walked quickly up the steps and through a front door. He was tall and distinguished, with peppery hair and ramrod bearing.

Before walking through, he looked each way up the street, checking for something. Waterman could clearly see Salt's face, creased in agitation. He opened the front door but did not step inside. Instead, he held it and nodded towards the car.

'Watch this,' said Swift, looking up at Waterman.

The rear passenger-side door opened and another man stepped out onto the pavement. He was smaller in stature than Salt, and elegantly attired in a suit. Waterman had a flash of a tidy moustache and heavy brows as he ran up the stairs and through the door Salt was holding open.

'His name is –' started Swift.

'Puipin,' cut in Waterman.

Swift nodded in surprise. 'Yes . . . He runs a security firm with heavy ties to the French government.'

'So, what's your conclusion?' asked Waterman.

Swift hesitated, arranging his thoughts before responding. 'Puipin is a private citizen and a foreign national. What's the chairman of the JIC doing meeting with him? It raises questions.'

'Puipin is also Salt's ex-wife's cousin,' said Waterman. 'I've met him before, at an event about a year ago.' Waterman stood upright and stretched his back. 'There's no red flag here. Not yet.'

'The meeting isn't in Salt's diary,' pressed Swift.

That halted Waterman. Like most key personnel in the military intelligence community, Salt was required to keep a thorough diary noting all of his meetings. A meeting with the principal of the firm Détente would certainly have to be in the diary, even if the man was a relative. There was too much in Salt's head for his day-to-day whereabouts to be unaccounted for. Waterman pulled on his beard, thinking.

'It could be an oversight. Sometimes diary entries are made after the event,' he said at last, without much conviction. The idea of Charles Salt forgetting something was an alien concept.

Swift looked uncertain. 'If that's not enough, what are you looking for?'

Waterman checked his watch and swore. He began to walk towards the door, then stopped and gave his instructions to Swift. 'Proof.'

Waterman thought about the lapel pin. The audio recording. The USB stick. It was a treasure trove of intelligence. How much more was there? And how often would a foreign power be offered clandestine audio files from within Britain's highest circles of power?

It wasn't just the recordings. In a way, they were just the smoke. The gun was Salt. In modern history, there had never been a whistle-blower or defector as high-ranking as Charles Salt. Blunt, Burgess and Maclean had been agents; Edward Snowden was a private contractor; Katharine Gun was a translator. All were in their own trenches, but Salt stood on the mountain top. There was not one British secret to which he did not have access.

With the tectonic plates of power shifting around

the world – Britain's tilt to America and away from Europe, the ascent of China, the destabilization of Russia – an asset like Salt would have players scrambling over themselves to offer him asylum.

Waterman was surprised that France had come out as the frontrunner. But maybe that was not surprising. Post-Brexit, France and Germany were competing for moral leadership of the EU. Germany was the industrial powerhouse, but France was stronger on the political stage. And an asset like Salt would enhance their security network.

He could see the chess moves now. But there was still one thing Waterman didn't understand. What was the prize for Salt? He had inherited wealth, so money had never been an issue. Salt had made serving his country his life's purpose. What had he found of higher value to trade all that for? Until Waterman had the complete picture, he would be making no intuitive leaps in the investigation of Charles Salt.

47

Riz and McBride were still sitting in silence in the IT room of BusLine when Riz's phone rang. He answered. It was Davies, advising him to check his secure email.

'They have the names of the deceased,' said Riz to McBride, after hanging up.

Riz opened the secure email inbox on his smartphone and saw a host of emails waiting for him. Most were from Shaw. A famed Luddite, it was a testament to how seriously he was taking this case that he was sending emails. Usually all his comms were via calls.

Most of the emails were one-line updates on other branches of the investigation: the ordnance report on the Victoria bomb, Simon Lang's personnel file from the MoD, Scotland Yard circulating the phone records from the iPhone. There was never more than a ten-minute gap between the emails.

Riz ignored Shaw's emails for the moment and searched for the one from Pam Smith that Davies had said just arrived. Riz noticed that there were, in fact, two. The first had arrived an hour ago, headed 'Victoria LOD'. The other, more recent, had arrived only a few minutes ago: 'Cambridge LOD'.

Riz opened the earlier email. It was addressed to a bespoke copy group that had been created called

'Victoria Task Forces'. There were at least fifty names on the list, all law-enforcement and terror-security professionals.

There was no cover note from Pam Smith, just a Word document attached. Riz opened it. The document was a graph, with a list of surnames in one column, first names in the next, with others devoted to gender, nationality, age and occupation.

He scanned the list. Tourists, office workers, a few retired people. One mother and her child. He tried to stem the empathy he was feeling. He wouldn't be of any use to anyone if he let his emotions overcome him. He opened the older email from Smith and looked at the attachment.

'That's interesting,' he muttered.

'What is it?' asked McBride, standing up and walking over to him. Riz pointed to a name on the Victoria list of deceased and then a name on the Cambridge list. McBride peered at the screen.

'Someone from the MoD was killed in each explosion,' said McBride, eyebrows raised.

Riz nodded. 'Not just that. They were both MoD police.'

The MoD police was a civilian special force. Riz knew little about it, other than that its role was primarily to protect MoD assets, principally marine fleets and nuclear installations. He knew it was small, around two thousand officers. Given the absence of any MoD assets near either of the blast sites, the chances of an officer from the division being among the dead at both suicide-bomb attacks today seemed too much of a coincidence.

A new email from Shaw popped into the top of Riz's inbox. He tapped it and scanned the contents. It was addressed to Pembroke and, this time, only the MI5 task force was copied. Shaw got straight to the point. He'd been in contact with the MoD regarding their two fatalities and their responses had been terse. Just a confirmation of the officers' employment and when they joined the MoD. It wouldn't even confirm whether or not the men had been on duty at the time of the bombings. The MoD had a reputation for being tight-lipped, but the fact that it wouldn't be more cooperative on the day bombs were exploding across the country was a little shocking to Riz. Shaw added a note that he'd conducted his own enquiries and found something of interest: both policemen were listed as having Enhanced DV status, which was highly unusual for front-line MoD police. Riz felt a quickening of his pulse.

'Could this help track down Adrian Lang?'

Riz looked up and saw McBride staring at him. Gazing into those expectant eyes made him realize he was far from London. Too far. He had to get back to the investigation. There wasn't much more he could do here.

'Can you print still frames for me of the last ten seconds of the footage? Here,' said Riz, handing him his business card. 'You can email them to me at this address.'

If McBride was disappointed about their newfound partnership splitting up, he didn't show it.

48

Shaw surveyed the people in front of him. The situation room on the seventh floor was designed for internal conferences, with a capacity of almost three hundred. The room ran the entire length of the north side of Thames House. Dimpled bomb-resistant glass windows looked out over the street, where a line of poplar trees obscured the view of the building opposite. People were still trailing in, making a detour to the coffee station at the back, where most of the other attendees still stood making conversation.

They were all there: MI5, Scotland Yard, GCHQ, the MoD, the Office for Security and Counter-Terrorism and the Joint Intelligence Organization. It was the largest cross-agency cooperative effort since the 2005 London bombings. And, as the acting operational head of the task force, it fell to Shaw to take the lead in the meeting.

This should have been the finest moment of his career. For once, he had been in the right place at the right time. But the email he had received from an anonymous sender an hour ago was crowding out everything else in his mind. He had been caught in the jaws of the great whale, despite all his efforts to conceal himself. And, as if that wasn't bad enough, the picture was haunting. Unshaven, dressed like a young offender on day leave, his face, in the glowing light of the screen, looking unhinged as he leered at the thumbnail pictures onscreen. If that picture ever got out, his career would be over.

He'd steeled himself for the knock on the door after receiving the email. But an hour had passed and the knock had never come. The anonymity of the communication also suggested he was getting a reprieve.

Waterman was sitting in the front row. Shaw avoided his eye but he knew Waterman was behind this. Only he had access to the computing power required to remotely switch on built-in cameras in antiquated desktops in seedy web cafés in south London.

Shaw had closed the account immediately and had reset his phone to its factory settings, scorching the earth around him. But there was still one connection to the website that he could not eliminate: Waterman.

And Waterman was sitting in front of him now, less than six feet away. Shaw clenched his jaw in a vain battle to stop a flush rising to his cheeks. The embarrassment was the least he had to suffer. There would be a reckoning. Maybe now, maybe later. But it was coming. The briefing could be the beginning of it. A sword hung over his head that only he and Waterman could see, and the open forum would be an effective way to wring concessions from him in front of the entire intelligence community.

Shaw checked his watch. It was time to start. He took a deep breath and stood up. 'Ladies and gentlemen, we're going to start in one minute.'

His booming voice brought their conversations to a faltering stop. He watched them as they filtered down the rows to take their seats. He turned his mind to business. This wasn't going to be easy. Each of these agencies had their own agendas and objectives, their own scores to settle. The MoD had already clammed up on the two MoD police killed today. And he knew GCHQ was keeping its own secrets too, at least one being his own. That fact alone reminded Shaw that no two secrets were the same. His job today wasn't to exert pressure to make sure all intel was pooled. Transparency was never good for the intelligence community, even among themselves. Some secrets were best kept, and others needed more baking, waiting for the right moment to reveal them.

'Thank you,' announced Shaw, projecting to the back of the room. The murmurs drew to a swift conclusion and soon there was only the sound of people shifting in their seats.

'Two bombs. The bombers brother and sister. And one sibling still at large.' Shaw turned sideways and pointed a finger at the poster-length photo of Adrian Lang that glowered at the room from the easel on which it rested.

'Adrian Lang. Thirty-four years old. Ex-armed forces. Like the other two, of no fixed abode.'

He turned and stepped towards the back wall. It was designed to be one huge board for presentations, its slick, glossy surface functioning as both a whiteboard and a canvas on which evidence and other photos could be fixed with magnetized strips. The entire wall was covered with photos of the deceased from both bombings, as well as maps of Victoria station and Trumpington Street.

'By mid-afternoon today, he will be the subject of the largest manhunt in modern British history.'

Shaw's voice rose as he warmed to the subject. He knew from his time as a captain leading his own platoon that every briefing was also a pep talk. People weren't machines. They needed inspiration. Some emotional charge that could become a connective tissue between them, binding them together in a common purpose after they left the room.

'Shortly before this meeting started, the Security Service and JTAC raised the threat level to critical. This is the highest in fourteen years. Maximum security measures are now in place. The armed presence at sea and airports has been tripled. Our friends at GCHQ are searching for any voiceprints that might exist for Lang, whether from intercepts or possible appearances on public media. If one is found, the voiceprint data will be sent to Predator drones, currently on flight patterns above key cities in England, to seek matches from any mobile intercepts. That face,' he pointed to Adrian Lang's photo again, 'is being displayed on at least five thousand electronic billboards around the country. And MI5 and Scotland Yard are rebuilding as much as they can of the last movements of Lang these past few days – any army buddies he may still be in contact with, the occupational health workers who last helped him, any dossers who may have seen him on the streets.'

A hand rose.

Shaw's insides roiled as he nodded to the front row. 'Director Waterman.'

Waterman stood and turned to address the others. 'Thank you. There's only one sibling left, and we have no reason to believe there are any other accomplices, which means the chances of intercepts are low. But plans like this leave traces. They always do. Adrian Lang's target is part of a pattern, and if anyone in this room has any new intel regarding the bombings today, GCHQ is lead on the patterning process.'

'Anything else?' asked Shaw, trying to keep the dread out of his voice.

Waterman shook his head and took his seat, to Shaw's considerable surprise and relief.

Another hand was raised and a bald man in the police uniform of a detective superintendent stood up. 'Do we have any direct evidence on Adrian Lang implicating him in this cell?'

Shaw's confidence was returning and he nodded as the man spoke. It made sense that it was a copper who asked this question. More bombs had exploded in Britain today than in Baghdad and this plod was worried about Lang's civil liberties. Shaw maintained a perfectly neutral face as he answered. 'As of now, no one has claimed responsibility. We have found no manifesto. No suicide note. What we have are two siblings, two bombs, home-made IEDs that took experience to build, and a missing sibling with the same background and experience as the dead bombers. The two incidents were close enough together today that there is reason to assume that, if there is a third incident, it will take place today as well. Rest assured that we are not leaving any stone unturned, but as of now, finding Adrian Lang is our first priority. That's the end of the formal overview. We'll take briefings now from the individual agencies.'

Shaw walked around the desk and sat in the front row, surrendering the podium to the next person.

At the end of the row, a woman Shaw recognized as MoD answered her phone and cupped her hand around her mouth as she spoke in a whisper. Shaw watched her balefully as she got up and moved in a crouch along the line of chairs to the exit.

There was little doubt in Shaw's mind that the MoD was keeping something from the task force. He understood the delicate art of secrets, especially in their profession, but something about the MoD's responses to his request for information today felt suspicious. The Langs had been armed forces after all, which made them ex-MoD employees. Along with the fallen MoD policemen today, that made the ministry the key intel source for the task force, and it was giving away precious little. It was hiding something, and Shaw would bet it had something to do with the two MoD men killed.

'I'd like us to work together on this.'

Shaw looked over to see Waterman had moved to the seat next to his. 'I'm not putting your girl Eden back.'

'And I'm not asking you to. I'm here to give you something. You've been looking into the two MoD men killed. According to my intel, they worked for the Close Protection Division of the MoD police force. Body men. And both men were on active duty.'

'Who were they guarding?' Shaw was curious, despite himself.

'I don't know yet. But I might have a way to find out. I'll share the intel when I have it.'

He looked at Shaw pointedly, the unspoken question hanging in the air. Shaw considered. People rarely, if ever, surprised him. And yet there was something about Waterman's demeanour that suggested no advantage was being pressed. He was getting a reprieve. There would be no quid pro quo. And that act made Shaw more inclined to cooperate than anything else. Finally, he nodded.

'So will I.'

49

Professor Matthew Broad looked around the spacious amphitheatre. It was a full house today. Almost three hundred. He recognized his undergraduate and postgraduate teams. They made up about a quarter of the audience. They all had their laptops open, the same look of studious intensity on their faces. It pleased him that the faces he did not recognize shared the same expression, although in their cases it was one of perplexity, as if they had stepped into the wrong lecture hall. He would have preferred his lectures not to be open: lectures generally moved at the speed of the slowest student. But since the book had come out, he'd achieved something of a celebrity status at the university.

'But how does that change for compounds that are covalently bonded?'

After asking the question, he looked around the room. His postgrads were checking for raised hands. The question was a gentle lob up for them. Broad enjoyed playing this game, asking questions only the initiated could answer, weeding out the others. If it was up to him, his lectures would only be to the top students in his postgrad class. The rest were dead weight. Even the undergrads.

One of his most promising students raised his hand. 'It would depend on the causation principle involved.'

'Exactly,' confirmed Broad.

Most of the audience were looking around uneasily now. He had already lost them.

Broad looked in annoyance as the door of the lecture hall opened. There was a large sign outside the door forbidding entry while he was speaking. It was one of the conditions he had agreed with the university.

It was Margaret, his close-protection officer. It was a surprise to see her there. She had become so adept at shadowing him that he mostly forgot about her. She was the soul of discretion. But she was now standing at the front of the lecture hall, with every eye turned to her.

Margaret nodded at him, a request to talk. In the middle of a lecture. Broad could feel his face turning red with anger. He had not wanted the blasted woman to follow him around and only agreed once the MoD insisted. They had said he would never know she was there, except when he needed her most. And here she was, barging into one of his lectures.

'What is it?' he asked, showing his anger in front of the assembled hall.

'Can I have a word, Professor?' Her voice was calm and professional, as always.

Broad took a deep breath and stepped to the side. He noticed that Margaret was holding out her smartphone to him. He looked down at the screen. The BBC News website had one headline across it in a huge font, describing the Cambridge bus attack.

Margaret whispered something in his ear. Broad looked up at her in surprise and nodded.

'Ladies and gentlemen, I have to cut this lecture short.'

Broad walked to the lectern, grabbed his papers, then went quickly through the door into the corridor.

Margaret was waiting for him. Her jacket was thrown back, displaying the empty holster attached to her belt. The Glock 17 it usually carried was now in her hand.

50

Sara stood in front of the mews house, waiting. Not one of the homes on the cobbled street near St James's looked occupied. Most had their curtains drawn and no interior lights appeared to be on.

She checked the house number Waterman had given her, confirming she was at the right address, and glanced at her watch. She'd been waiting half an hour and calls to Waterman's mobile had bounced to voicemail.

She knocked on the door again and this time a whirring sound came from the ceiling. She looked up to see a camera swivel towards her. The door opened automatically and she stepped inside.

The interior was composed of one living space, with steel stairs leading to a balcony area under a wide skylight. It had bleached-wood floors and several desks piled high with papers and empty mugs. As seemed to be ubiquitous with GCHQ's work spaces, several digital monitors were mounted on one wall, feeds of news channels playing across their screens.

'Sorry I'm late. Got tied up at a meeting. I hope you found it without too much difficulty.'

She looked up to see Waterman walking down the staircase from the upper floor. He was carrying a sheaf of papers in one hand.

'Just the right amount of difficulty,' replied Sara. 'I don't suppose you want people turning up here unannounced.'

'Too right. It's normally chaotic, but I've dismissed the staff for half an hour.'

Waterman motioned her to a large conference table in the far corner. He hesitated. 'So, how are you?'

It didn't seem like an empty question. He looked at her with genuine concern, and she considered her reply. In the last week, she'd been drugged, stabbed and almost killed by a bus bomb, but the only thing that stuck in her mind was the faces of those she'd saved. She wouldn't want to be anywhere else. Her life finally seemed to have purpose.

'I'll be better once we've found Adrian Lang.'

'Quite right.' Waterman took a seat on the far corner of the table. Sara sat down opposite him. He placed two slips of paper between them. Sara reached over and pulled them closer to her.

'There's been a development. Those are the LODs – lists of the deceased – from Victoria and Cambridge today. Look at the highlighted names.'

One name on each list had a fluorescent yellow line running over it. Their ages were different, but their employer was the same: the Ministry of Defence.

'The MoD is keeping mum about why each man happened to be at the site of the explosion.'

'But it's tough to keep secrets from GCHQ, I presume,' said Sara.

'We know they were bodyguards,' replied Waterman, 'and on active duty when the bombs went off.'

Sara frowned and looked back at the list of the dead at Victoria station. A smattering of students, a waiter, a researcher, a retired stockbroker, a couple of academics, a solicitor. None leapt out as requiring an armed MoD protector. She turned to the Cambridge list. More students, a handful of academics, some factory workers.

'So, who were they guarding?' asked Sara.

Waterman frowned. 'The MoD is refusing to disclose anything, even to me.'

Sara looked up at him. He was gazing at her levelly. She was getting to know him better. She hadn't been brought here to be caught up on the investigation. He expected her to tell him something. Something from these pages.

'I'm sorry,' said Sara. 'I can't really do much with just a page of type. I need photos, or an item of theirs. Something with a personal connection. Just a name isn't . . .'

Waterman nodded. 'OK. I thought maybe . . . Vincent Shaw is getting me photos of the deceased. I'll show them to you as soon as I have them. MI5 has confirmed the Cambridge bomber was Penny Lang, Simon's sister – they're working with the police to try to piece together her life before today. All of the Lang siblings struggled after they were decommissioned. Eventually went off the grid. Police are checking the hostels around Cambridge to see if Penny stayed in any of them.'

Waterman pulled out a photo from the sheaf of

papers and placed it on the table. It was of Adrian Lang. The expression was haughty, a face that stared blankly at the camera with the same detached eyes that Sara had seen in the holiday picture.

'This is Adrian Lang's MoD photo. Like Simon and Penny, he served in the army. Saw active duty. Had trouble fitting back in when he returned to civilian life. A few arrests for public-order offences. Seems like he's the most rough-and-tumble of the three. Dropped off the map around nine months ago. Shaw and the joint task force are pulling out every stop to find him. But my hopes aren't high. We have no idea where he's going to strike. We don't know enough about him to predict his next move so, unless he makes a mistake, we may not know until the bomb goes off.'

He reached out and let his fingers rest on the photo's surface. 'I've been racking my brain to understand how you can do what you can do. I'm a believer. That's probably the best word to describe something you can't prove or explain in rational terms. Belief. And you might be the person who can make the difference now.' He dropped his voice. 'Can you tell me anything about where this next bomb is going to go off?'

Sara stared at the photo, her stomach twisted in knots. Memories of the sights and sounds she'd seen when she'd first connected to Adrian Lang's face returned to her. For the first time in this last week, they had made her doubt her own power.

She pulled the photo closer to her and let her fingertips rest on his face. Her peripheral vision began to black out and the darkness spread quickly around her. Faint sounds receded until she seemed to be standing in a void. A familiar sense of vertigo seized her and she reached out a steadying hand to the edge of the desk.

The same images flashed again in her mind. A series of low-slung, single-storey prefab huts sat on a single asphalt top. A grim campus of some sort, an island set in the middle of a sea of endless green. Above, a pavement-grey sky.

'Can you tell me what you're seeing?'

'It feels like a military facility,' said Sara. 'But, strangely, the atmosphere seems festive. There are families and children, as well as uniformed soldiers. I see balloons. Somewhere a band is playing.'

The vision was strange, carnival-like. Like a children's party in a prison. As if two different visions were colliding in the same mental space. Once again, Sara scoured the scene for clues but nothing stood out. No clocks to mark the time, no distinguishing buildings, no curious landmarks. Other than the festivities, everything about the place seemed drab, as if the intention when it was designed was to ensure the eyes of anyone who passed outside would slide off it.

Then the events that had spooked her last time she had touched the photo began to unfold. A crack, like thunder, went unnoticed by most of the families milling around. Then a column of smoke rose from one of the buildings. The explosion itself was curiously anti-climactic, something that happened out of shot, away from and unnoticed by the happy crowd.

A few glanced at the smoke, then cries of alarm rippled through the throng, rising above the band's lilting melody. Soldiers ran between buildings. The frame speed of the drama began speeding up. The civilians were being ushered out of the main gates through human cordons of uniformed soldiers. In her vision, they moved too quickly, their limbs jerking as they pulsed forward. And then the jerking increased in speed and became violent. More and more fell down, arms and legs spasming, backs arched, hands clawing at their throats. In only a few seconds, they were all lying still on the ground, their bodies twisted into macabre shapes. A balloon bounced in the air, its string tethered to the fist of a dying boy. The child's hand unclenched, releasing the string. The balloon floated up, over the barbed-wire fence that surrounded the compound, over the field, up, up, over the next field and over the nearby town, where hundreds of bodies lay motionless in the streets. The balloon kept drifting, higher and higher, with more towns spread out beneath it, all with bodies littering their streets.

Sara broke contact and stepped away, struggling to find her breath.

'What did you see?' asked Waterman.

Sara wondered what to say. The bomb that had gone off had seemed to be a local event, with few, if any, casualties that she could see. It was nothing like the other two bombs, whose destructive effect was immediate. Whatever caused thousands to die didn't even seem connected to the explosion. How could she communicate something to Waterman when she was unsure of what she had seen?

'The images are confused this time,' she said, at last. 'There are too many layering into each other. Do you have anything else of Lang's? A personal item?'

'No, but we'll try to find something,' said Waterman. She could tell he was disappointed. She wished she could give him more. Maybe there was a way to see something from these names. She let her finger run on the paper, staring at each of the columns until the letters and numbers disassociated from their meanings into senseless shapes. Nothing came.

'We'd better get you out of here,' said Waterman, finally, looking at his watch. 'Riz Malik contacted me. Said he wanted to see you. I told him to wait outside. He should be there now.'

He stood up and walked back towards the stairs, his attention now elsewhere.

51

The BMW was waiting on the cobbles when she opened the front door to the mews house. The passenger window powered down, revealing Riz, leaning over the seat.

'Hop in.'

'I thought I was banished from the front line,' said Sara, stepping in. For some reason, despite the circumstances, she couldn't stop herself smiling when she saw him.

'You're still banished from the front line,' said Riz. 'But the front line just moved. Everyone's concentrating on finding Adrian Lang. I thought you might help me with another line of enquiry.'

'A second front, you mean?' prompted Sara.

'Exactly.' Riz smiled, pressing down on the accelerator and propelling the car forwards.

The pub wasn't too far from Victoria station. Close enough that there was a knot of protesters standing at the bar, a ONE LOVE placard resting on the floor. Riz motioned to a table at the back of the room, a discreet distance away from the nearest afternoon patron.

'Do you want a drink?'

'Aren't you on duty?' asked Sara.

'It's been quite a day,' replied Riz. 'It may only be four in the afternoon, but no one would judge you for having a stiff drink.'

Sara shook her head. 'Just water. Don't let me stop you, though.'

Riz went to the bar and returned a short time later with a large glass of water and a tumbler filled with a copper-coloured liquid. The peaty odour wafted across the table to Sara, bringing back memories from her twenties: drinking herself into a stupor to stop the voices in her head.

'So, what's the second front?' asked Sara, after taking a sip of her water.

Riz unzipped the front of his jacket and pulled out his phone. He tapped out a number on the lock screen and flipped his index finger across it a few times.

'I've got two things for you. Both loose leads. There might be something to them, or there might not.'

As he talked, Sara watched him closely. Was she really the resource he needed right now, in the middle of a bombing campaign? Or had personal reasons led him to her? As unlikely as the latter sounded, she found herself hoping it was true. She was enjoying the interplay with Riz. She sensed he was attracted to her. And she was attracted by his attraction. Which in turn seemed to increase her attraction to him. A feedback loop that seemed to be binding them closer by the hour.

'This is a still of Penny Lang's face, just before she blew herself up on the Cambridge bus . . .' He was pointing his iPhone towards her. She leant forward to get a better look. It was a fuzzy close-up, taken from above, of Penny wearing a khaki combat jacket, staring three-quarters away from the camera.

'As best as I can tell,' continued Riz, 'that's some sort of burn mark on her face.'

An S-shaped dark shadow a few inches wide ran from above her eyebrow, down the side of her temple, and vanished under her ear.

'And this is a sketch of Simon Lang, by a Scotland Yard artist, from a description of one of the squatters at the Circus.'

Riz flipped his finger across his screen, dismissing the photo and replacing it with a sketch of a man standing naked, his back towards them. He was muscular, his back wide and bulky. A black shadow ran in a straight diagonal line from one shoulder-blade to the top of the opposite buttock.

Sara shrugged. 'They were both in the armed forces. They're probably combat wounds, right?'

'Wrong, actually,' said Riz. 'I checked their discharge files, which the MoD actually agreed to disclose. Neither was injured in combat. Whatever these burn marks are, they received them after they were decommissioned.'

Sara nodded vaguely. There wasn't much she could do with the information, other than try to connect with the photo and the sketch he was showing her. And she knew from experience that the connection would bring visions of the bomb but nothing more.

'What else do you have?' she asked.

Riz took back his phone and swiped it several times.

'Shaw sent the phone logs for Simon Lang's iPhone. Take a look.' He tipped the phone towards her. On the screen there was a photo of a phone bill, with a string of telephone numbers in a neat column. The same two numbers kept recurring all the way through.

'I'm guessing those are Adrian and Penny's numbers. Did you find Penny's phone?'

Riz shook his head. 'Must have been on her. Look at this one, though.' He pointed to the only non-recurring number on the list. 'I tried it. Listen to this.'

He dialled it, then put the call on to loudspeaker. The phone rang and rang, then rolled over to a voice message.

'Hello, you have reached Core Service Solutions. There is no one here to take your call, but if you leave a name and number, we will call you back.'

Riz hung up just as a sustained beep signalled that the recording was about to begin.

'Core Service Solutions?' asked Sara. 'It sounds vague.'

'I agree,' said Riz. 'There's no mention of it on the web. Which takes some doing, these days.'

'And it's the only number that Simon Lang called that didn't belong to a sibling?' asked Sara, holding his eye.

Riz nodded. 'It's registered to an address in London. In Putney.'

'So, what do you think it is?'

'Normally, I'd bring Special Branch with me on this one. Possibly an AFO team. In case it was an accomplice or ordnance supplier. But I don't think that's necessary here.'

'Why?'

'Because Companies House has the shareholders listed. It turns out one of them is the MoD.'

52

Sara stared through the swishing windscreen wipers.

'That's three twenty-seven Putney High Street,' said Riz, pointing ahead of him. 'The door is between the bank and the sofa shop. Looks like an office.'

Sara opened the car door. The air felt freshly ionized after the shower and, notwithstanding today's attacks, the street was bustling, the pavements packed as people ran errands and shopped. They crossed the road and stepped into the doorway. Several bells were mounted on a single white casing, with the names of the businesses adjacent to each buzzer.

'OK, follow my lead,' said Riz, reaching for the bell at the top.

His finger was about to press the button when Sara reached for his sleeve and pulled it back. 'We need answers right away,' she said. 'If MI5 is asking, we might scare them.'

'What are you suggesting?'

'Let me go,' said Sara.

'They're going to be just as reluctant if GCHQ is asking,' countered Riz.

'You've seen I can get results. Trust me.'

Riz mulled it over, then nodded. 'I'm going to wait down here. Any trouble, call.'

Sara shook her head, pointing to the camera lens mounted in the doorbell casing. 'Probably best wait in the car.'

He gave a reluctant nod. After he left, Sara rang the bell. A pleasant, professional voice came through the speaker.

'Core Service Solutions. Do you have an appointment?'

Sara leant closer to the speaker. 'I'm a walk-in.'

'Are you or were you a member of the armed forces?'

'Yes,' said Sara, reacting quickly.

The door buzzed and clicked open. Sara walked into a tiny vestibule with steep carpeted stairs leading up. Before she closed the door, the filtered voice came through the speaker again. 'Top floor.'

It was three flights up. The doors of the other premises were closed. The whole building felt empty. The only sign of occupation was fresh trail marks on the stair carpets, which suggested they'd been hoovered recently, and the absence of any mail piled near the doors.

When she reached the landing at the top, the door was open and a woman in her twenties was waiting for her, a bland, professional smile on her face. 'I'm Amy,' she said, holding out her hand. 'Nice to meet you.'

Sara looked at the hand, and then at Amy, before reaching out and shaking it firmly.

'Are you all right?' asked Amy, after a few seconds. Sara was still gripping Amy's hand and, from the expression on Amy's face, must have looked unsettled. She let go.

'I thought I'd lost you for a second.' Amy waved Sara in. 'It's probably the stairs. They can make you quite light-headed.'

The interior of the office was drably corporate and under-furnished. A grey carpet, black desk and black chair in one corner, and a large armchair in another. In front of the armchair a glass coffee-table was spread with magazines, and, on the desk, a stack of papers, neatly arranged.

'How did you hear of us?' asked Amy, looking more closely at Sara.

Sara weighed her response. From the connection with Amy a few moments ago she knew one thing for sure. Amy was not connected to the bombings. When Sara shook her hand, she had been briefly launched into a blizzard of suburban activity – noisy school runs, shouted encouragement from the touchlines at sports events, shopping expeditions and family dinners, then endless office tasks, arranging meetings, checking forms, making appointments. If this office was somehow part of the bombings, then Amy was oblivious to it.

'Veterans' circles,' said Sara, vaguely. She looked around. 'What do you do here?'

'We're an agency with one client. The client wants to support those who have bravely served in the armed forces and might need extra support in readjusting to life after the army.' The words tumbled out of her with the uneven spacing of memorized phrasing. 'You just have to fill in some forms and, if you qualify, we put your name forward. They pay five thousand pounds for cooperation.'

'Cooperation?' echoed Sara. Amy's words sounded like they were trotted out several times a day verbatim. 'Who is the employer?'

'It's a research institute,' said Amy with a smile, not willing to be drawn any further. 'Would you like to apply? We're pretty selective. Word of mouth only. Just sign these.' She reached into the top drawer of the desk, pulled out a stack of papers and handed them to Sara.

Sara took the papers and leafed through them. The first was a non-disclosure agreement, meaty enough that it ran to almost ten pages. The next few were consent forms for the release of medical files. 'I'm still not exactly sure what I'm signing,' said Sara.

'The client is in research and development. Drug development. They're looking for test subjects for human trials. It's all very hush-hush. That's why you need to sign these.'

'Would it be possible to have a glass of water first?' asked Sara.

Amy nodded, pleased. 'Of course. Just one moment.' She picked up an empty glass from a shelf near the desk and walked to the back of the office, opening a door and disappearing inside. Sara caught a glimpse of a mirror and a fridge through the open door. There was the sound of a tap running.

Sara stepped closer to the desk and looked at the pile of papers. It was a variety of correspondence, mostly bills. Keeping one eye on the door of the kitchenette, she searched through it.

Near the middle of the stack, she saw a printed medical record. She scanned it quickly.

In the kitchen, the tap stopped running.

The patient's name was at the top of the form. James Gastrell. And, below, an address.

She pulled the page out and walked quickly to the door. She was halfway down the stairs when she heard Amy's voice.

'Hello?'

53

Waterman tapped the MI5 briefing note in his hand as he walked across the car park. He could see Salt's car parked near the fence, about a hundred yards away.

He struggled to compose himself. This was the first meeting since he had ordered the Code Blue investigation on his former boss. Notwithstanding his leadership position at GCHQ, he was an expert at intercepts, not at dissembling. Unlike Salt, who had been director general at MI5 before his lateral move to GCHQ. He wondered whether Salt would know something was wrong from his demeanour. There was no other option, though. Salt was the only other person who would know about the MoD protection officers, and this was intel Waterman needed.

Waterman pushed aside his doubts. There was little purpose to them. He couldn't change his mind and walk away. Salt was likely watching him from behind the tinted windows.

He took an unobtrusive breath and yanked on the door handle.

Salt was sitting in the far seat. He was dressed impeccably as always. He noticed Waterman looking at the red carnation in his lapel.

'The Victoria silence,' said Salt, by way of explanation.

Waterman nodded awkwardly, trying to keep his eyes off the flower, and the pocket of Salt's shirt.

Salt looked at him patiently. 'You wanted to see me?'

Waterman nodded, steeling himself to keep it together. He would have liked nothing more than to blurt out everything to Salt now and ask him to explain himself. 'Yes,' he said, rubbing his beard protectively. 'I read the file. Based on the presence of the protection officers, our working theory is that their charges were the actual targets. But the names of the charges are redacted, even in my copy. Only two copies have the names shown.'

'Mine and the PM's,' said Salt.

Waterman could feel his blood pressure rising again. No matter how high one rose in the ranks, one step further was required for full access to the truth.

'You've entrusted me with Sara,' Waterman said slowly, 'so, within these walls, just tell me . . . what is going on?'

Salt regarded him for a moment, his mind clearly turning over at speed. Finally, he nodded. 'I can't tell you everything. Just some of it. And what I say can't go anywhere further.'

Waterman didn't say anything in response. He wasn't there as a private individual, and was not in a position to make any personal promises. If what he was told might impact the defence of the realm, then he was duty bound to take it further, no matter what personal assurances he had received. But Salt knew this as well as Waterman.

'Project X-ray,' said Salt.

'I've never heard of it,' said Waterman.

'No one has,' said Salt. 'It doesn't exist, officially. It was launched two years ago. Commissioned by the PM. Overseen by the MoD. The Americans fund part of the budget. The rest is taken from a number of other official projects, and hidden in budget-line items with innocuous category headings. X-ray is led by three scientists. Two were killed in today's bombings. The MoD have taken the third into hiding. Lang will never get to him.'

'What is X-ray?' asked Waterman.

'It's a research project. Decommissioned soldiers were the test subjects. The Langs were part of the pool.'

'But why do the Langs want to kill the scientists behind Project X-ray?'

'The Langs were paid for their services. And the risks were explained to them. But, they clearly remained aggrieved.' Evidently realizing more questions were coming, Salt continued, 'That's all I can tell you, Robert. You need to concentrate your efforts on finding Lang. He's still dangerous. The positive news is that the third scientist is safe.'

'What about Sara? She's still working on the case.'

'That's fine,' said Salt. 'Keep her focused on the search for Lang. But I don't want her anywhere near Project X-ray.'

'As you once told me,' said Waterman, 'I can't control her.'

343

Salt turned towards Waterman and dropped his voice. 'Project X-ray is more important than Sara Eden. It needs to be kept from her at all costs. For her safety as much as anyone else's.'

'What does that mean?'

'It means,' said Salt, with finality, 'that when it comes to Project X-ray, even Sara Eden is expendable.'

Sensing the meeting was over, Waterman nodded and reached for the door handle.

'Robert, one more thing before you go,' said Salt, his voice softening. Waterman looked back and saw Salt motioning towards the door. 'Shut that for a second, please.'

Waterman sat back in his seat, waiting for Salt to continue.

'I've been thinking through my future plans. This pact with America has . . . changed things. I haven't made any final decisions yet, but I'm not sure I'm in it for the long haul.' Salt looked distinctly uncomfortable as he spoke. Waterman's skin prickled. 'I just want you to know . . .' His voice trailed off as he searched for the right word. Waterman wanted to say something, but his mouth was so dry his tongue seemed fused to the roof of his mouth. 'I just wanted you to know, if I do leave, you were . . . the best of the lot.'

Waterman's face flushed with embarrassment. He shouldn't be vulnerable to praise from a suspected traitor, but such was the influence of Salt on him that he couldn't help it.

'I was taught by the best, sir,' he replied, before he

could stop himself. He nodded awkwardly and opened the door.

'Send my regards to Valerie,' said Salt. 'You have a good one there.'

Waterman shut the door and walked quickly across the tarmac to the building.

54

The pub looked like vacant property. Windows were boarded up, a metal sheet covered the front door, and a single iron bar protruded above it, the last remaining part of the wooden sign that once hung in front. The only evidence of occupation was a skinny teen, spider web tattoos covering his neck, standing near the door, pulling on a cigarette held in a cupped hand, the tip like an angry firefly. After he took the last drag, he flicked it into the street and pulled the front door of the pub open. The inside looked like a bear cave. Pitch black.

Riz looked at the medical report Sara had swiped from the office of Core Service Solutions. They were parked in a side alleyway, looking out onto Du Cane Road in White City.

'That's the address James Gastrell listed. He's the publican.'

'That's a pub?' asked Sara.

'Kind of,' said Riz. 'Places like this exist outside central London. They don't make their money from beer. They're usually police no-go areas. A bust would get ugly very quickly. Too many casualties, on both sides. Not worth it for the amount of drugs likely inside.'

'So, what's the plan?'

'We go in together this time,' said Riz.

They left the car and crossed the road. Riz stopped in front of the door and held Sara's eye. 'Ready?'

Sara nodded and pushed open the door.

It took her eyes a few seconds to adjust to the interior. It was a single windowless room, lit only by low-wattage bulbs fixed high up the wall, soaking the edges of the space in a dim light. She could vaguely see shapes in the shadows, huddled together like wolves on the edge of a clearing.

'Think you're in the wrong place, darling.'

The bartender was big, even for the White City area, where bartenders tended to be recruited more for their muscle than mixology skills. His voice didn't match his size, but was nasal, reedy, the words struggling through his battered nose. Sara couldn't see him clearly, even though he was less than a few feet away: the diffuse light took the edges off everything inside. She took a step forward, into the edges of the perimeter of pearl light that illuminated his features. His face was like a battered war zone, a living text to a violent history, the legacy of beatings, given and received, covering the surface.

Light flooded the room and Sara turned to see Riz standing silhouetted at the open door. He stepped inside and walked to the other end of the bar, pulling up a stool.

'I'm looking for James Gastrell,' said Sara.

The whispered conversations around the edges of the room stopped, leaving only the faint sound of traffic outside.

In her peripheral vision, she could see one of the shadows rise and move to the door, standing like a sentry by it. Sara held up her hands, looking around the room. 'I don't want any trouble.'

'What do you want with James Gastrell?' asked the bartender.

Sara walked to the bar and took a seat, directly in front of him.

'I want to talk to him about Core Service Solutions,' she said.

The bartender leant closer towards her over the bar.

'Are you a friend of theirs? CSS?' Before she could answer, he seemed to come to a conclusion and jerked his head to a door behind him.

'He's in the back. This way.'

Sara looked at Riz, who gave a minute shake of his head. The bartender walked along the narrow gangway between the bar counter and the wall, pushing the door open and coming through. He didn't hold the door, and it flapped shut behind him. Sara could see Riz slide unobtrusively a few feet along the bar until he was standing not far from the back door.

Sara's heart was pounding. Bright eyes studied her in the dark from the corners of the room. There was still silence around her, everyone watching the drama unfold, biding their time. She walked behind the bar and followed the bartender's footsteps. She could feel the sticky floor under her boots as she walked. With a last sideways glance at Riz, she pushed the back door open and walked through.

She was in a darkened corridor, lit only by the natural light from a transom above what looked like the rear exit door at the end. There were two doors off the corridor, and on her left, she could see scuffed stone stairs heading down into a murky cellar.

She inched forward, letting her eyes adjust to the darkness, when a huge hand grabbed her by the collar of her jacket and pulled her off her feet, yanking her through one of the open doorways. She was in a musty storeroom, mildewed crates stacked high around her. The bartender put both his hands around her neck and lifted her off the ground, ramming her back against the wall.

'You tell those fuckers at CSS I'm never going back,' he rasped.

Sara's hands flew up to his, her fingers desperately kneading the pulpy flesh at the base of his palms and wrists, looking for a way to break his grip. But his fists were stone, impossible to move. As his flesh pressed to her neck, images pummelled her mind unbidden. Tracer fire lighting up a night sky. Rows of writhing bodies screaming in pain. The dazzling white work surfaces of a lab. A single naked flame burning from a Bunsen.

'I'll show you pain.'

She kicked wildly, beating her heels against the wall behind her, then aimed one foot, then another, at his groin. The impact had little effect, and each kick shifted her weight down, tightening his grip around her neck. She could feel herself losing consciousness, her vision blacking out while the images increased in intensity.

A crash nearby shifted the bartender's focus and she saw a shape launch itself at him. The meaty hands released from her neck and she fell, suddenly feeling a sharp ripping pain in her side. On her knees, she pressed a hand to her hip bone. Her palm was slick with blood.

She looked up at the section of the wall where she had been pinned. A thick, stout-looking nail was sticking out, a makeshift coat hook of sorts. Her blood now covered it like a lacquer.

Riz and the bartender were grappling. Riz straddled the other man, who was struggling to lift himself from the floor. Riz pulled his elbow back and cannoned a fist into the tip of the bartender's nose. His knuckles landed with a wet crunch, blood splattering from the man's nostrils onto his mouth and chin. Riz seized the advantage and drew back again, landing a second knockout punch in the same place. The bartender howled and his legs flopped down. Riz raised his fist once more and paused, waiting to see if a third strike was necessary. The bartender opened his eyes and grinned, revealing a blood-soaked mouth of broken teeth. He reared suddenly, tipping Riz over onto the floor. The temporary advantage Riz had secured had gone. The bartender's brute strength was on display now, flipping Riz easily over and pinning him down with one hand.

Sara stepped quickly out of the room and walked to the connecting door to the bar. There were two deadbolts on her side and she slammed them shut. The last thing they needed now was an invasion from the main area.

She stepped back into the storeroom to see the bartender squatting on Riz's chest, two huge fists throttling Riz. Ropy chords stuck out from Riz's neck, as taut as tendons and his face was turning puce red.

Sara looked around her. A row of bottle necks stuck out of a crate near her feet. She grabbed one and lifted it back, swinging it in one full rotational axis across the front of the bartender's forehead. The bottle smashed on impact, spraying him and Riz with liquid and glass fragments. The bartender's eyes rolled up into his head and he tipped over to the side, releasing his hands from Riz's throat. Riz sat upright, holding his neck and coughing.

A furious thumping was coming now from the connecting door to the bar. A multitude of hands were beating on it. The splintering sound of wood rose above the noise.

'We don't have long,' said Sara, clutching her side. She reached down and picked up another bottle, uncorked it and upended it on the bartender's face. His eyes remained closed. He was still out cold.

'I'm guessing this is James Gastrell,' she said, kneeling next to him.

Riz got up and came over, still rubbing his neck, where thick bruise marks were already appearing near the base. He leant over the bartender, raised his hand and aimed a hard slap at his swollen face.

Gastrell shook awake with a start, his eyes instinctively screwed up in pain. When he opened them, his first response was fury, a leftover, as if the cache of his brain hadn't cleared. He tried to scramble up, his elbows working frantically, his face pinched in anger, but Riz dropped down easily, his knee landing with force on the man's chest. Gastrell gasped in pain.

'Core Service Solutions. Who are they?' asked Sara.

'Get off me.'

'Then tell us what we want to know,' said Riz, shifting more of his weight onto his knee.

'They experimented on me.' He spat out the words as if the violation was still fresh. 'On an army base. Buggers did this.' Gastrell pulled his T-shirt to one side and exposed his neck. A thick burn mark ran from his collar bone towards his chest.

'Where is the base?' asked Sara.

'Porton Down.'

55

'It sounds like you've just had an announcement of imminent flight,' said Swift.

He and Swift were in Waterman's office, on the ground floor of GCHQ, looking out over the inner grass quad. Waterman was pacing back and forth, his head tucked down, his beard pressed onto his chest. The next step in a Code Blue operation would be to hand over the file to Stephan Cowan, the head of MI5. Such a move would likely destroy Salt's career, whether or not a formal investigation concluded there was treachery. Salt had too many enemies in Thames House, and it was likely that word of the investigation would be leaked. Waterman stopped in front of the window and stared out. It was a cold, windless day.

Swift had connected his laptop to the outsized monitors on Waterman's far wall. His fingers danced over the keyboard of his computer as a video appeared on the screens.

'Here's what we have so far: your personal witness of Salt recording your conversations, video footage of him taking off-book meetings with a member of a French defence firm, and a potential admission he's about to fly. It's a lot of circumstantial evidence. Maybe it's not definitive proof, but . . .'

'Valerie,' said Waterman, his eyes still trained on the quad.

Swift looked at him in confusion. 'Sorry, what?'

'He called my wife "Valerie",' said Waterman, turning around at last. 'He's known Susie for ten years. A man with something close to an eidetic memory got my wife's name wrong.'

Swift shrugged. 'If he's planning what we think he's planning, he's probably under a lot of pressure.'

Waterman shook his head. 'That man thrives on pressure.'

Swift seemed at a loss as to the relevance of Waterman's line of thinking. 'What do you want to do about the Code Blue?'

The older man kept tugging at his beard, his eyes unfocused. Finally, he looked at Swift. 'That building in Mayfair where Salt met with Puipin. I want to see the CCTV on any other doors to the building for an hour before and after their meeting.'

56

'The next question is how we get into Porton Down,' said Riz, slipping his phone into his pocket. 'It's huge. Miles of fence posts. Only guarded intermittently. I've got a pair of bolt-cutters in the boot. I say we find a blind spot in the perimeter cameras and cut our way in. I've just texted Shaw for clearance. It's worth a try.'

They were standing on the pavement next to his car, one block from the pub. The frenzy of the last twenty minutes was still pulsing through Sara, making the swish of cars passing on the main road sound almost feral. Adrenalin crackled through her senses, bringing her peripheral vision into bright perspective and imbuing the colours around her with a febrile energy. Everything still seemed like a potential attack.

'Are you OK?' asked Riz, looking at her with concern.

She snapped back to the present. 'Yes, I'm fine.'

'Let's see the wound.'

Sara pulled up her blouse. Dark red blood pulsed from a flap of skin the size of her thumb, just above her hip bone. He peered at it closely, assessing it with a professional detachment. After a few beats, he stood up, went to the driver's side of the car and opened the door.

'Flesh wound,' he said dismissively.

Sara laughed at the sudden flip. She could tell he was trying to defuse the situation.

'Doesn't really compare with this,' said Riz, once they were both seated and the doors were closed. He hauled up his polo shirt, exposing his bare stomach. It was flat and hairless, the abdomen of a teenager. A thick welt ran from his belly button in a straight line up to his sternum.

'Stumbled into a cell in Bradford by mistake. One of them stuck me in the belly button with a screwdriver and ripped me up to here.'

Sara did her best to look unimpressed. She pulled up a leg of her trousers to the knee, pointing to a jagged trough in her skin that ran all the way along her calf muscle. 'Marie Belter, with a home-made shiv. An argument over who got the bed by the window. We were eleven.'

'God, your childhood sounds even rougher than mine,' said Riz. He leant over her and popped open the glove compartment, pulling out a half-bottle of vodka and a thick wad of napkins, each stamped with a fast-food logo.

'I don't drink, so that better be to sterilize the wound,' said Sara, wincing.

'It's not, actually,' said Riz, unscrewing the top and taking a deep chug from the bottle. He gave her a cheeky smile, then tipped some vodka onto the napkins, letting the liquid soak through. The sweet-sour paraffin smell filled the car.

Sara stared at the vodka bottle. It had been six years since she had drunk alcohol but she felt like she needed something to ground her. Her senses were still fizzing.

Riz put the bottle down carefully near the hand-brake. He then fished in one of his pockets and pulled out a thin tube. Before he could open it, Sara took it from his hand and read the label. 'Superglue?'

Riz nodded. He reached for the edge of her blouse, then stopped himself, looking up at her, eyebrows raised. *Is this OK?*

'I might need a shot of this first,' she said, reaching for the bottle.

Before she knew what she was doing, she upended it and took two big gulps. The spirit hit the back of her throat like acid, a wave of euphoria following, and she burst out laughing.

'Damn. Pace yourself,' said Riz.

Sara lifted up the blouse to expose the cut again. Blood ran along the waistband of her trousers and soaked the top of her leg. Riz pressed the napkins to the wound and then rubbed in a circular pattern, clearing the blood from the area. The vodka had done what she had hoped, muting the experience of their connection.

'So, how long have you been in the service?' he asked. His face was so close to hers, she could smell his breath. Vodka and peppermints. He lifted her blouse a little higher, exposing the bottom edge of the scar from her attack in the drains.

'Ten days now,' replied Sara.

Riz gave a little laugh. 'Some pretty good scars for just over a week's active duty.' He lifted the bottle again and poured a measure over his fingers. He pressed the wound as he squeezed a line of glue across the two flaps of skin.

'Just need to keep my hand here while this sets.' He lifted his head until his face was only inches from hers. There was a slight tremor in his voice.

Sara didn't look away and they stared at each other. The air felt thick inside the car. Sara's eyes shifted to his mouth, then back up to his eyes, and their heads moved towards each other at the same time.

Riz kissed her hungrily, his hand reaching behind her head, fingers lacing into her hair and gripping it in a bunch, his other hand still connected to the bare skin of her hip. Sara moved her head as urgently against him, feeding on him.

The images that tumbled into her mind when her lips pressed against his were stretched and distorted, the sounds compressing as if they were played in slow-motion. A snarling dog. Children screaming in an enclosed space. A struggling body being lowered onto a large sheet of plastic.

'Wait,' said Sara, pushing him off. She lifted the vodka bottle again and took another hit of the sting-ing, viscous liquid. She wanted him, but wanted the experience on its own terms. A physical connection. She wanted the veil lowered, to let him keep his mys-teries to himself.

Riz took the bottle from her and had another deep

chug. Then they launched themselves at each other again. Riz moved his hand to her neck and began to tug her leather jacket down across her shoulders.

'Here,' breathed Sara, pushing him off so she could shrug off the jacket. Then they collided again, the passion ratcheting up.

'Wait,' said Sara again, opening her eyes and pushing him off.

'What?' he asked, breathing hard.

She looked up and down the alleyway. It was empty.

'OK.' She laughed, pulling him back towards her.

A buzzing sound cut through their laboured breathing.

'Hold on a minute,' gasped Riz, lifting himself off her and sliding his hand into his pocket. His phone was ringing. 'It's Thames House,' he said, looking at the caller ID.

He answered the phone, keeping his eyes on hers as he spoke in monosyllables. His chest was still heaving and his pupils were dilated, thick black pebbles locked onto her. 'Yeah . . . Yeah . . . OK, thanks.'

After he had ended the call, Riz pressed the phone meditatively to his mouth, a study in casualness, the moments before the call seemingly forgotten. Once again, it was pure theatre and Sara couldn't help enjoying it. She was privately grateful for the interruption. The frenetic energy of the fight had triggered something she would have preferred to remain dormant for now. She lifted herself back up in her seat and adjusted her clothing.

'Did you get permission?' she asked.

'Yup,' said Riz, twisting the key in the ignition and putting the car into drive. 'Bit of a surprise, but he says the MoD can't hide their secrets for ever. We're off to Porton Down.'

57

Salt sat in the back of his car, looking through the window at the front steps of the Mayfair terraced house. He'd been at the game long enough to develop an intuition for when he was being followed. They were closing in, although he knew they hadn't joined all the dots yet. They couldn't have, because he hadn't joined them himself.

It was impossible to know how long he had left. It could be a week, but it could also be days.

He pulled up his overcoat collar and opened the car door, walked quickly across the pavement, up the steps and through the front door.

A series of doors led off the chessboard marble-floored lobby, as well as a corridor leading to the back. Salt followed the corridor and pressed the call button for the tiny lift.

The top floor housed the converted eaves of the townhouse, with a lower ceiling than that on the ground floor. Low enough that Salt had to incline his head slightly as he walked along the plush carpet. He opened the door at the end of the corridor without knocking.

A fresco covered the far wall and gilded accents ran along the edge where the ceiling met it. Long couches ran along the near and opposite walls. The room had a plush, domestic feel, like the drawing room of a stately home. The only evidence that the space was in fact an office waiting room was the spray of magazines covering the coffee-table. The silence felt snug and the only sound was the ticking of the carriage clock on the mantelpiece.

There was never anyone else in the room. It wasn't an accident. Salt made sure of it. He made the appointments himself.

Only this time there was.

He was sitting on the couch, reading *Country Life*, his huge beard and mass of long, shaggy hair in direct contrast to his tailored suit.

Salt knew his own reaction had given him away. A shiver of surprise, then resignation. A curtain fell away permanently, exposing him for the first time to the man he had trained to be his replacement.

'How long have you known?'

'Not long,' replied Waterman, closing the magazine and laying it on the coffee-table. 'We pulled footage of the back door. Puipin was the cover, but we saw who was smuggled in the back too.'

The door on the other side of the reception room was half open and they could both see the consulting room beyond.

'He's the best there is,' said Salt. 'But I couldn't meet him in Harley Street. You'd have found out. So, Alain offered to arrange a meeting here, in the spare room of his building.'

Salt walked over and sat on the opposing couch.

'What's the prognosis?' asked Waterman.

'Not good, I'm afraid,' said Salt. 'Forgetting started about six months ago. It's deteriorated rapidly since then. I've been recording most of the meetings to help me remember. I've kept the files at home, on a private server, air-gapped. But it's getting more difficult to hide.'

'I'm sorry,' said Waterman. He looked genuinely distraught. It gave Salt a little hope.

'I'd like to stay as long as I can.'

Waterman stood up and held out his hand. There was an expression of friendship on his face that Salt hadn't seen before. Salt stood up as well and took the offered hand. He knew what the answer was as well as Waterman did.

He was done.

58

The drive out of the city was laborious. The road system of central London had been chopped into numerous blocks, with uniformed policemen in sleek yellow jackets flagging down cars and peering inside the windows. Adrian Lang's face stared down at Sara and Riz from each of the electronic billboards on the Great West Road. The sky took on a metallic tint as the sun dipped into it. Riz listened to the radio, media reports rotating from coverage of both bombings to talking heads speculating about likely suspects, to thought pieces about jihadist influences within Britain. Occasionally, Riz made or took calls, the Bluetooth piping voices through the car's speakers, projecting unseen presences into the space.

The mad passion of half an hour ago had receded, replaced with an intensity of purpose. Sara's mouth still had the brackish taste of vodka, and the alcohol was making her eyes heavy. She let them close, the sounds around her lulling her into sleep. When she woke up, the cityscape had thinned out, green fields now hugging either side of the six-lane highway.

'We're almost there,' said Riz. He took the next exit and followed the main road for a few miles before turning onto a lane. They were in the middle of nowhere, with little to relieve the endless green fields that stretched out in every direction. In this unleavened landscape, the sky seemed more expansive than it did in the city, a vast, grey estate pressing down on top of them.

'I feel like I've been here before,' said Sara, almost to herself.

'Really?' asked Riz. 'You must have come to Porton Down, then, because there is absolutely *nothing* else here.'

Sara didn't want to tell him she'd never been to Porton Down. Or anywhere near this part of the country. But she was becoming increasingly sure she had seen this place before. Twice.

Riz flipped on his indicator and turned left. 'OK,' he said, under his breath. 'Let's circle the place first and look for vulnerabilities.'

About fifty yards ahead, a sentry post stood by the side of the road. A high perimeter fence skirted an army base built on a hill. At the crest, drab one-storey huts clustered around a large, central parade ground. The hairs bristled on Sara's neck as she took it all in. Everything was exactly as she had seen it when she had connected with Adrian Lang's photo. This was the compound from her vision. Riz powered down his window as the car slowed in its approach.

'That's weird,' said Riz. 'There's no barrier across the road. Nor any sentry.'

Sara followed his look. Up ahead, something was lying on the asphalt.

'Oh, shit,' said Riz in a whisper.

A body lay half in and half out of the sentry post. Uniformed. A rifle still in its hands. A thick puddle of blood on the tarmac near it.

As the car approached, Sara saw the stump of the barrier protruding from the base of the gate. A few yards ahead, the snapped arm lay in the grass by the side of the road.

'Hold on,' said Riz, pressing the accelerator to the floor, causing the car to shoot forwards up the hill. They pulled out their phones and began dialling.

The radio cut out as a ring tone played through the speakers. Then Shaw's voice was piping through them.

'The MoD have reported Porton Down is under attack . . .'

'I know,' responded Riz, gripping the steering wheel tightly as the car reared under the acceleration. 'We're here now. This must be Adrian Lang's target.'

Sara tried to tune out Riz and Shaw's voices. Waterman picked up her call on the first ring and was talking right away.

'Are you at Porton Down yet?'

'How did you know?'

'Shaw told me. Sara, this is important. Do not approach Lang. Do you understand? Find Professor Matthew Broad. He's the last of three scientists. Broad's lab is in Hut C. It's Lab Four. Let MI5 deal with Lang. Get Broad out of there.'

Sara hung up just as the car crested the hill and drove onto the flat tabletop of the base. A high-sided lorry, the name of a rental company stencilled on the side in bright orange letters, sat in the middle of the road ahead of them, the driver's door wide open.

Riz pulled the car into a sudden stop, throwing them both forwards into their seat belts.

People were running in every direction, civilians and service personnel. Mothers gripped their children tightly to them as soldiers shouted indistinct orders and guided them to the rear of the base.

'What are civilians doing here?' asked Riz, looking around incredulously.

'It's family day,' said Sara, almost unconsciously. It was playing out exactly as she had seen when she'd connected to Adrian Lang's photo. Bunting was strung between the huts; banners with hand-painted signs hung over abandoned stalls in the parade ground; soldiers carrying brass instruments sprinted across the asphalt.

'How do you know?'

Riz was talking to her, but she was elsewhere. This was where it started. A stream of events that ended with thousands dead.

'Sara.'

She looked at him, coming out of her daze.

'Lang is after a scientist called Matthew Broad,' she said, at last. 'I know where he is.'

Riz unbuckled his belt and opened his door. 'You find him. I'm going to look for Lang.'

59

Sara ran against the tide of people, searching the sides of the huts she passed. Each one sported a spray-painted stencilled letter on its end wall. She passed T. Then S. Then R. She pivoted and ran diagonally across the square, briefly elbowing through the mass of families still fleeing. She rejoined the row of huts that ran perpendicular to the row she had just left. A soldier in combat gear ran towards her, carrying a rifle with both hands.

'Get out of here, now! We're clearing the area.'

Sara looked around her. She saw a stencilled F on the hut next to her.

'I'm with MI5,' she said, running around him and continuing up the path between the huts. More soldiers were running towards her, rifles pressed to their sides.

'This area's being evacuated. You have to leave, now!'

Sara ignored them and kept running, her eyes searching the huts' exterior walls. Then she saw it. Hut C. Stone steps led to a door. She pulled it open and went inside. She was standing in a long corridor that ran to the rear exit on the far side. The corridor was at least a hundred feet long. Four doors led off each side.

She ran down the corridor checking the signs as she ran, finding Lab 4 at the end. She knocked on the door with a series of furious raps.

'Professor Broad. My name is Sara Eden. I'm not going to hurt you. I'm here to take you to safety.'

Several seconds passed, then a series of bolts was shot. A sucking sound accompanied the opening of the door, which was several inches thick and rimmed with an insulation layer of rubber. It opened a crack and a face peered through.

'Get in, quickly.'

Sara stepped through, then watched as Broad closed it and began the elaborate locking process.

The lab had no windows. The space was composed of four long workbenches, with chemical-testing paraphernalia covering every square inch of the surfaces. Each workbench was covered with a thick Perspex box, and in the side of each box were two large openings from which protective gloves hung. Broad was a slight man in his fifties, with a short, neat moustache and a pair of gold-rimmed glasses worn tightly to his face. He had on a white biohazard suit. The helmet sat on a nearby counter.

'He's here, isn't he?' There was something fatalistic in his voice, as if the event had always been inevitable. As he walked back into the middle of the lab, she noticed he had a limp. His right leg was rigid, and he pulled it along with him in a rolling gait.

Sara nodded. 'Yes, Adrian Lang's here. But I'm going to take you to safety. Is there another way out?'

Broad nodded and walked towards the far wall. He crouched awkwardly, his frozen leg jutting out at an abrupt angle to his torso, the other bent and curled underneath him, and pointed to the outline of a hatch in the floor. 'It leads to a crawlspace below. Didn't want to use it until I knew it was safe to leave.'

He tried with difficulty to lift himself back off the ground. He pressed one palm flat on the floor, reached out and gripped her hand with the other.

'Can you lend a hand, please?' He shifted his weight onto her arm and used her to lift himself up. As his bare skin pressed to hers, a series of images pummelled Sara's mind. She broke contact with him and stepped back in alarm, causing him to fall backwards into a heap on the floor. 'Be careful,' he barked.

Sara looked around her, as if noticing the lab for the first time.

'What is this place?'

Broad rolled onto his hands and knees and crawled to a nearby workbench, using the side to lift himself. His face was red, although it wasn't clear to Sara whether this was due to the physical exertion or his rising temper. 'Whoever you are, I can promise you it's above your clearance level.'

Sara walked to the nearest workbench. A cage the size of a shoebox was flush to one of the Perspex walls. Inside there was a rodent wheel and an inverted water bottle with a nipple on one end. A skull and crossbones logo was stamped on the bottle, just above the words 'DANGEROUS CHEMICALS'. Two mice lay on the floor of the cage, still. Black, thick-ridged burn marks covered the majority of their body surfaces.

'What are you doing? You don't have clearance.'

Sara ignored him and placed her hands into the glove-holes. Directly in front of the gloves, a pump connected to a spray mechanism positioned over the cage. She pressed the pump once, a single squeeze. A fine mist spritzed into the cage, falling gently on the dead bodies of the mice.

'What's in the spray?'

60

A sudden volley of shouts came from outside in the corridor. Broad flinched and backed away, moving towards the far wall. Sara walked towards the door, listening. She could hear Riz's voice.

'Adrian, stay back! Stay back!'

A voice replied. Calmer than Sara had expected. A faint North Country lilt softened the edges of the words.

'Get Broad out here now. No one else needs to be killed.'

'Sara, are you inside?' Riz's voice was close. He must be standing on the other side of the door.

'Yes,' replied Sara.

'Keep Broad against the far wall,' said Riz. 'He's got a suicide vest.'

Sara looked back towards Broad and the cold, clinical testing boxes on the tables. She leant against the door and spoke loudly to project her voice.

'Riz, the two MoD men today. They were protecting scientists. A three-person team for a secret project called X-ray. Broad is the third. They're weaponizing chemicals.'

'Are you mad?' Broad had stood up and was staring at Sara with disbelief. 'Whose side are you on?'

Riz was silent for several seconds before speaking. 'No, that's not right. Britain signed a convention. We destroyed our stockpile.'

'So has Russia,' said Lang. 'Officially. Yet they're still using them. Chemical weapons are no different from nuclear. If one superpower has them, others must.'

The memories of what Sara had seen when he grabbed her hand were still pulsing through her: the same images she'd seen before. The floating balloon, the dead littering the high street, corpses piled high. For the first time, she realized the location could have been anywhere. Anytime. It was the future deployment of X-ray.

'We have to stop this, Riz,' she said at last. 'What Broad is developing here doesn't discriminate between civilians and soldiers. Thousands of innocents could be killed.'

Riz's voice rose in surprise.

'Sara, we work for military intelligence. We are not decision-makers.'

Sara stared at Broad.

For some reason, the words of Christian came back to her now. *Be a messenger for others or use the future for yourself.* He was the last person in the world whose advice she ever thought she would follow. Broad stared at her, shock and disgust on his face.

'You can't seriously be thinking . . .'

Sara shook her head, as if to dismiss her thoughts. She walked across the length of the lab towards Broad, who flinched as she approached. She then crouched by him and lifted the edge of the trapdoor. 'Come on, let's get you out of here.'

Broad looked at her with consternation, then nodded grudgingly. 'I'm glad to see you've come to your senses.'

61

Sara crawled on her hands and knees out from under the hut. Broad followed her, his right leg ploughing a trail in the dirt behind him.

'Where's your car?' asked Sara, after they had stood up and were a few feet clear of the building. The sounds of panicked mass retreat had died down around the base, replaced by volleyed shouts of mobilizing troops. Broad pointed to the chain-link perimeter wall nearest them.

'Just on the other side of Hut E.'

He began half running, his speed hampered by the bulky suit he was wearing.

Sara hesitated, looking back at the hut. Riz was still inside, keeping Lang at bay.

'C'mon!' shouted Broad.

Sara took a final look. At that moment, two squads of soldiers appeared from different directions, running towards the hut, dispersing into smaller units as they approached, fanning around the building to close off all exits.

'Lang's inside!' shouted Sara. 'Along with an MI5 officer.'

A soldier with sergeant stripes veered towards her.

'We'll take it from here. Get Professor Broad to safety.'

Sara looked over towards Broad, who had stopped and was urgently swiping his arm to signal her to catch up. She followed him through the gaps between two huts and out onto an asphalt stretch where about twenty civilian cars were parked in three rows. Broad looked in dismay at them as he limped along the first row.

'They're all punctured.'

Sara saw that every car was sitting low to the ground, the frames resting on the rims of the wheels, the tyres flopped uselessly to the side.

'Lang must have done this,' said Broad, running to the next row of cars. 'To stop anyone . . . Here's my car. Thank Christ! He didn't touch it.'

He fumbled in his pocket for his keys and pressed the fob, causing the front and rear lights to flash once. He pulled the driver's door open and flopped inside, scrambling to put the key into the ignition. He seemed to have forgotten about Sara: he slammed the door and threw the car into reverse. The car surged backwards. Sara watched as Broad drove along the road towards the rear gate of the base.

Sarah heard gunfire behind her and turned and ran back to Hut C.

A clutch of soldiers was standing near the stone steps leading to the rear door. She pushed through them, climbing the steps and walking through the open door. Several soldiers stood inside the corridor. At the far end, she could see Riz with another soldier, while a third crouched beside the body of Lang.

'I don't get it,' said Riz, as she approached.

Lang's body was lying in a pool of blood. He was face down, and the crouching soldier flipped him over.

'What is it?' asked Sara.

Riz pointed to the suicide vest.

'It's a dummy. The liquid's water.' He looked up at Sara in confusion. 'Why would he kill himself, for noth–'

He was interrupted by a deafening crack that caused everyone in the corridor to bounce down into a reflex crouch. Shouts echoed off the walls as voices shouted, 'Cover!'

Bodies immediately started moving, running down the corridor and through the exit door. Riz and Sara followed them. The first thing they saw was a column of white smoke rising from the other side of the opposite hut.

They moved with the group of soldiers, half running, pausing at the corners of the huts to peer around the sides, until they were standing next to the lines of parked civilian cars.

What was left of Broad's car was just outside the rear gates of the army base. It was little more than a smoking chassis, black with soot. The rest was spread over a wide radius.

62

Waterman scanned the last page of the email.

It had been a long journey with Sara, albeit in an accelerated time frame. He had gone from wary sceptic to committed believer in less than a week. The speed of his conversion had surprised him. But, despite his highly analytical mind being able to challenge every rational link in a chain, his senses could not deny what he had witnessed. Time and time again, Sara had been able to provide critical intel based only on physical touch. For all the computing arsenal Waterman had at his command, it was beginning to dawn on him how much of an asset Sara Eden could be. Finally, he understood the level of Salt's zeal and why he had pursued the family down the generations.

Waterman had been trying to suppress his sadness at the loss of his mentor. It had been less than a week, but the emotion was still within easy reach. His relief that Salt had not betrayed his country was profound. Because if Charles Salt could do so, what hope was there for any of them? But the reality of Salt's condition, brought home for Waterman by several hours on the internet researching early-onset dementia, soon blew that relief away. The man who had guided

Waterman's career would soon be in retreat from not only the security services but also from life.

It was for this reason that Waterman hoped he could honour his mentor by green-lighting Sara, Salt's long-cherished project, into active duty. Which made Salt's final recommendation to Waterman before his official retirement so perplexing. Waterman had reread the email three times now. Salt had sent it from his private email address, with a recommendation that both the sending copy and the receiving copy should be deleted after reading. The email was brief and to the point, and the conclusion was that the Sara Eden project should be terminated with immediate effect.

Waterman checked his watch. If he didn't leave now, he was going to be late. He logged out of the program, then opened a drawer and pulled out a pair of thick, translucent gloves. He stood up and walked out of his office into the wide corridor that led to the lifts.

He understood Salt's concerns, which were laid out with characteristic clarity. 'In the final analysis,' Salt had written, 'you will have to accept that controlling Sara Eden is not an achievable mission objective. And that level of volatility could put the mission, and lives, at risk.' For all Sara's training and natural power, she was still an ingénue, and Salt's first indictment against her was that she was vulnerable to petty politicking, as had been the case in her interaction with Shaw. But her being flat-footed in office politics was not the main issue. Salt's main anxiety related to the fact that her success during the operation in The Hague was a direct result of her disobeying two direct orders from Water-man. Salt's conclusion was that, ultimately, Waterman would need to get comfortable with the fact that Sara could at any time go rogue.

Waterman walked to the lifts and pressed the call button. A lift arrived and he took it down to the eighth floor. His mind was still churning as he walked along the cool, dark corridor. Salt's words always had a powerful effect on him, even though this time they were delivered from beyond the professional grave. He would likely never see his mentor again. It was difficult, if not impossible, to socialize with those outside the intelligence community. In Waterman's line of work, relationships tended to be made with those of like security clearance, and the disclosure of Salt's diagnosis had terminated his access to intelligence at any level. As a result, it was difficult for Waterman not to treat Salt's email with a reverence akin to how he would treat a last will and testament.

She was waiting for him when he entered the low-ceilinged conference room. The bruising on her face she'd received from the fight in the storm drain was almost gone, but he knew from her medical report that she still had a mild concussion from the bus explosion, and her fight with Gastrell had required ten stitches. He'd never have known it to look at her. She sat on the other side of the table, her hands folded on her lap, her legs crossed, calmly watching him as he stepped into the room.

The monitors around were all on, each displaying a

different surveillance photo of the same person. She was an aristocratic-looking, expensively dressed woman with flat-ironed, jet black hair. In most of the photos she was stepping into or out of a private jet.

'The MoD is on the warpath about Lang,' said Waterman, sitting in the chair opposite her.

'What was it doing with chemical weapons?'

Waterman exhaled quietly. He considered potential misdirects. Subtle responses that might push Sara in the wrong direction. The information was top secret, after all. And if it came out that he'd passed this intel to an agent without clearance, well, that would really push the MoD over the edge. But as he looked at Sara, he realized it would be pointless to lie. Her abilities made secrets impossible. Her question was just a courtesy, giving Waterman the chance to tell her before she found out anyway.

'They were developing a hybrid version of anthrax. And an antidote in parallel, one that could be given to British troops if they were caught in the blowback. The MoD needed test subjects to be exposed to the hybrid and then to receive the antidote. Ex-soldiers were thought to be more likely to be loyal and keep the confidence.'

'And what's X-ray's status now?'

'Dead.'

Sara said nothing for a few seconds, then looked up at the television screen. 'Is this the next project?'

Waterman nodded. 'I'll tell you about her in a moment . . .'

Nothing could dent his respect and admiration for Charles Salt, but some risks were worth taking. Especially when the potential rewards were so high. But before he took the risk, there was one question he needed answered.

'First, I want to ask you about what happened at Porton Down.'

Sara waited, her expression open. 'You read my report?'

'I did. It's clear now that Lang posed as a decoy to get Broad to escape in his own car. The bomb was fixed to the undercarriage of the vehicle.'

He hesitated. He didn't want to ask the next question, but his rational mind couldn't help ticking over, searching for logical connections everywhere, even in the illogical power of his new asset.

'There was only one question I had . . .' He faltered. Some part of him almost didn't want to know. 'You never mentioned in your report whether you ever touched Broad.'

She didn't break eye contact when she responded, 'If I had, I'd have seen the bomb.'

Waterman held her eye for several seconds, then nodded. It was a yes or no question, and her conditional response had done little to dampen the concerns that Salt's email had implanted in his mind.

'Sara, when we started, I was not a believer. I am now. I think you could be the most valuable agent and resource we've ever had. But if we're going to work together, I need to know we're going to be on the same page.'

Sara nodded emphatically. 'Absolutely. I want what you want.'

'And what's that?'

She stood up and walked to the nearest monitor, looking closely at the surveillance photo.

'To neutralize the threat. And protect the innocent.'

Acknowledgements

Thank you to:

- my wonderful agent, Luigi Bonomi, for his invaluable help from start to finish
- my fantastic editor, Jillian Taylor, for always pushing this book to be the best it could be
- the brilliant copy-editorial team at Penguin, including Hazel Orme and Nick Lowndes, for getting the copy right so the story could flow through
- my wonderful parents, who encouraged me to start writing and who have inspired me my whole life
- my children, Ethan and Daisy, for being the ultimate distractions at the beginning and end of each day
- and profound thanks to my wife, Shannon, for her love and support, for coaxing me through doubt and sticking points, for making the good ship float while I am writing, and for saying yes in The Last Book Shop.

He just wanted a decent book to read ...

Not too much to ask, is it? It was in 1935 when Allen Lane, Managing Director of Bodley Head Publishers, stood on a platform at Exeter railway station looking for something good to read on his journey back to London. His choice was limited to popular magazines and poor-quality paperbacks – the same choice faced every day by the vast majority of readers, few of whom could afford hardbacks. Lane's disappointment and subsequent anger at the range of books generally available led him to found a company – and change the world.

'We believed in the existence in this country of a vast reading public for intelligent books at a low price, and staked everything on it'
Sir Allen Lane, 1902–1970, founder of Penguin Books

The quality paperback had arrived – and not just in bookshops. Lane was adamant that his Penguins should appear in chain stores and tobacconists, and should cost no more than a packet of cigarettes.

Reading habits (and cigarette prices) have changed since 1935, but Penguin still believes in publishing the best books for everybody to enjoy. We still believe that good design costs no more than bad design, and we still believe that quality books published passionately and responsibly make the world a better place.

So wherever you see the little bird – whether it's on a piece of prize-winning literary fiction or a celebrity autobiography, political tour de force or historical masterpiece, a serial-killer thriller, reference book, world classic or a piece of pure escapism – you can bet that it represents the very best that the genre has to offer.

Whatever you like to read – trust Penguin.